# Steady and Strong

## ITALIAN STALLIONS
### BOOK SEVEN

### MARI CARR

Copyright © 2024 by Mari Carr

All rights reserved.

No part of this book may be reproduced in any form or by any electronic or mechanical means, including information storage and retrieval systems, without written permission from the author, except for the use of brief quotations in a book review.

No part of this book was written using AI.

Cover Design: Qamber Designs

Cover Photography: Wander Aguiar

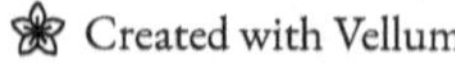 Created with Vellum

# Steady and Strong

It's a win-win-win situation.

Luca has resigned himself to a life as a bachelor. He's watched all the Morettis fall in love, but nothing's ever clicked for him. Until Harper...and Conor.

Former super model Harper has spent too much of her life living up to other people's expectations of her. Perfect hair, perfect body, perfect boyfriends. For the first time ever, she's able to forge her own path. New career, no more diets, and—hopefully—a relationship with a man of her choosing, one who sees past the pretty face to the person inside.

Conor has spent his entire life lost in the shadows, the forgotten Russo, but he's decided it's time for that to change. After all, both of his older brothers have found love. He's determined it's his turn, and that resolve gets a little push in the right direction when a new investment means he'll be working with the man he's always had a crush on. But if he likes Luca, why does he suddenly have feelings for Harper too?

*Chapter One*

"**U**n-fucking-believable."

Conor Russo stood on the sidewalk, watching as his latest investment went up in smoke...literally.

The street was blocked by the three fire trucks and nearly a dozen firefighters working to save what was—hopefully still—going to be his restaurant.

Well...his and Harper Branson's restaurant.

Conor still couldn't quite believe he was going into business with one of the most recognizable faces in the world. A former supermodel, Harper had graced the cover of countless magazines, and she'd spent years as the face of Siren's Smile, one of the most popular perfumes on the market. Images of her—and that famous siren's smile—consistently showed up in television commercials, on billboards, the sides of city buses, and on endcap displays at the local grocery store.

He and Harper had formed a partnership nearly a year ago, their plan to open a high-end restaurant here in Philadelphia. In early November, they'd found the perfect property in a prime location of the city and had decided rather than rent the restaurant space on the bottom floor, they'd simply purchase the entire three-story building outright.

The building that was currently on fire.

Conor had only met with Harper in person a handful of times, the last time being when she drove from New York City to tour the three different properties he'd narrowed down as their top choices. Since he lived in Philadelphia, he'd taken the lead on finding the real estate for their endeavor. They'd both agreed that this one was ideal for their plans, so they'd signed on the dotted line.

The rest of their meetings had been done over video conference calls as she completed her coursework at the Institute of Culinary Education in New York, as well as finished the last of her modeling contracts. Now...here they were, mid-April, at the very beginning stages of this new business endeavor, and it was all going to shit.

Conor rubbed his chest, trying not to let his anxiety get the better of him.

Tonight was supposed to be a small celebration as Harper was, at last, ready to move to Philadelphia full-time to become an active partner in the redesign and reconstruction of their future restaurant—Harper's Dining Room. The name was perfect, as Harper was known for her pleasant, girl-next-door appearance *and* attitude. Her entire brand was wrapped around her friendly nature, the idea for the restaurant name born from the fact that she was the type of person you'd like to share a meal with.

Conor glanced down the street and saw Luca Moretti talking to one of his friends, Kayden Gallo, a cop on the Philadelphia police force. Kayden was clearly on duty, in uniform and serving as crowd control for the gawkers hovering nearby to watch the action.

Kayden had parked his cruiser sideways at the end of the block to prevent thru-traffic, which was probably causing a lot of headaches in other parts of the city as this was typically a busy thoroughfare on Saturday nights, when the restaurants and bars in the area were hopping.

The police barricade felt unnecessary considering no one

could drive through with all the fire trucks parked in the street, blocking both lanes.

Conor wasn't surprised to discover Luca here. After all, he was the contractor on the restaurant reconstruction job, and the two of them had planned to meet tonight—right now, in fact—with Harper. Conor had been en route to the meeting when he'd gotten the call from the alarm company that a smoke detector was going off and the fire department had been alerted.

Their original plan had been for Luca to give him and Harper a tour of the building, showing them what physical progress the construction crew had made thus far. Since work on the restaurant had only started a week earlier, all that had really been accomplished was gutting the first floor completely, maintaining the retaining walls, while taking the entire place down to studs.

Luca looked over, spotted him, and gave him a quick wave. Conor nodded once, then glanced away, turning his attention back to the building, shaking his head in disbelief once more.

Prior to their acquisition, the bottom floor of the building had been a pizza parlor, though that business had been closed for nearly six months. The top two floors had been sectioned off to create six small apartments—three on each floor. Upon purchasing the building, they'd honored the remainder of the leases of the current renters but didn't re-up them. The last person moved out a few weeks ago.

Thank God. He would hate to think of someone losing all their possessions in a fire. He glanced at the upper floors, slightly relieved to see that the flames didn't appear to have made it that far.

He and Harper had been delighted to find the building, located in Old City, a part of Philadelphia well known for its trendy restaurants, fashionable boutiques, and eclectic galleries. It was a popular tourist attraction, but it also pulled in quite a lot of local foot traffic as well.

Conor glanced at his watch, then ran his hand through his

hair anxiously. Harper should be arriving soon. This was going to be one hell of a welcome to Philadelphia for her.

He'd called her immediately after receiving word that the fire alarm was going off, aware she was on the road and not checking her messages. Conor had foolishly told her it was probably nothing, that the alarm had most likely been triggered by dust from the demolition.

So much for that theory.

He needed to warn her before she arrived because this was going to be one hell of a shock. However, before he could pull his phone out of his jacket pocket, he caught sight of her walking toward the building. Her wavy, long blonde hair was pinned up in a tight ponytail and she was wearing sunglasses even though dusk had come and gone, giving way to night. He suspected the shades were less for eye protection and more an attempt to remain unnoticed.

That was a pointless endeavor. Even if Harper hadn't been famous, people would still notice her. She was a breathtakingly beautiful woman with electric-blue eyes, high cheekbones, a curvy figure, and legs that went on for miles. Those legs were currently framed in tight blue jeans paired with a plain, lowcut white T-shirt, chunky silver jewelry, and covered with a soft black leather jacket. On anyone else, it might look like a regular outfit, but Harper wore it like a work of art.

A quick glance in the opposite direction proved that Luca had spotted her as well. Harper and Luca had never met in person before—tonight was going to be their first introduction—though Luca had been involved in most of their video conference calls since being hired as contractor.

Conor couldn't quite believe he was working with the Moretti brothers on this project. God knew that was something that would have been unheard of when his grandfather and father had been alive.

The Russos and Morettis had participated in a four-generations-long feud that had included everything from infidelity to workplace sabotage to sketchy loan sharking to high school rivalries. It seemed the animosity had finally ended with Conor's generation—he and his brothers, Matt and Gage, as well as Luca's large clan of brothers and cousins attempting to make amends.

The rift began to be repaired when Gage had married Penny Beaumont, whose brother, Rhys, was in a strange sort of throuple relationship with Tony Moretti and a young single mom, Jess. Gage's marriage had opened the door to more interactions between the two families and had led to Tony and Matt—who'd legit hated each other since their senior year of high school—burying the hatchet just a month earlier.

Of course, their newfound peace was also helped along by the fact Matt had fallen in love with Liza Moretti, Luca's cousin.

The last few weeks, Conor had found himself receiving invitations to countless Moretti social events, like happy hours with his brothers and their new group of friends as well as a standing lunch date the Moretti men had every Wednesday at Paulie's Diner.

So far, he'd turned them all down because he wasn't entirely comfortable with this new norm. In truth, he'd preferred the years when his path rarely crossed that of the Morettis. It hadn't been hard to avoid them the past fifteen years or so, as Conor rarely left his office in his night club, Enigma. For the most part, he didn't travel in similar social circles and his day-to-day routines didn't overlap those of the Morettis in any way.

Though to be fair, his solitary routine didn't overlap with those of *anyone*.

As for Luca serving as contractor...Conor had Gage to thank for Moretti Brothers Restorations winning the bid to refurbish the building and create Harper's dream restaurant. Not that it was much of a bidding process.

For the first time in his life, Conor offered a job based on nepotism.

A couple of weeks after Thanksgiving, he'd been invited to join Gage and Penny—as well as Rhys, Jess, and Tony—for dinner. Typically, Conor would have offered an excuse and stayed home, but for some reason, he'd accepted that night, too fed up with eating takeout alone.

During the meal—which had been very laid-back and enjoyable—Gage had asked Conor how things were going on the restaurant project. Conor had told them about purchasing the building and their plans for the renovation, complaining about how the construction company he'd hired had backed out just a few days earlier.

For the next hour, he and Tony had dominated the conversation, discussing his and Harper's vision. Conor had gone into detail as he described the building, which Tony was familiar with, claiming it used to be his favorite pizza joint.

One thing led to another and before he knew it, he found himself offering Tony and his brothers the contract right there at the table, and Tony—mercifully—had promised to fast-track the project, even though Moretti Brothers had a waiting list of future clients.

Conor realized nepotism wasn't the right word. There was no denying Moretti Brothers Restorations was the best construction firm in the city, but given their families' past hostility, Conor had never worked with them, even after his father passed away. Considering Russo Enterprises did a great deal of construction in and around the city, they'd been shooting themselves in the foot by not hiring the Morettis all along.

This restaurant was their first foray into a Russo/Moretti professional relationship since the original rift four generations earlier. Conor suspected his brothers as well as Luca's family were very interested in the success of the partnership, as it would potentially open the door to more joint ventures, which could be profitable for both companies—Russo Enterprises as well as Moretti Brothers.

While Conor hadn't had any qualms offering Tony the job that night at dinner, he wasn't sure he would have been quite so quick to do so if he'd known Luca would be the actual contractor —not Tony—and their primary contact at Moretti Brothers.

Primarily because he and Luca had a tiny bit of a past, one that still, all these years later, brought up some latent, misplaced jealousy and embarrassment. He wasn't able to shake those feelings, even though the incident had occurred nearly twenty years earlier.

The worst part was, he was pretty sure Luca didn't have a clue anything had even gone down between them.

Much to Conor's chagrin, back in high school, he'd been wildly attracted to Luca, who had unwittingly been the first person to break his heart.

And now...they were working together.

Fucking. Awesome.

It had been easy to forget Luca existed when they never ran into each other, and for most of his adult life, mercifully he'd had no more than half a dozen "Luca sightings." During those run-ins, they'd done little more than say hello and move on.

Ever since beginning work on this project, Conor had managed to avoid in-person meetings with Luca, instead dealing with the man behind the camera on his computer, and always with Harper and one or two of Luca's other brothers in attendance as well.

Conor watched as Harper got closer, her attention focused solely on the building. Black smoke was billowing from the broken front windows as two firefighters directed a powerful stream of water from their hoses, dousing the flames.

Before Conor could call out to her, Harper pulled out her phone, tapping on it for a minute or two.

"Hey, Conor."

He looked over to discover Luca approaching him, also taking note of Harper on her phone.

"Did you warn her?" Luca asked.

Conor shook his head. "She knew about the alarm, but I

didn't have a chance to call back and tell her it wasn't just a glitch."

"Shit," Luca muttered.

Harper must have felt their gazes on her because she looked their direction, tapped her phone a couple more times, tucked it away, then gave a quick wave as she headed toward them.

"Hello, Conor," she said as she stepped up to him. "Guess the dust theory didn't pan out."

Conor grimaced. "It did not. Not exactly the welcome to Philadelphia you were expecting." He reached out to shake the hand she offered.

"Not even close." Then her gaze traveled to Luca. "Well, hey, there you are. Luca Moretti...in person," she said genially.

"Hello, Harper," Luca replied, with a smile that was too charming for Conor's peace of mind as his cock—the asshole —twitched.

Aaaaand this was why Conor had avoided meeting with Luca in person. He did a terrible job holding his libido at bay around the man.

Harper offered a handshake to Luca as well. "It's nice to finally meet you face-to-face."

"I wish it was under better circumstances," Luca said, as all three of them turned to look across the street.

Conor didn't see flames anymore, which gave him hope that perhaps the fire was out. If it was, it appeared it had been contained to the first floor. Not that that was necessarily good news. There would still be significant smoke damage to the floors above. God only knew how long this was going to set them back on the project.

"Do we know what started it?" Harper asked.

Luca shook his head. "Not yet."

"You were here this morning, weren't you?" Conor asked Luca. Though it was a Saturday, Luca had mentioned putting in a half day in hopes of turning the corner on the demolition phase and moving them toward the actual remodel. "You mentioned at our meeting yesterday you planned to do something with the electrical wiring." He, Luca, and Harper had held a quick video call, touching base on their plans for this evening, including the tour of the building, followed by a late dinner.

Luca nodded. "I did say that, and I was here earlier."

Conor gave him a very pointed look. "You don't think perhaps something went wrong with whatever you did?"

Luca scowled and crossed his arms. "What are you saying?"

"Seems like a pretty big coincidence, wouldn't you say?"

"You think I set the fire?"

Conor sighed. "Don't you?"

"No. I don't."

Conor wasn't sure how Luca could discount that question so quickly. Surely, he didn't think he was infallible. "How can you be so sure?"

"Because I know how to do my damn job."

Conor felt something inside him snap. There were too many aspects of this project that were pushing him out of his well-established comfort zone. Taking on a business partner, working with a famous model, and having Luca thrust back into his life left him feeling edgy and...well...itchy. Like he was walking around every day in a scratchy wool sweater that was too tight.

Conor raised a hand, gesturing to the building. "All I'm saying is it seems highly suspicious that the very day you start working with the electrical wiring, we have a fire. What else could have started it? The place has been gutted."

"I inspected the existing electrical wire, checked the GFCI outlets, and it was all up to code," Luca insisted. "I don't know what started it, but it wasn't me."

"Must be nice to be so confident," Conor muttered, hating himself the second the words left his mouth. He wasn't a fighter by nature, so he wasn't sure what he was doing.

Luca's features darkened. "How do I know this isn't another attempt by the Russos to destroy the Moretti reputation?"

Conor scoffed. "Jesus Christ. Do you seriously think I'd burn down my own building just to make your company look bad?"

Luca shrugged. "It wouldn't be the first time the Russos have pulled underhanded crap to ruin my family. I thought we were beyond all that feuding families shit, but maybe we aren't."

"I had nothing to do with this," Conor insisted.

Luca didn't look convinced. "You've got insurance on the building, right? And it's not like you're hurting for money. Like you said, the place was gutted, and the work has barely begun. Not much to lose that you couldn't recoup easily enough."

"You've gotta be kidding me!" Conor was livid. From the corner of his eye, he saw Harper watching them, her gaze traveling from his face to Luca's and back again like a spectator at Wimbledon. "That's an outrageous accusation."

"Is it? I mean you were awfully damn quick to point the finger at me."

Conor put his hands on his hips. "So now you're accusing me of insurance fraud to get even?"

Luca stared at him, completely unrepentant. "You accused me of incompetence. Doesn't feel so good, does it?"

Conor should have seen this coming. While his brothers had been more than ready to put their stupid generations-long hatred toward the Morettis to rest, both men thinking with their dicks and hearts rather than their heads, Conor hadn't been quite so convinced, wondering if there was simply too much water under this particular bridge.

The problem was Conor and his big mouth, offering the job on a fucking whim, after a rare, enjoyable night out. He never did that. And once the horse was out of the gate, he couldn't call it back because Gage and Matt believed Russo Enterprises working with Moretti Brothers Restorations felt like the next logical step in cementing the peace between the two families. Which meant, he was stuck trying to sort out old-as-shit emotions regarding Luca as well as fighting back some next-level arousal...all while dealing with a ticking time bomb in his head.

His anxiety had been sky-high all day as he approached this meeting.

Luca had been handsome and charming as hell in high school, and those characteristics had only grown since then. Which was why Conor should have held the company line and gone with another construction crew. Now he was standing here, starting to feel the too-familiar pressure on his chest that told him he was in danger of suffering a panic attack, but he couldn't walk away in the midst of this mess, couldn't resort to his old tried and true.

Escape.

*Fuck.*

This... This was why he kept to himself, maintained familiar routines, avoided stressful situations.

His panic attacks had begun when he was much younger, the first hitting when he was twelve. His mom had been going through one of her dark periods, her mood sending her to bed for days. Conor hadn't been able to concentrate enough to study for one of his tests because he hated it when Mom disappeared to her room. While she was in the house physically, mentally she had checked out, and none of them were allowed to talk about it, expected to act as if everything was normal.

Dad had read Conor the riot act for getting an F, calling him an embarrassment, reminding him that Russos didn't fail. Then he'd sent Conor to bed without dinner. In his room, he had succumbed to a heart-thumping, chest-tightening, trembling pain that was unrelenting. He'd curled into a ball on the floor, fighting to breathe, certain he was suffocating to death.

At the time, he'd wondered how long it would take before anyone found his dead body. When he finally managed to catch his breath, he'd crawled into bed and slept for twelve hours straight. He hadn't understood what had happened that night, but he was nothing if not resourceful.

Always a reader, he'd gone to the school library and checked out a book on mental illness, terrified that perhaps he was suffering from the same thing as his mother. It had been the first time he'd been able to attach a name to his mother's illness.

Depression.

The library book had contained a wealth of information on not only depression but on panic attacks as well.

Conor had been too ashamed to admit his own mental illness to his mom or brothers, so whenever he felt the telltale shortness of breath or the constriction of his chest muscles, he—like his mom—took to his room, hiding there until the worst of it had passed. It worked for him because he'd always been a big reader, so his family never thought anything of it, always assuming he had his nose buried in one of his books. They'd begun to refer to him as a loner, and he preferred they believe that rather than know the truth.

In the business realm, he was a no-nonsense ball-buster, a man capable of getting exactly what he wanted as long as he held all the power, all the control. He'd never mastered the art of teamwork.

However, none of that confidence translated to his personal life. Because when emotions came into play and things got tough, Conor was very adept at disappearing.

Working with Moretti Brothers *was* a smart business decision, Conor knew that. The problem was it crossed into a gray area with Luca involved because the work and his fucked-up feelings were overlapping.

He rubbed his chest and tried to take a deep breath, hoping neither Luca nor Harper noticed. "This was a bad idea, Luca. I'll admit, I had my reservations about the two of us working on this project together and this proves that it was a mistake."

Luca rolled his eyes. "Fucking hell, Conor. That didn't take long."

"What didn't?" Conor asked.

"You finding a way to avoid working with me. You've been pulling this shit since high school. I don't know what the hell I did to you, but enough is enough. What is it about me that bugs you so much?"

Conor didn't know how to reply to that. He'd always felt as invisible to Luca as he did to the rest of the world. It never occurred to him that Luca might actually recognize the distance Conor had kept between them all these years.

Before he could respond, another Moretti approached.

Aldo, Luca's cousin, was one of the firemen fighting the blaze. "Hey, Luca, Conor. Thought I'd let you know the fire is out."

The Moretti family was a large, tight-knit group, and Conor had come to learn that every relative seemed to know what every other relative was doing, so it was no surprise Aldo knew he and Luca both had ties to the building.

"That's good," Luca said.

"It was mostly contained to the kitchen in back. The fire marshal is walking through right now to determine how it started. Might take a few hours, though."

"How bad is it?" Luca asked.

"Well, someone with a higher pay grade than me—the code inspector—will have the final say-so, but I don't think there was a significant amount of structural damage. That'll be a good thing in terms of moving forward with construction," Aldo explained. "Unfortunately, the code inspector works a nine-to-five, so I wouldn't look for any decision on that until next week...if you're lucky."

Luca placed his hand on Aldo's shoulder and gave it a squeeze. "Thanks, man. That sounds like as good a news as we were going to get."

Aldo smiled, then turned his attention to Harper. "Just wanted to take a minute to say I'm a big fan, Ms. Branson," he said, his white teeth shining bright when contrasted by the black soot on his handsome face. The Morettis were graced with damn fine Italian genes, every single male in the family undeniably attractive, every woman beautiful.

"Please, call me Harper," she replied, batting her eyes and flashing the fireman a gorgeous smile of her own, thanking Aldo for his help in fighting the fire. Conor didn't know her well, but it didn't take a genius to see she was flirting with the man.

Aldo headed back across the street, but before Conor and Luca could continue their argument, another man approached, this one with a McDonald's bag and a large soda.

"Ms. Branson? Wow! It really is you. When your name and order came across the app, I thought it had to be a joke."

Harper turned around, lighting up when she saw the guy, who was blushing. "You found me. I wasn't sure you would, considering all I offered you was 'sidewalk outside a burning building' and the street name."

The Door Dash driver laughed. "I figured if it really was you, it wouldn't be that hard. All I had to do was walk toward the fire trucks."

She reached into her purse and pulled out a ten-dollar bill, handing the tip to him. "Thanks so much."

"Do you think I could take a selfie with you?" the delivery man asked.

"Sure," Harper agreed, and the two of them smiled widely, mugging for the camera as the young guy snapped the pic with his phone.

"Wicked. Enjoy your food." He waved as he walked away, clearly thrilled to have met a celebrity.

Harper carried her food over to the curb, plopping down and opening the bag. Pulling out a burger, she opened the box, taking a huge bite and moaning loudly. "Oh my God. This is the best burger I've ever had."

Distracted by her behavior—and grateful for the brief reprieve from his argument with Luca—Conor stepped over to her. "That's a Quarter Pounder with Cheese, Harper," he said, as she continued to shove the burger into her mouth. "I promise you, this city is filled with countless burgers that are much better."

She snorted. "I've had an *almond* since yesterday at

lunchtime. Not to mention the fact I've been on a crash diet for the last month in the lead-up to this morning's photo shoot."

Luca dropped down next to her on the curb. "An almond? As in *one*?"

Harper nodded. "I needed to lose twenty pounds prior to this shoot. I only managed to drop fifteen. So, after much discussion this morning—which is why I got here so late—the photographer decided to go with beauty shots."

At his and Luca's blank expressions, she explained. "From the neck up. Which means all my dieting was for naught. Fuckers," she grumbled.

"Let me get this straight," Luca said. "You show up here, discover your building is on fire, and your first thought was to open up the Door Dash app and order McDonald's?"

"Yep," she replied as she ate the last bite of cheeseburger, licking ketchup off her fingers. "Wasn't sure dinner was still going to happen, and I was too hungry to wait anyway."

"Jesus," Luca muttered. "Did you chew that thing?"

Harper laughed. "It's called inhaling for a reason."

Conor had been surprised when Harper contacted him out of the blue a year and a half earlier. She'd gotten his name through the friend of a friend, who had kindly praised him as an excellent restauranteur and a great contact about the city, since she'd set her sights on Philadelphia for her venture.

He'd hesitantly agreed to a phone call, not expecting much to come of it. He'd never taken on a business partner before, preferring to be the one who called all the shots when it came to his investments. However, one conversation in, and he'd been instantly taken by the woman, who wasn't anything like he had expected.

When he'd learned a supermodel wanted to open her own restaurant, Conor had assumed she was just looking for a way to capitalize on her name once the modeling gigs began to dry up. He'd gone full stereotype in his mind, expecting a rich, spoiled, vain diva. What he'd gotten was a woman who matched her brand perfectly. She was down-to-earth, witty, and she'd proven herself to be intelligent and hard-working as well.

He'd been impressed to discover that she was going to culinary school, not just to study cooking but to also earn a degree in restaurant management at the Institute of Culinary Education. She was keen to learn everything she could, and after a fifteen-minute conversation, he'd genuinely believed her when she said working as a chef in her own restaurant was her dream job.

Conor had always thought she was drop-dead gorgeous, but as he got to know her better, he realized she was even more beautiful inside.

"Did you get fries?" Luca attempted to peek into the bag.

Harper slapped his hand away. "Refer back to my earlier statement about one almond."

Conor didn't like looming over them, so he took a seat on the curb next to Harper.

"So," she said after taking a sip of soda. "Let me see if I've got this straight. We're currently dealing with a burned-out building, incompetence, *and* insurance fraud."

Neither he nor Luca responded. Conor felt like an ass for his earlier allegations. Luca hadn't been wrong when he'd accused him of looking for a way out. That was exactly what he'd intended.

"And a lifelong family feud," she added.

Luca grimaced, while Conor rubbed his jaw, but again, neither of them answered.

"Fine. We'll tackle all that shit later. First things first. Because there's a more important issue to address," she said.

Conor wondered what the hell could be more important than the fire and he and Luca being at odds.

"What can you tell me about that gorgeous firefighter?" Harper nodded her head toward Aldo as she pulled out a large order of fries with a shit-eating grin.

Luca laughed. "He's my cousin, Aldo, and he's got a girlfriend." Then he pointed in Aldo's direction, where he and Kayden were standing close, talking. "And a boyfriend."

"Damn," Harper mused. "That's hot as shit." She tipped the carton of fries toward Luca, who grabbed a couple and shoved them in his mouth quickly.

Then she offered them to Conor. He sighed, taking one and eating it. He couldn't recall the last time he'd had McDonald's, though he knew he was counting in years, not months. Regardless, it was a damn good fry, so he reached for another.

Harper stuffed three fries into her mouth as she stared across the street at Aldo and sighed heavily. "Sounds like we're all having a shitty night. I could use a beer."

Luca exchanged a glance with him before talking to Harper. "Me too. There's a quiet pub next block over. That cheeseburger looked good. Might get one of my own if you'd like some company."

Harper perked up. "Oooo...a pub sounds good. Do you know if they serve dessert? I could go for a piece of pie or cake or maybe an ice cream sundae."

Luca chuckled as he clutched his heart. "Beer and dessert? Harper, you are my kind of woman."

Harper leaned toward Luca and bumped her shoulder against his in a friendly manner. Conor swallowed hard, struggling to sit here and watch Luca and Harper flirt with each other. This was probably the point where he should excuse himself, let the two of them—

"What do you say, Conor?" Harper asked.

She was giving him that famous smile, and Conor felt the first tingles of...something he should *not* be feeling for his new business partner.

Then Luca looked at him in such a way that Conor knew the other man expected him to turn down the invitation. Maybe he was even *hoping* that he would. It felt like a dare Conor couldn't resist.

If he was smart, he'd bail.

On fucking all of it.

The pub and the project.

Luca continued to stare him down.

*Russos aren't weak.*

*Russos don't fail.*

Those words were the mantra that had played in his head for most of his life. Always spoken in his father's voice.

For the first time in forever, Conor didn't want to escape. He was tired of being alone. Tonight, he wanted to be a part of something, even if it was just burgers and beers at a pub.

"I'm in."

Those two words elicited two very different reactions from his partners. Delight on Harper's part, disbelief on Luca's.

"Great." Luca stood and dusted off the seat of his jeans, drawing Conor's attention to his very sexy ass. "I'll go tell Aldo we're heading out together and get him to call me when the inspector figures out what started the fire."

Conor rose as well, offering a hand to help Harper up as Luca jogged across the street to talk to his cousin.

Harper tossed her trash into one of the city bins, the two of them standing next to each other on the sidewalk as they waited.

When Luca returned, he asked, "You two ready?"

Harper nodded and the three of them walked together to the pub.

As far as nights went, Conor had to admit, this one had been un-fucking-believable.

And it wasn't even over yet.

# Chapter Two

Harper walked between Conor and Luca as they headed to the pub, discreetly trying to take stock of the two men. She'd met Conor in person before and had gotten to know him a little, so she felt a bit more comfortable with him. He was a tall, handsome man, his medium-brown hair cut stylishly, longer on top, shorter in the back and on the sides. He had a well-trimmed beard that she found ridiculously sexy. He wasn't overly muscular, though he was fit.

During their previous meetings, he'd always worn a bespoke suit with solid-color silk ties—as if a pattern would simply be too wild for him. Everything he wore screamed wealth, though she didn't think that was his intent. Instead, it felt as if he'd discovered his style at some point in time and just stuck with it for ease and comfort's sake. Tonight, he'd broken the pattern, but only barely, opting for black dress slacks and a crisp white button-down shirt, sans tie, which meant he'd left the top two buttons undone, giving her the tiniest peek at his throat and sternum. No visible tats on the straitlaced businessman. No surprise there.

While she'd seen Luca on the computer screen, he'd been relegated to one tiny square during the video chats. The man really needed a lesson in backlighting because the window behind his desk meant he'd always been more silhouette than detail. That small square hadn't kept her from figuring out the guy was built with a capital B, but she hadn't realized just how large he'd be...or how fucking gorgeous.

She wasn't a short woman—five-eight before heels—but his size dwarfed hers, something she'd rarely experienced. Luca's broad shoulders, thick arms, and calloused fingers revealed a man who worked with his hands, and worked hard. His skin was a darker tan than Conor's, though both men boasted of Italian genes, which had granted them that lovely olive skin tone she loved.

Luca also sported a beard, but his was thicker and more unruly than Conor's, though his hair was shorter. Luca was probably one of those guys who owned his own set of clippers and he just slapped on the same guard every time and went for it in front of his bathroom mirror.

While Conor was dressed up, Luca wore loose-fitting jeans that were almost too well broken in and a basic black T-shirt that wasn't overly tight. She hated those men who bought their shirts a size too small thinking it made them look more buff. Luca didn't have to resort to smoke and mirrors because he was the definition of strapping.

She had noticed tattoos peeking out of his shirt sleeves during their meetings, but she hadn't realized quite how colorful or extensive they were. Luca had full-sleeve tats on both arms, intricate, heavy patterns in black, gray, and red. She'd always been a sucker for tattoos, and Luca's looked utterly lickable.

They'd just turned a corner, the sign for the pub Luca had suggested halfway down the block, when her phone rang. Harper pulled it out of her purse and sighed. It was her first night of freedom and she kind of wanted to keep it that way. For a moment, she considered letting the call go to voicemail, but she knew Bradley Renner, her manager—former manager—was probably just making sure she'd arrived okay.

"I need to take this," she said to Luca and Conor, who politely moved a few steps ahead of her, giving her some privacy. "Hey, Bradley."

"Hello, Harper. I wanted to see if you got there safely."

"I sure did," she replied. "Traffic was a beast getting out of the city, but once I hit Jersey, it let up."

"That was my fault," Bradley admitted. "I'm still not sure we should have gone with headshots. Maybe I should talk to the client and see if—"

"The client was perfectly happy with the shots we got."

For most of her career, she'd deferred to her ambitious manager because their goals had lined up. She'd wanted to be a supermodel, and he'd wanted to get her there. It was the perfect working relationship.

"You're right. They were happy. I'm dropping it." She could hear the smile in his voice.

"Wow. I'm seeing real growth here, Mr. Perfectionist."

Bradley chuckled. "Haha. Is everything good with the restaurant?"

"Yep," Harper lied. There was no way in hell she was telling Bradley about the fire. He would probably take it as some omen that her new venture was destined to fail.

As soon as she thought it, she felt guilty. Yes, Bradley had worked overtime to convince her to change her mind once she decided to leave modeling, but when she graduated from culinary school, he realized how serious she was, and since then had been her biggest cheerleader—after Mom and Luna.

"The restaurant is absolutely perfect. Everything is terrific."

She noticed both Luca and Conor slow down a bit, Conor even glancing over his shoulder at her. So much for privacy.

She gave him a one-shoulder shrug and a no-big-deal look, and he turned back around. "Listen, I'm on my way to dinner with Luca and Conor. My contractor and business partner," she clarified, though she'd said their names to Bradley before. "Why don't I call you in a week or so when I'm more settled and we can chat longer?"

"Okay," Bradley said. "Sounds good."

"Talk to you soon."

"Goodbye, Harper."

"Everything okay?" Luca asked as they walked inside, and a hostess led them to a booth near the back. It was a Saturday night, and the pub was doing a great business.

"Yep. Just the standard 'did you get there in one piece' call from my former manager. We've been in each other's faces since I was fifteen, him always hovering over me like a mother hen, so I guess old habits die hard." She slid into the booth, unsurprised when Luca followed her in, Conor claiming the bench seat opposite. She'd gotten the sense early on in their video chats that Luca Moretti was a charmer, a true ladies' man.

Why wouldn't he be? The guy had the face and body to back up those actions. Harper would have to be dead not to notice the sex appeal that oozed from him, and she was *not* dead.

Luca placed his arm along the back of the booth, turning his body slightly toward her, while giving her a sinfully seductive smile.

She was amused by his flirting, but she wasn't susceptible to it.

After too many years as a model, living a life most people only dreamed of, she'd been the recipient of every kind of flirting known to man. She'd had men wine and dine her, cover her in jewelry, surround her with dozens and dozens of roses, attempt to seduce her with their handsome faces and sweet words and a whole bunch of other shit that wasn't real.

Harper had been kicked enough in the love department to know she would be smart to give it a wide berth while she focused her energy on opening the restaurant.

If anyone were to look at her Wikipedia page, they'd see what might look like an impressive list of former lovers—a rock star, a billionaire, a couple of actors, even a prince. What *wasn't* on the page was the ugly truth behind every single one of those "power couple" romances.

Nowhere did that story of her life include the pain she'd gone through at the hands of men who had broken her trust.

"What can I get you?" the waitress asked as she stopped by their table.

"I'll have a PBR," Luca said. "And a cheeseburger and fries." Glancing at Harper, he added, "Someone was stingy when it came to sharing theirs."

She laughed but offered no apology, and even though she'd plowed through the Quarter Pounder, she was still hungry. "Do you have onion rings?" she asked the waitress, who nodded. "Great. I'll have an order of those and a vodka tonic."

"I'll have a cab sav," Conor said, before pointing toward Luca. "And another cheeseburger with fries."

The waitress left to fill their order, and Harper leaned back, sighing deeply.

"Still hungry?" Luca asked.

"I've been hungry my entire life, on a diet since before I learned to walk."

Conor winced. "That sounds miserable."

"It's why I wanted to go to culinary school. Too many years of living without. I decided after modeling, I'd never diet again. Food has always been uncharted territory, literally the forbidden fruit, and the more time I spent without it, the more I craved it. A few years ago, my mom got me a gift certificate to do one of those two-hour cooking classes with her. We made tamales and loved it so much, we signed up for three more classes."

What Harper *didn't* say was, that initial class happened after she'd collapsed following a photo shoot. Mom's eyes had been opened wide to the stress Harper had been putting on herself, and she'd put her foot down—with Harper *and* Bradley—insisting that her grueling schedule be pared down.

Harper hadn't exactly been grateful with Mom's interference at the time, but looking back now, she was fairly certain Mom had saved her life. Harper had been pushing herself to dangerous extremes, and the collapse had been her wake-up call.

"After those classes, I became obsessed with cooking." Harper had gotten very good at sharing this abridged version of her life, repeating this same tale to countless reporters and late-night TV hosts after announcing her retirement from modeling. No one, with the exception of herself, Mom, Bradley, and the medical staff at a private hospital, knew about her collapse. "One night, I was out with my best friend, Luna, and she asked if I'd ever considered going to culinary school. Just like that, the light went on, and I suddenly knew what I wanted my future to be."

The waitress returned with their drinks.

Conor raised his glass of wine. "To second careers. For what it's worth, I think you'll be an amazing chef."

Harper smiled, tapping her glass against his, then Luca's. "Thanks."

Luca took a swig of his beer. "You know, if you're interested in learning more about cooking Italian food, I can introduce you to the OG of pasta."

"OG of pasta?" she asked with a laugh. "Sounds like there might be a waiting list to meet someone that important."

"I've got an in," Luca said, his wide grin infectious. "Nonna loves to cook and loves to *talk* about cooking. Her eggplant parmesan is the greatest food on the planet. Takes her days to prepare it, so we usually only get it on special occasions. My brothers and I swear we want it to be our last meal before we die. Because one bite of that, and anyone would die a happy man."

Harper didn't know Luca well enough to know if he was joking about the invitation, but she wasn't about to turn down the offer. "I would love to meet your nonna. Italian cuisine was one of my favorite things to make at the institute. I bet she has all the old-school tricks when it comes to homemade pasta."

"You bet your sweet ass she does," Luca said, grinning. "And believe me, I have no ulterior motives. None at all. I mean...obviously if you make the eggplant parmesan, you'll need someone to sample it, and while I don't like to brag, I *am* known for being a humble, giving man, so I volunteer as tribute."

Harper snorted. "I must admit, you do seem quite humble, and it would be a very selfless act, eating your favorite food as a favor to me."

Luca leaned back, his arm still resting along the bench behind her as he sighed dramatically. "Just the kind of man I am."

"Homemade pasta sounds like a lot of work," Conor murmured.

Harper got the impression he didn't like their contractor flirting with her, which made sense. For the immediate future, Luca was basically their employee.

Conor struck her as the kind of guy who did not mix work and play, but he didn't know her well enough to know she was in no danger of succumbing to Luca's charms.

"No good Italian nonna would buy noodles in a box." Luca crossed himself as if simply using the words "noodles" and "box" in the same sentence was a sacrilege.

Harper leaned back, sighing blissfully, as it finally sank in that she was here. She'd done it, made the switch from model to chef. This moment had been the light at the end of the tunnel for so long, she'd started to think she would never make it. "I can't tell you how happy I am."

"Happy?" Conor asked, clearly surprised, given the way the night had gone.

She waved her hand. "I mean the fire thing sucks, but it sounds like the building is okay. Hopefully this won't set us back too far."

"From what Aldo said," Luca chimed in, "we should be okay."

Harper smiled at him, then looked back at Conor. "As for being happy, I was referring to finally being here in Philadelphia. Tonight is the first night of the rest of my life. I've been counting down to this day for years."

"Really?" Luca asked.

"Yep. Because I'm doing exactly what I want to do."

Luca frowned. "You didn't want to be a model."

Harper wasn't sure how to answer that question. Of course, she had the standard line, the polished one, but when she spoke, those weren't the words that came out.

"Modeling wasn't exactly a choice I made. It's not like I said I want to grow up to be a model. It was just what I was. My mom put me in a beautiful baby contest five seconds after I was born, then in pageants. That evolved into commercials, then photo shoots, then walking the runway, followed by big contract deals. I did love it. All the attention, the traveling. It was exciting, and then…"

"And then?" Conor asked.

Harper's answer to *that* wasn't simple…and it occurred to her she'd taken this conversation too far off course. "It wasn't," she admitted. "There was a lot of pressure to always be perfect, always be *on*, always be spotlight-ready. My manager had created a very definite Harper brand, and I was expected to live up to it."

"Girl next door," Luca added.

She rolled her eyes. "Yep. Harper Branson, the fresh-faced, smiling, pleasant, upbeat girl everyone wants to be friends with."

Conor frowned. "I don't mean to upset you, but we've had a lot of conversations, and you do strike me as a very positive person."

She laughed. "To be honest, I am. Bradley didn't mold a bitch into a nice girl. He worked with what he had. The trouble is, it's hard to always be happy, you know? I have sad days just like everyone. Or days where I was stressed out and preoccupied. Or even just days when I got out of bed on the wrong side and felt grumpy. I had to smile through all those days."

Luca took a sip of his beer. "That would suck."

"Yep. I had to weigh a certain weight, smile that smile, and be the person everyone expected rather than the person I was that day." Harper picked up her drink and took a large gulp, just to stop herself from talking. "Wow. That was a lot of oversharing for the first night. Sorry about that."

"I don't mind," Luca said sincerely.

She gave him a grateful smile, chalking up her loose lips up to the fact she was overtired from the long, traffic-riddled drive here, over-giddy—she hadn't lied about how good that Quarter Pounder tasted—and uncharacteristically comfortable with these two men, who were essentially strangers.

In her mind, they represented the realization of a dream, so she was acting way too familiar with them, too quickly. "Anyway," she said, aware it was time to change the subject, "I just realized I was ready for the next big challenge, for something different."

If there was one thing she'd learned the hard way, it was to play her cards close to her chest. Being a celebrity came with a price, one that meant well-meaning friends weren't always as sincere as she thought, using her renown to make money by selling her story to the tabloids or to steal a few minutes of fame for themselves. Which was another reason why she was surprising herself by being so open and honest. "I guess what I'm just trying to say is that I'm really happy to be embarking on this next chapter in my life."

"I'm glad we're going to be a part of it," Conor said.

Harper had picked up bits and pieces of her dinner companions' personalities through their Zoom meetings, things like Luca's charm and wit, and Conor's serious nature and intelligence. Luca laughed easily and she'd enjoyed his sense of humor as much as she was impressed by his expertise and vision when it came to bringing her dream restaurant to life.

Conor, in some ways, was Luca's polar opposite. Managing to provoke a smile from Conor felt like a bigger deal, more like an accomplishment, because he didn't smile much. Not that he came across as grumpy or miserable. He was a brilliant businessman, and while they were partners in this venture—fifty-fifty—he'd felt more like her mentor this last year, answering her countless questions about running a restaurant and about the city. He was patient and kind, though a bit too quiet for her rather boisterous personality.

What she hadn't picked up on during any of their previous conversations was the tension that seemed to simmer between the two men. That hadn't been apparent over Zoom at all. To be honest, she never would have guessed Luca and Conor had any association prior to this project. She'd thought they were strangers when the work had begun, so discovering some long-standing feud and deep-seated animosity had taken her by surprise.

She was tempted to pick up the conversation Aldo, the gorgeous firefighter, had interrupted earlier, but she decided to wait until after the onion rings were delivered. She was still hungry and didn't want to take a chance they'd both storm off. She hated eating alone.

However, she *was* going to address it because Harper had been the type to let sleeping dogs lie in her past—always deferring to Bradley, her mom, her clients, her fans—but she was turning over a new leaf in Philadelphia. She'd spent the first twenty-nine years of her life, tiptoeing around everyone's feelings at the expense of her own. Those days were over.

She was hopeful whatever had transpired between them, Luca and Conor could clear the air. She wasn't interested in dealing with two men at each other's throats throughout this entire project, so they needed to make peace. Perhaps it was the stress of the fire that had provoked the argument and now that things didn't seem quite so dire, cooler heads would prevail.

"How far back do you think the fire will set us?" she asked Luca when the silence at the table drifted a bit too long.

Luca took a quick swig of his beer. "No way of knowing before the code inspector checks out the building. If there's minimal structural damage, then hopefully we can get right back to work. Sounds like the kitchen took the worst of it, but there will be smoke damage throughout and that's a bitch to deal with."

"Nothing on the top two floors had been touched, and since the plan was to gut them once the restaurant renovation was complete, we've lost nothing there," Conor added, before looking in Harper's direction. "You sure you don't want us to move the timeline up on the apartment overhaul? Maybe we could hire a second construction company to tackle that project."

Luca frowned. "We have other crews, one of which is near the end of their current project. Once they're finished, I can move them over to work on the apartment above. And if you're tied to the current timeline as far as the restaurant goes, we can always hire temps, get more people in place to complete the work."

Conor nodded. "Let's talk about doing that," he said to Luca, before turning back to her. "Otherwise, you could be in that hotel for a while."

Harper shook her head. "My number one priority is finishing the restaurant, getting it up and running. You've set me up in a beautiful hotel suite with a kitchenette and comfortable living area, so it's not like I'm roughing in. Unless—"

Conor held up his hand. "You can stay in that hotel as long as you need. That's not a concern on my end. I just want to make sure you'll be comfortable."

"I'll be fine," she reassured him. "Thank you."

When they'd purchased the building, Harper had expressed an interest in taking over the top two floors for her own living accommodations. She'd been happy when Conor had readily agreed. During one of their countless phone conversations, they'd discussed construction timelines, which indicated—pre-fire—that she didn't need to sign a full-year lease on an apartment.

Conor had surprised her by coming up with an easy, flexible solution. Russo Enterprises owned several five-star hotels in the city, and he'd offered to set her up in one of the suites for the duration of the construction work. The offer had been too good to pass on. So she'd put her furniture in storage, and her car, currently parked two blocks over, was packed to the gills with her clothing, toiletries, and other personal items she couldn't live without until her apartment was ready to move into.

"You didn't tell your manager about the fire," Conor pointed out.

"Yeah, that wasn't a conversation I wanted to get into. It's taken some time—a lot of it—to get my manager on board with my career switch," she said. "I mean, obviously he's taking a hit money-wise by losing me as a client, so it makes sense. He owns his own agency, but I brought in the lion's share of the revenue. Twenty percent of seven-figure deals is sweet. Twenty percent of five figures is less so."

"I guess I can see where he'd be sorry to lose you," Luca murmured.

Harper blew out a long breath. "Bradley was rather insistent that the clock hadn't run out on my modeling career, and even when it did, he was ready for the next phase."

"Which was?" Luca asked.

Harper groaned. "Television."

Conor had lifted his glass to take a sip of his wine but stopped midway. "Do you act?"

She snorted. "God, no. I wish I did because acting in an actual show would be better than Bradley's ideas."

Luca grinned. "Do I want to ask?"

"He thought I would make a great judge on one of those competitive talent shows. Or I could be a celebrity on a reality show. Can you see me living in Big Brother's house? Just the prospect makes me want to throw up. I have no interest in doing anything like that."

"I don't know," Luca said, his shit-eating grin letting her in on his joke before he launched it. "Now that you've gone to culinary school, you could try to score yourself a show on the Food Network, maybe become the next Martha Stewart or Pioneer Woman."

She pointed her finger at Luca. "Never say those words again," she said, feigning an angry voice, though the fact her lips were quirking up at the ends gave her away. "I don't mean to bitch about Bradley. To be honest, while it took him some time to come around, he's actually been really supportive the last few months, interested in the restaurant and my plans for it."

"I'm glad to hear that," Conor said.

"I've spent the first twenty-nine years of my life under a spotlight. Now I'm ready to spend some time in the background, or more specifically, in the kitchen, making culinary masterpieces."

Luca lifted his beer, tapping it against her glass. "Sounds like a plan."

The food arrived, so they dug in, their conversation turning to easier things, like Luca's insistence that Harper—now a Philadelphia resident—change her sporting team allegiance. He hadn't liked hearing she was a Yankees fan at all. Of course, she was sort of overplaying her devotion to the team simply to get a rise out of him. Watching paint dry held more appeal to her than sitting through an endless baseball game.

Conor hadn't chimed in once during their discussion, so she assumed he didn't care for sports any more than she did. Something he confirmed when he changed the subject and started talking about the latest book he was reading.

Harper had just wiped the grease off her fingers after devouring the greatest onion rings she'd ever eaten—God, she really had been starving—when Luca's phone rang.

Glancing at the screen, he said, "It's Aldo." He answered immediately, all of them anxious to know what had started the fire.

"Hey, man. What did the inspector find?" Luca listened for a moment, his brows furrowing. "How the hell did that get there?"

Harper exchanged a glance with Conor, who was clearly as confused as she was.

"Of *course* I didn't put it there. It's a construction site. Jesus, I don't use space heaters anywhere."

*Space heater?*

"A squatter?" Luca said, clearly repeating something Aldo had said. "I guess it's possible. Today was our first break in the weather. It's been downright cold the last few nights, but there was no indication that someone had broken in when I was working this morning. Was there any sign of forced entry?"

Luca listened for a moment, then sighed. "Oh, I see. Okay. Yeah, thanks for letting me know." He ended the call. "I guess you guys heard."

"The fire was caused by a space heater," Conor clarified.

"And you didn't put it there," Harper added.

"I didn't. Apparently, it was found in the cellar beneath the kitchen. I've only been down there once—when we did the initial walk-through on the building a couple of months ago."

"I haven't been down there either," Conor confessed.

Harper considered the cellar. It had been pretty bare bones, the pizza parlor that had owned the building prior to them using it the same way she intended to.

As storage.

It was one of the places they hadn't intended to do any renovations.

"I only put in a few hours today, knocking off at noon since it's Saturday and I knew we were meeting later tonight. I wanted to do a full inspection of the wiring, and that's easier to do when there aren't a bunch of guys around," Luca went on to explain. "Didn't have a chance to check out the cellar below. Didn't consider it a top priority."

"Inspection," Conor said. "*Just* an inspection?"

Luca smirked. "It took several hours, so I didn't get around to starting any of the new wiring we'd discussed."

Conor sighed. "I see."

"Aldo suggested there might have been a squatter?" Harper asked.

Luca nodded. "He and the fire marshal think that maybe a homeless person had set up a nest down there. No way to tell if there'd been a forced entry because the fire destroyed any evidence of that."

Conor rubbed his forehead. "There's not exactly a shortage of homeless people in Philadelphia. It's probably not a bad guess."

"Yeah. According to Aldo, Kayden said there's been a record high as far as break-ins this winter. He said it's not uncommon for homeless people to seek shelter in abandoned buildings. The pizza parlor's been closed for a while now, so that wouldn't have gone unnoticed."

"Maybe not, but you and your crew have also been working there for a week," Conor pointed out.

Luca grimaced. "True. But, like I said, we haven't gone down in the cellar and there's only an outdoor entrance to it. If someone had found a way in, they could be sleeping there at night and hightailing it out before we start work each morning. At least now you know it wasn't an electrical issue." Luca gave Conor a pointed look. "As for the other thing..."

Conor rolled his eyes, though there wasn't any heat behind the expression. "I did not set a fire with a space heater for insurance money or to destroy the Moretti reputation."

It had been obvious to Harper back at the restaurant, and again now, that Luca hadn't really believed that either.

"Okay," Luca drawled. "I believe you."

Harper wasn't sure, but it looked like a tentative peace was shifting into place. Or it *had*. Until she opened her big mouth.

"Looks like you were both wrong. Only thing left for you to do now is kiss and make up."

It felt like an innocuous enough statement, a humorous one that she'd expected to break the tension.

Boy, was she wrong.

Conor froze, staring at Luca in a way that...

*Oh.*

*Well.*

*Wow.*

"Um," she murmured, feeling very much like she'd just stepped into a big pile of shit, while Luca appeared oblivious to the hornet's nest she'd just kicked.

Meanwhile, Conor completely shut down. She'd never seen anyone go so utterly...blank.

Then he rubbed his chest while glancing down at his phone. "It's later than I thought. I need to stop by Enigma to grab some paperwork before heading home." He suddenly resembled the rabbit in *Alice in Wonderland* who was late for a very important date. Especially when he slid out of the booth and pulled his wallet from his back pocket. Sliding out several twenties, he tossed them in the middle of the table. "That should cover my share of the tab."

And hers, and probably Luca's too, she considered, as she counted the twenties.

"Conor," she started, but he'd already tucked his wallet and phone away.

"I'll call the code inspector on Monday, see if I can grease a few palms to get him to the construction site sooner rather than later." Conor didn't make eye contact with her or Luca.

She felt like she should say something but realized she would probably be wiser to keep her mouth shut until she got to know these men better. She'd already shoved one foot in there. She didn't want to go for two. Hungry or not.

"Okay." Luca took Conor's hasty retreat in stride. Until Conor rubbed his chest again, the action capturing Luca's attention, then he studied Conor's face—hard.

There was some history at play between these two men that felt like more than family animosity.

Conor glanced at Luca, his poker face slipping slightly, the tiniest glimmer of...pain?...sadness?...flashing in his eyes.

Luca's expression softened. "You don't have to run off."

"I'm not running," Conor said too quickly, almost breathlessly. He didn't bother to say goodbye as he turned and left the pub.

"I..." Harper started, only two words felt right, though she didn't know why. Regardless, she said them. "I'm sorry."

Luca turned her direction. "For what?"

She gave him a rueful smirk. "I was hoping you wouldn't ask me that because I have no idea."

Luca—God bless him—laughed, the tension of the past few minutes dispelled.

"Don't feel so bad," he said. "I'm feeling the need to apologize too."

"To Conor?"

He nodded. "Yep. And like you, I have no idea why."

# *Chapter Three*

Luca glanced at the big-screen TV behind the bar and realized he wasn't as into the Phillies game as his drinking buddies were.

Typically, he was an early riser, even on the weekends, as Saturday and Sunday were the only time he could get his personal chores done. He'd lived alone for a decade in a two-bedroom apartment that wasn't particularly large, but big enough for him. And while he wouldn't call himself a neat freak, he also wasn't a fucking slob like his brother Joey. As such, he always dedicated a few hours of every weekend to mundane shit like laundry, vacuuming, dusting, and scrubbing the damn toilet.

Yesterday had been a wash as far as doing chores because he'd opted to put in a few hours at the construction site, doing an inspection of electrical wiring in the restaurant. A task that had been a big waste of time, considering it had all gone up in flames hours later.

He'd intended to tackle the housework today, but he'd had an uncharacteristically slow start to the morning, lying in bed until well after ten, something unheard of in his life. His alarm went off at five a.m. every weekday, and while he didn't set one on the weekends, he was still up and out of bed by at least seven.

So the fact he couldn't drag his ass out of bed told him last night's events had bothered him more than he'd realized. After Conor practically sprinted out of the pub, he and Harper had remained for another hour, the two of them chatting easily. She was an interesting conversationalist, capable of telling very entertaining stories. She'd kept him in stitches as she shared some of her past experiences, discussing some of the catfights between models, laughing about practical jokes she'd played—and had played on her—then she described some of the more outlandish outfits she'd had to wear.

After a while, they'd wound up talking about some of their favorite vacations. While she'd adored Paris and Lake Como and Portugal, Luca's travels had all been on American soil, as he'd been steadily working his way through seeing as many National Parks as he could. He admitted to his love of hiking and camping, while Harper looked thoroughly horrified by the prospect of sleeping on the ground and walking up mountains.

When Tony had shown up at the office a few months earlier, informing Luca, Gio, and Joey that they'd landed a job working on Harper Branson's restaurant, Luca had quickly dibsed the role of project manager.

Because...it was *Harper Branson*. He, like half the men in the world, had fallen a little bit in love with her over the years based simply on that smile, which was even better in person.

Luca had lived in Philadelphia his entire life, so the opportunity to work with an actual celebrity, someone who was practically a household name, had been too exciting to pass up. And while Harper *was* incredibly beautiful, last night he'd become an even bigger fan, not based on her looks but her personality.

His plans to tackle his chores today fell apart completely when his brother Joey called and invited him to join him and his best friend, Miles, at a sports bar for a pitcher of beer, some wings, and the Phillies game. Before he could put his adulting hat on, staying in to do the laundry he was going to regret skipping come Wednesday when he ran out of clean boxers, he agreed.

Now, in hindsight, he could see it had been a mistake because his head wasn't in the game—literally. Too many things were burrowing under his skin and bugging the crap out of him.

"All I'm saying is I thought we'd have more say-so on the guests."

Luca listened with half an ear as Miles bitched about something regarding the show.

Joey had landed a gig as host of a cable show, *ManPower*, a couple of years earlier. The highly successful show was where he'd met Miles, the two men cohosting together. It had been a great pairing, not just in front of the camera but behind as well. Miles and Joey had become the best of friends, and sometimes it was hard for Luca to remember a time when Miles *wasn't* around.

Luca, his brothers, and his cousins were very close—best friends in addition to relatives—and over the years, other men had cracked into their Moretti inner circle. Men like Tony's roommate, Rhys, Aldo's and Gio's best friends, Kayden and Rafe, respectively, and now Miles. There were very few sporting events Luca watched alone, and he was grateful for that camaraderie.

*ManPower* was similar to Mike Rowe's old show, *Dirty Jobs*, with each episode featuring a person who demonstrated how they built or fixed or created something cool.

The powers that be behind the show had scheduled some less than entertaining guests the season before, something that had driven Miles up the wall. He'd been pushing for more power in regards to selecting the guests, but with only moderate success so far.

Joey shrugged, clearly not as annoyed as Miles. "They've taken input from us before."

Miles rolled his eyes. "We're filming an episode with the executive producer's brother-in-law, who makes birdhouses and catios for this season."

"What the fuck is a catio?" Luca asked.

"A screened-in porch for a cat," Joey responded.

Luca chuckled, then poked the bear, aka Miles. "I think that sounds kind of cool."

Miles sighed. "So far, the only show they've planned that sounds moderately interesting is that family-run brewery in Northern Virginia."

Joey grinned. "The brewery is awesome. I talked to one of the guys who owns it, Levi Storm. Said we're going to be interviewing their brew master, Lou. If all goes well, this is probably where my hosting career will end because working at a brewery as a job? Yeah. Screw the show and the construction gigs. That's gotta be the epitome of career choices."

Miles smirked. "Your business would fail in a matter of months, due to you drinking all the profits."

"I can see it now," Joey said, ignoring his best friend, waving his hand slowly in front of him as if revealing an image of his future. "Me and my beautiful wife, Emma, would settle down on a little farm, making beer and babies and living the good life."

"Still think you're going to marry Hermoine, huh?" Luca joked. Joey was absolutely in love with Emma Watson and had been for years.

Miles groaned as Joey wiggled his eyebrows. Miles had a tendency to roll his eyes every time one of their gang of friends mentioned their significant others—real or imagined. Most of Luca's relatives and friends had settled down in the past year or two, which meant he, Joey, and Miles—the last remaining bachelors—were forced to spend time with a lot of guys who were head over dicks in love.

"You and I can name at least twenty people between us who would be more interesting than the brother-in-law. We met him once, remember? The guy with the obnoxiously loud laugh."

Joey winced. "Oh shit. Is that him?"

Miles nodded. "I vote we put together a list of serious guests and present it to the executive producers," Miles grumbled.

"That's a great plan. And let me just say, I think it's cute you think we're going to get a say-so." Joey lifted the pitcher, filling up his mug and Miles's, before starting to do the same for Luca. He frowned when he realized Luca hadn't taken more than a couple of sips. "You okay, bro?"

Luca managed one nod before sighing heavily.

"Are you that upset about the fire?" Joey asked. "Because I talked to Aldo this morning and he really doesn't think the damage is that bad. He said if we get the green light from the code inspector, we could probably be up and running again by the end of the week."

"It's not the fire," Luca started. "Or at least not *just* the fire. We'd done little more than gut the place, so while the cleanup is a pain in the ass, it would have been a hell of a lot worse if we were also dealing with destroyed appliances and furniture. Shit, the place had been stripped down to bare bones—the drywall ripped out so that the beams were exposed. I kinda think that's why the fire didn't do that much damage. There wasn't a hell of a lot left there to burn."

"True," Joey agreed. "So stop letting it ruin your Sunday. Enjoy the game."

Luca and his brothers had all been employed right out of high school by Moretti Brothers Restorations, the company started by another pair of Moretti siblings, Uncle Renzo and Luca's dad, Frank.

After Renzo's passing due to a heart attack, Dad slowly began to turn more and more of the running of the business over to Luca, Gio, Joey, and Tony. Nowadays, Dad's capacity within the company was almost exclusively in an advisory role, as rheumatoid arthritis made it too difficult for him to work construction anymore.

Tony, the oldest, had taken on the position of figurehead for the company, overseeing most of the managerial tasks. He still worked onsite as well from time to time, but as the company began to grow and take on more jobs, Tony's days of wielding a hammer grew fewer.

When Joey had first gotten the network job, they'd all been

thrilled for their brother, but there'd been some growing pains as the roles shared by four brothers in the business had been reduced to three. Joey's time with Moretti Brothers was now limited to less than half a year, as he spent the rest of his time touring the country to film the show. He was home now on one of those breaks, so he was splitting his time between working with Luca on the restaurant renovation in the morning before heading over to help Gio at his current worksite.

Luca and Gio served as the primary onsite project managers, along with several other men who'd risen through the ranks over the years, as it wasn't unusual for the company to be working a half dozen jobs at the same time, with at least that many more on their waitlist. Business was booming.

"I can't believe we've been here nearly an hour and you haven't touched on what we really want to know." Miles reached for a wing from the platter in the middle of the table. "When are you going to tell us about Harper, man?"

Luca chuckled. "She's more beautiful in person."

"Oh damn," Miles said, leaning back. "I'm so fucking jealous. That woman has starred in way too many of my—"

Luca held his hand up to cut the other man off. "Spare me the details." Now that he'd met Harper, it bothered him to think about how many guys used her as spank bank material because she was a hell of a lot more than just a smoking-hot body. "She's a really cool person, funny and open, and my God, can she fucking eat."

Miles and Joey laughed.

"Seriously?" Joey said. "I thought models lived on shit like celery and diet pills."

His brother wasn't too far off the mark. "That was true for Harper for a long time, but remember, her next career is going to be as a chef. She said cooking classes and culinary school opened her eyes to a whole new world as far as food goes."

"Good for her," Joey said. "Life's too short to be hungry all the time."

Harper would probably have a run for her money if it ever came to an eating contest between her and his second-oldest brother. Luca had watched Joey polish an entire large supreme pizza and a dozen wings on his own, and still bitch about there not being dessert.

"Agree." Luca took a drink of her beer. "Last night was the first time we've met in person, but I can tell she's going to be great to work with, unlike—"

"Gwen Baxter," Luca and Joey said in unison.

A couple of years earlier, Moretti Brothers had the misfortune to work with one of Philadelphia's haughtiest, most entitled socialites. Tony had been the contractor on the job, and she'd made his life a living hell for months, burning up his phone with texts and calls that fluctuated between irrational demands in terms of the renovation to obnoxious sexual come-ons.

Luca had harbored some tiny concerns the same might hold true with Harper—not the come-ons but the demands. Regardless, he'd decided to take the risk because working with her had felt like a dream come true.

"I'm glad Harper's cool," Joey said. "But that doesn't really explain why you're sitting here like someone just ran over your puppy."

"Harper isn't the only person I'm working with on this job."

Joey nodded slowly, the light going on. "Ah...Conor Russo. I have to admit, I was surprised when Tony sprung it on us that Moretti Brothers and Russo Enterprises were working on the same team for the first time in what? Seventy? Eighty years? I know there's a tentative peace, but I'm not convinced jumping into business together is the wisest way to test it."

Joey had been out of Philadelphia more than he'd been in it the last couple of years, so he'd been absent for a lot of the bridge building that had occurred one tiny brick at a time between their family and the Russo brothers.

"I don't think this has anything to do with the families," Luca said. "Just me and Conor. Not that *that's* anything new."

Joey frowned. "I don't remember you having a beef with Conor."

"Beef isn't the word I'd use to describe it because the truth is, I don't have a problem with the guy."

"Does that mean he has one with you?" Miles asked, his brows furrowed in confusion. It was a testament to just how good a friend Miles had become, given the way he found it hard to believe someone wouldn't like Luca.

"Apparently. It started back in high school, though I don't have a fucking clue why. We were in Spanish together when I was a junior. Conor, the brainiac, was in the same class even though he was a sophomore. We sat beside each other almost the entire year, and I actually thought we were friends. Then we got partnered up on a Spanish project toward the end of the school year. We hung out in the library after school every day for a week 'working' on it." He air-quoted the word working, which cracked his brother up.

"Let me guess," Joey said. "Your version of working was screwing around and acting like a jackass until the librarian threatened to kick you out."

Luca tapped the tip of his nose to let Joey know he got it in one. "Like I said, we were having a good time together and then—boom. One day I go to Spanish class and find out Conor got the teacher to switch up the pairings."

"Why would he do that?" Joey asked.

Luca shrugged. "Probably because he's smart as shit, and I was crap in Spanish. No doubt he realized he'd be carrying me on the project and asked for a new partner."

"*No hablo español*, eh?" Miles joked.

"The only phrase I bothered to learn was '*no sé.*'"

"What's that mean?" Miles asked.

"I don't know," Luca replied. "Or at least, I think it does."

Joey snorted. "I understand why Conor switched partners."

"Yeah, but it wasn't just that. He changed seats in the class, taking one all the way across the room. It was like we were friends and then...everything flipped, and he avoided me like the plague."

"That's weird," Miles mused.

For a while, Conor cutting him off so abruptly had really bothered Luca. Mainly because he'd liked Conor, and he couldn't figure out what he'd done to the guy. But then school ended and summer started, and Luca had forgotten all about him. Because he had a driver's license, a summer job earning decent money, and at least four hot girls to spend that cash on.

He and Conor didn't have any classes together his senior year, so their paths never crossed. He spent his last year in high school working hard to maintain the C average that would keep him out of the doghouse with his dad and dating at least half the volleyball team—at different times. So he didn't have time to worry about a guy who, for all intents and purposes, had disappeared from his life.

It was strange when Luca thought about it now because in some ways, it almost felt like Conor had switched schools, even though he hadn't. After that broken Spanish partnership, he stopped seeing Conor in the hallways and at lunch. After graduation, Conor faded even further into the background, relegated to just a childhood memory.

"So is Conor being a dick or something?" Joey asked.

Luca shook his head. "No. We got into it about the fire a little bit, but even as we were barking at each other, I couldn't help but feel like we were fighting about something else. When Tony told me Conor had offered us the contract, I was surprised, but kind of pleased because I figured it meant whatever problem Conor had with me was over."

"And now you don't think it is?" Miles wiped barbeque sauce from his fingers, a pointless endeavor, considering he reached for another wing the second he put his napkin down.

"I don't know. I get the feeling he picked the fight as a way of severing our working relationship. Which makes no sense because I thought the three of us—me, Harper, and Conor—had been working well together up until then. I'm mean, as well as you can over Zoom."

Miles leaned closer. "And you're sure you didn't piss him off over something else? Steal the girl he liked or something? From what I hear, you were a big hound dog back in high school."

"That's the pot calling the kettle black," Joey muttered to his friend. "The stories you've told me…"

Miles rolled his eyes. "I seem to recall you matching me story for story."

Luca chuckled, pointing at Miles. "You two really are the perfect duo. You're the Tom to his Jerry. The Bullwinkle to his Rocky. The Ron to his Harry."

"I'm not fucking Ron," Miles grumbled. "And stop trying to change the subject. I'm just saying there must be something more than you being shit in Spanish," Miles insisted. "It had to be a girl, or maybe you got picked for some team or office that he wanted."

Joey chimed in. "Matt got pissed off when Tony won class president and the quarterback position on the football team."

Luca shook his head. "It couldn't have been anything like that because we weren't on any teams or in any clubs together. I swear the only time we were ever together was in that class. I don't think I stole a girl he liked, but…" He shrugged. "Maybe."

Joey shook his head. "Nah. I don't think that's it. I'm pretty sure Conor is gay…or maybe bi."

"Seriously?" Luca frowned. "I never got that vibe. Why do you think that?"

Joey grinned. "Because the dude was practically eye-fucking you at Chives a month ago, when Gage and Penny announced they were having a baby."

Now *Luca* shook his head, not so much because he disagreed but because he was shocked. He sat there for a minute, replaying all of his and Conor's interactions in Spanish class and in the library that week with this new information.

Then he recalled that night at Chives. Luca had forgotten his phone, and when he'd returned, Conor had been the only person left in the restaurant. Luca had bent over to retrieve his cell from the bench seat of the booth, where it had fallen out of his pocket, and when he turned around, he thought he'd caught Conor checking out his ass. He'd dismissed it, thinking it ridiculous.

But maybe his brother was on to something.

"How in the hell would you have noticed something like that?" Miles, the straightest straight man on the planet, asked him.

Joey snorted. "Because I've looked at hot guys the same way."

"Fuck off!" Miles replied, aghast. "Seriously? You get hard-ons from looking at guys?"

Luca knew the look in Joey's eyes very well. If his brother had one true talent—after taking a perfectly clean house and making it an absolute shithole within minutes—it was getting under Miles's skin.

"Yep," Joey said, popping the p.

Miles considered that for a minute. "You ever get hard from looking at me?"

Joey burst out into loud laughter. "I said *hot* guys, Miles."

Miles crossed his arms and scowled. "Yeah, well, let me save you some time. I'm not interested. Never happening."

"Never say never," Joey taunted.

The two men were distracted from their play fight when the Phillies scored a run.

"Hell yeah!" Joey yelled as he and Miles high-fived, their attention focused on the game once more.

Luca was glad for the reprieve, as it gave him time to consider Joey's belief. Luca, in high school, was pretty much as straight as Miles was now, so it wouldn't have been surprising if he didn't pick up on Conor's attraction to him, if that really was the case.

But when he played over some of their interchanges in class and in the library...

Maybe Conor *had* been flirting with him.

The problem was, even if Conor had come out and expressed

an interest, Luca knew how it would have ended. He would have rejected him.

Now, though…

Shit. This hesitation, this questioning, was all Gio's fault. Maybe it was the twin bond. That strange mental connection he shared with his brother. Luca swore he and Gio were capable of not only knowing if the other was in trouble but also sharing emotions. Gio was clearly unwittingly transferring his feelings to Luca. Because there was no denying that since Gio had settled down with Keeley *and* Rafe, Luca was overwhelmed by the desire to find a similar happily ever after.

A commercial came on, and Miles turned back to him. "So what are you going to do if it turns out Joey is right and Conor has the hots for you?"

Luca shrugged.

Miles had been about to devour another wing, but he froze with the piece of chicken halfway to his mouth. "Wait—would you go out with him?"

Luca didn't respond, playing that question over in his mind.

"The fact that it's taking you so long to answer must mean you're really thinking about it," Miles stated. Then he looked over at Joey. "Would *you* go out with a guy?"

Joey laughed and slapped Miles on the shoulder. "Why do you assume I haven't already?"

Miles stared at his best friend for a full minute before shaking his head. "Jesus. I thought you were joking about the hard-ons and hot guys. Just when I think you can't surprise me any more, you always find a way to take shit to the next level. Must be something in your genes because I've never met a family more open to just about fucking anything."

"Hang on," Joey said. "Do you mean *fucking* anything or fucking *anything*?"

The three of them laughed, but Luca had to concede that Miles had a point.

Luca was one of five kids. He had his brothers, Tony, Joey,

and Gio, and a sister, Layla. Three of his four siblings had settled down with not just one partner but two. While his oldest brother, Tony, shared Jess with Rhys, the two men weren't *together* together. The same didn't hold true for Luca's twin, Gio.

Gio and Rafe lived together in throuple bliss with Keeley, and there was no question it was a true ménage in every sense of the word. The same held true for Layla and her two guys, Miguel and Finn.

"Maybe it's time you took that stick out of your ass, Miles, and opened your mind to our way of thinking," Joey teased.

Miles crossed his arms. "No thanks. If I settle down, it's going to be the old-fashioned way. One man, one woman. And that's a big if."

"Boooring," Joey drawled, feigning a yawn, turning his attention back to the game, yelling at the umpire for making a bad call.

Luca pretended to watch as well, but the game couldn't hold his interest because Joey had introduced an entirely new wrinkle.

And it was one that didn't upset Luca.

At all.

# Chapter Four

Conor stood on the sidewalk outside the restaurant, studying the boarded-up windows. It had been just over a week since the fire, and the code inspector had finally given them the all clear, allowing them to return and declaring construction could continue.

It had also been a week since he'd succumbed to the worst panic attack he'd had in years. Conor kicked himself for making such a mess of things lately. He'd managed to keep the attacks to a bare minimum for ages by keeping his life simple, orderly...predictable.

So much for that.

He had a ticking time bomb in his head, and he needed to take that more seriously than he had been of late.

Luca had suggested Conor and Harper meet him this morning, so the three of them could walk through the building together to see how bad the damage was and to discuss next steps.

Conor hadn't seen or spoken to either of them since the night of the fire, when he'd run out of the pub like the hounds of Hell were nipping at his heels. He'd fallen back on his old tried and true.

Escape and avoidance.

Jesus.

If Conor had one true talent, it was making an ass of himself in front of Luca Moretti.

He'd been enjoying himself at the pub, the conversation between the three of them flowing easily despite his and Luca's earlier blowup. It had gotten even better—for all of a minute—when he and Luca had made amends after their ridiculous fight.

Then Harper had suggested they kiss and make up, and Conor had been thrust back to the high school library, to that moment when he'd been a second away from kissing Luca.

Even now, he couldn't think about that day without feeling like the world's biggest idiot. He'd harbored a serious crush on Luca since day one of his freshman year, so when sophomore year rolled around and he found himself sitting next to Luca in Spanish class, he'd had to pinch himself almost daily. Because Luca wasn't just hot; he was the coolest, funniest, most interesting guy Conor had ever known. They'd had a blast in class, and when their Spanish teacher put them together as partners on one of the final projects of the year, Conor felt as if he'd won the lottery.

Working with Luca had been even better than Conor had expected. There wasn't a lot of laughter in the Russo house, something Conor hadn't realized he missed until spending time with Luca. The two of them had spent a full week after school working on the Spanish assignment in the library, stealing as much time as they could before Luca had to go to baseball practice.

Luca had kept Conor laughing the whole time as he tried to speak Spanish, using an accent that sounded more Australian than Latino, saying all the wrong words. They hadn't gotten much work done, but Conor hadn't cared because he was spending time with someone who actually saw and liked him for who he was. Luca didn't hold back, complimenting him for being so smart, laughing at Conor's jokes, and best of all, wrapping his arm around his neck to roughhouse with him.

Fifteen-year-old Conor had been struck by first love, falling hard for Luca. So hard, he'd lost sight of who he was—and who he couldn't be.

He was a Russo; Luca, a Moretti.

While that didn't matter these days, back when Dad was still alive, it mattered a lot. Although, Conor was perfectly aware him falling for a Moretti would pale in comparison to him falling for a *guy*. Dad's misogyny was only bested by his outright homophobia. Conor shuddered to think about what Dad would have done if he'd learned his youngest son was bisexual.

*Russos aren't weak.*

*Russos don't fail.*

*And Russos sure as shit aren't gay either.*

At least not in his dad's world.

Conor had let himself forget—or perhaps ignore was a better word—that fact whenever he was with Luca because he was in love, and he'd thought...actually, he'd been *certain* the attraction wasn't one-sided, that Luca liked him too. He was young, inexperienced, and he'd mistaken all of Luca's attention as flirting.

At the end of that week in the library, he and Luca had ventured into the stacks in search of a book to fulfill the "print source" requirement of their assignment. Luca walked up behind Conor and reached above his head to grab a book off the shelf. Conor turned, unaware of how close Luca was standing. Conor could see the specks of gold in Luca's light brown eyes, could feel the heat of his breath against his face.

Conor's heart raced, thinking this was it.

The moment.

They were going to kiss.

Conor had shifted until mere inches remained between them, his eyes locked on Luca's too-inviting lips. Conor had licked his, so fucking excited. Then he'd closed the distance *and* his eyes, so ready for his first kiss—when a girl called out Luca's name.

Luca turned, grinning as Trina Paulson walked up to them.

Conor stood stock-still as Luca wrapped his arms around Trina, kissing her the way Conor had thought he'd meant to kiss *him*.

Luca introduced Trina as his girlfriend. Conor could only assume it was a new relationship because Luca had never mentioned her before, jokingly claiming just a few weeks earlier that he was "too young to settle down."

Trina barely glanced in Conor's direction, telling Luca he was going to be late for practice. Luca had given Conor a brief wave and a "later," walking off with Trina, his arm tucked tightly around her waist as she giggled at something he whispered in her ear.

Conor had stood by the bookshelf for several minutes after, certain he could feel every crack and splinter forming in his heart.

Devastation hit fast, but something worse came right on its heels.

Panic.

One didn't grow up in the Russo house without becoming an expert in distrust. Conor had foolishly thought himself above that petty emotion, until he realized he'd never truly let down his guard enough to offer someone his trust.

Until Luca.

What if Luca had been toying with him?

What if he'd led Conor on? Let Conor think he liked him, as a game, as a way to make Conor look like a fool?

What if he was telling all his teammates that Conor had almost kissed him, and they were all laughing at him behind his back?

What if what Conor had almost done got back to his *dad*?

Terror took over, and Conor had struggled to take a breath, his heart racing, his chest tight, so fucking tight. He'd never had a panic attack hit him so quickly, but the one he suffered that day took him down within seconds.

Conor had shoved all his shit into his backpack as quickly as possible, a cold sweat breaking out all over his body. Somehow, he'd managed to make it to the parking lot, where Gage was waiting to drive him home. Rather than deal with Gage's nonstop chatter, Conor had pulled a book from his bag and pretended to read.

He'd spent the entire ride counting every pounding beat of his heart and fighting overtime to keep himself from loudly panting for air. By the time they'd made it home, he'd felt so light-headed, gray spots were hindering his vision.

Luckily, his brother hadn't even noticed his distress. Conor had locked himself in his room for the rest of the night, fighting one of the worst panic attacks of his life.

Monday morning, he'd gotten to school early and begged his Spanish teacher to allow him to switch partners and seats, and for the rest of that year and the next, Conor became an expert in avoidance. He'd spent his entire junior year like a soldier on a covert mission, constantly scanning every hallway and carefully turning every corner, as if there were a sniper ready to take him down.

It wasn't until Luca graduated that Conor finally managed to relax. No word had ever gotten back to him that Luca had somehow played him, and no one seemed to know about that near kiss.

As the years passed, Conor was better able to see what had really happened that day. He'd fallen in love with a boy who hadn't fallen back, who hadn't even known Conor had feelings for him. He'd been as invisible, as forgettable to Luca as he'd been to everyone else in his life.

Since beginning work on this project, it had become clear Luca hadn't changed much since high school. He was still easygoing, funny, entertaining, charming as fuck. He was also still oblivious to Conor's attraction.

Thank God.

Conor had hoped the man had changed enough that he could fight this overwhelming desire. Unfortunately, if anything, it was stronger because—Jesus—this muscular, tatted, bearded bad boy version of Luca was impossible to resist.

"Hey, Conor."

He turned at the sound of Harper's voice, grateful she'd arrived before Luca. He watched as she shoved the last bite of what looked like a cream-filled donut into her mouth, before licking her fingers.

"Good morning, Harper." He forced the old memories away and put on what he hoped passed for a friendly smile. "How's hotel life?"

She shrugged. "Familiar. I'm no stranger to hotels after a lifetime of traveling for work."

"I admire your fortitude because I don't know how you managed to do that for so many years. I don't travel much for work, but after a night or two in a hotel, I'm always ready to get back home and sleep in my own bed."

"Do you live in a house or..." Harper asked.

"I have a penthouse apartment here in the city. I live on the top two floors of one of Russo Enterprises' high-rise buildings."

"All I'm hearing is you have a great view."

He nodded, then realized he'd been a terrible business partner. Harper was new to the city, with no friends, and he'd left her on her own for an entire week, without offering her a tour of the city or even company for a meal. "I have an excellent view. Maybe one night this week, you'd like to join me for dinner. I'm a terrible cook, but I'm wonderful when it comes to ordering takeout. Probably why I own two restaurants. Just stop in and grab the special and go," he joked.

Harper's eyes widened with excitement. "Orrrr, you could supply the view and the kitchen, and I can bring the ingredients to cook dinner for *you*. The kitchenette in the hotel is functional, but that's about it. I'm anxious to start trying out some new recipes so I can try to decide what to include on the menu once the restaurant opens. We can call it research."

Conor enjoyed Harper's enthusiasm. They hadn't known each other for long, but her positive outlook was the one constant from all their conversations. He was drawn to it in ways that he shouldn't be.

It was bad enough he had a hard-on for his contractor. Falling for his business partner would be the fuckup of all fuckups.

But he sort of liked the idea of Harper in his space, seeing his home. His loner status was wearing thin these days. He blamed his brothers. He'd spent the past few months hanging around two men who were so madly in love they couldn't see straight. Matt and Gage's happiness made it all too apparent how *unhappy* he was.

Harper made him smile, made the heaviness that never seemed to totally leave his chest lighter.

"I would love to do some research with you," he said, then he added a label he really shouldn't have. "It's a date."

"What's a date?" Luca said from behind him.

Conor turned, surprised Luca had managed to sneak up on him. Typically, his Luca radar was much stronger. Especially when his scent reached him. For a guy who did hard manual labor, he always smelled good, a combination of musk and sandalwood and something that was uniquely Luca.

"Hey, Luca," Harper said. "Conor is going to let me shanghai his kitchen this week to make dinner, since I'm going through cooking withdrawals in that hotel."

"Is that right?" Luca's grin widened. "You know, I've got a kitchen too."

Harper giggled. "I never would have guessed. It's so rare for homes to have kitchens."

"Don't tell Nonna that. She has two."

Harper's eyes widened. "She does not."

"It's not that unusual in Italian households." Then Luca bumped shoulders with her playfully. "But, full disclosure, that Italian thing skipped me, because I don't use my kitchen the way you would. Unless you prepare a lot of microwave meals or cans of soup."

Harper crinkled her nose. "Disgusting. Between you and Mr.

Self-Professed King of Takeout over there, I can see I have my work cut out for me. Tell you what. Why don't we work smarter, not harder? Maybe you could join me and Conor? He's promised an excellent view, and I can kill two birds with one stone, show you guys why it's better to dine than to simply eat."

Luca glanced his direction, and he looked almost... shit...hopeful?

The words "the more, the merrier" fell out before Conor could pull them back.

Internally, he groaned.

*Who the fuck are you right now?*

Conor was not the kind of guy who entertained people in his home. His dates—which were few and far between—happened in restaurants, and when sex followed, Conor either went to the date's home, or he took them to one of Russo Enterprises' hotels.

"Awesome. I'm really looking forward to it," Harper gushed. Like Luca, she had an easy smile.

Conor envied their ability to not only feel happiness but to project it to everyone around them. He didn't consider himself a miserable person, but he struggled with emotions—all of them, the good and the bad—so typically, he kept them buttoned up, locked away. The only people he felt relatively comfortable being himself around these days were his brothers, yet even with them, there were parts he kept hidden.

His close relationship with Matt and Gage was a fairly new development after nearly a decade of estrangement. For too many years, the three of them had been more business partners than brothers. They'd only begun reaching out to one another on a personal level after Gage fell in love with Penny, and those bonds were further strengthened when Matt opened up to them about the night their mother died.

He, Matt, and Gage hadn't had an easy childhood. Mom's struggles with depression became too much for her, and when he was nineteen and away at college, she committed suicide. Between losing her and dealing with their strict, judgmental, sadistic father, it was amazing he and his brothers were functioning members of society.

It didn't take a genius to figure out his upbringing had fucked him up. Not too long ago, Conor had suggested his brother Matt consider starting therapy. It was definitely "do as I say, not as I do" advice.

Not that Conor hadn't tried the therapist route.

He had. Many years ago.

But he'd stopped going because the therapist's only answer was drugs. Conor had seen what Mom's medicine had done to her. He'd rather suffer the occasional attack than live every day like a zombie. When the doctor kept trying to push the prescriptions at him, Conor stopped going.

"A home-cooked dinner by a real chef sounds great. Just text me when the two of you pick a night and I'll be there. I can bring the wine," Luca offered.

"Perfect," Harper said. "As soon as I get back to the hotel, I'm going to run through my favorite recipes, figure out something delicious to make us."

"As long as it's not Quarter Pounders with Cheese," Conor said in a deadpan voice, "I'll be happy with whatever you cook."

He was pleased when his comment made both Harper and Luca laugh, even though he'd only been half joking. For someone who was a classically trained chef, Harper seemed to have an undiscerning taste in food. Although, when he considered she probably hadn't gotten to indulge in those foods he considered kids' fare when she was younger, it made sense she'd want to try it all now.

"Well," Luca said, gesturing toward the front door. "Should we see what the damage is?"

While the glass had blown out of the large windows, the front door hadn't sustained any serious damage, the lock still functioning. Luca ripped down the caution tape stretched across the doorway, then unlocked and opened the door. They were all immediately assaulted by the overpowering smell of smoke.

"I have some guys showing up soon to set up large fans to combat that smell, air the place out. We're going to take down the boards in the windows and open the place up for a few hours this afternoon," Luca explained.

"Sounds good." Harper stepped inside behind Luca, Conor following. The room was dim, thanks to the boards, the only light provided from the open front door.

"Here." Luca raised his hand, and Conor spotted the crowbar that he hadn't even noticed before. "I might as well do this now, so we can get some light in here." He used the crowbar to pry the board away from one of the windows, and Conor took the opportunity to admire Luca's muscular arms. He was wearing a plain navy-blue T-shirt, his tattoos visible beneath the sleeves.

Conor had never considered himself a tattoo kind of guy, his past male lovers more like him—professional businessmen. There hadn't been a single blue-collar bad boy, a regret Conor hadn't realized he even had until Luca reappeared in his life, and he let himself wonder just how far those tattoos stretched. Were they only on his arms, or did they continue on his chest, his back, and, God help him, his thighs?

Conor forced himself to look away, but a quick glance at Harper proved she'd just been giving Luca the same scrutiny. She looked his way, then gave him an unapologetic grin and a wink that told him he'd caught her, and she did *not* care.

He huffed out a soft laugh, wishing he had her confidence.

Once the boards were removed, Luca tossed the crowbar down on top of the large sheets of plywood. "There. That's better."

Slowly, the three of them made their way around the space. The smoke damage was significant, but Conor realized Luca hadn't exaggerated when he'd said there was precious little to burn.

"We'll obviously have to replace a lot of the beams that were fine pre-fire," Luca explained. "And I'm going to be starting from scratch on the electrical rather than adding to the existing. The ceiling and flooring are going to have to be completely replaced rather than us working with what was here, but that's not dire because we'd already planned to do that in the dining area."

They continued walking, passing through the part of the building that would serve as the dining room into what was going to be Harper's large kitchen. "This was where the fire started, so as you can see, the damage here is bad. We're lucky the structural damage was limited, but cleaning all this up is going to set us back on the original timeline."

"How far back?" Harper asked.

Luca shrugged. "Best-case scenario? If we can get all the materials we need now, that we previously *didn't* need, two to three weeks. Worst case...a month or more."

"Ugh," Harper groaned.

"Yeah," Luca said. "We're going to do everything we can to keep as close to the original plan, but—"

"We understand, Luca," Harper said, placing her hand on his forearm. "Obviously, none of us anticipated some squatter would accidentally set a fire with a space heater."

"Once we get the cleanup from the fire done and work begins again, I think we should put some security measures in place to make sure no one else breaks in," Conor added.

"Agreed," Luca said.

Conor had already given it some thought. "I have a company I use with my other businesses. I'll reach out and get that set up."

"Great," Harper said. "It sounds like we have a plan. Now... who's hungry? I passed the cutest little coffee shop on the way here with the best donuts."

"Didn't you just have a donut?" Conor asked.

"Yeah, but there was a coconut one I really wanted to try and I'm still hungry. It'll be my treat," she added to sweeten the deal —literally.

Luca chuckled. "That sounds good to me. I should probably hang out here and wait for my crew, since I took down the boards, but I could meet you—"

He didn't bother to finish as voices from the front of the building called out his name.

"Never mind," Luca said. "Sounds like they're here. Let me give them some directions and then we can head out."

Harper and Conor watched Luca walk toward the front, where three men were hauling in large fans.

"Does he know?" Harper asked, and Conor realized he'd been checking out Luca's ass—and she'd busted him.

"Know?" he asked, hoping she wasn't asking what he thought she was.

"Luca," she said softly. "Does he know you've got feelings for him?"

Conor frowned, ready to deny, deny, deny. "What makes you think—"

"The way you look at him," Harper said, cutting him off. "The way you walked out of the pub the other night when I suggested the two of you kiss. It's obvious the two of you have a past. Care to share with the rest of the class?"

"We don't have a past."

"Then why did Luca say you picked that fight the night of the fire so you wouldn't have to work with him?"

Conor had been holding his own counsel for so long, he didn't know how to talk to someone about anything personal.

"He doesn't know how I feel about him," Conor said quietly, not because he was afraid of Luca overhearing but because his throat was closing. "At least...I don't think he does."

"Why don't you tell him?"

He raised one shoulder. "It's not that easy."

"Because of a family feud."

Conor shook his head. "No. That's ancient history."

Harper didn't respond, just looked at him, patiently waiting for him to answer her question. He didn't know how.

"I don't think...he'd be...interested. I'm pretty sure he swings toward women."

Harper glanced to where Luca stood, talking to his crew, then turned back to him. "How can you know that unless you ask?"

Conor had spent so many years clinging to the fear of his father's anger and his young-boy heartbreak, he hadn't even considered asking Luca out, now that they were adults.

"That wouldn't be a smart thing to do. We're going to be working on this project for months."

"Right," Harper agreed. "Months. Not forever."

"Harper—" he started.

"I'm shutting up," she interjected. "Well, I will after I say one more thing. Life's short, Conor. Too short. We only get one, so we should at least try to live without reservations, without fear, and do whatever it takes to find happiness."

It was good advice, but there was something about her tone. "Speaking from experience?"

She nodded. "I spent the last few years living a life that didn't truly make me happy anymore. I tried to convince myself I was, that I'd just hit a bump in the road because I'd always loved modeling. But when it became less joy, more grueling, I knew I needed to make a change. Problem was, it felt like doing so would hurt the people I cared about."

"Your manager?"

She nodded. "And to some extent, my mom. Mom's dream when she was younger was to be a professional ballerina. She never made it, so when my modeling took off, it felt like she was living vicariously through me. Not that she was putting pressure on me. The truth was, she was very proud of me, and during those early days, when I was still underage, Mom traveled everywhere with me and it was an amazing adventure.

"It was sort of the same thing with Bradley. He'd just started his agency when he signed me. My career and his business grew together, side by side. For so many years, our goals were aligned and it was a great partnership. But there's a limit to how much you can squeeze into twenty-four hours, something I was slow to figure out, and something Bradley *still* hasn't figured out. By the end of my career, I was starving myself, working with my trainer four-plus hours a day, and traveling fifty weeks out of the year. One morning, I woke up, looked in the mirror, and didn't recognize myself."

Her words struck a vein with Conor because she'd always given the appearance of being confident and comfortable in her own skin. Knowing she struggled too made him feel less alone. He admired how open and genuine she was. "And now? You recognize yourself?"

Harper's smile was huge. "Nope. Because I'm just getting to know this new Harper. But, I can tell you that she loves the way she looks in the mirror now. Happy, free...always full," she added with a laugh.

"So you're taking your own advice." He gestured around at the restaurant.

"This is a dream come true. It's a new one, but it feels right. It fits better than the modeling ever did."

Conor could listen to her talk all damn day. She was positive and fascinating, courageous in a way he wished he could be. Now that she'd opened the door just a crack, he wanted to know everything about Harper.

He ran a hand through his hair. "I couldn't understand you talking about how happy you were your first night here. You have to admit, you walked up right in the middle of a shitshow, between the fire, and me and Luca going at each other."

She laughed. "It would have taken a hell of a lot more than a little fire to dim my happiness about being here, creating this with you." Harper spun around, and even though they were standing in the middle of a burned-out room, her joy touched him, sparked some in him. "Of course, I was pretty damn happy about the Quarter Pounder too."

He rolled his eyes, chuckling. "Come on, Harper." He held out his hand, electricity tingling along his spine when their palms met, her fingers curling around his.

Wow.

This was going to be a problem...because he was definitely attracted to both his partners in this venture.

Her words pinged around in his brain.

No reservations. No fear.

He didn't have a clue what it would feel like to live without those, but damn if he didn't want to give it a try.

"Ready?" Luca asked, as they walked toward him, his curious gaze taking in the fact they were holding hands.

"Yep," Conor said, with a lighthearted tone that sounded foreign coming from him. "Let's go get Harper another donut."

## *Chapter Five*

Harper juggled the large bag of groceries as she waited for the man at the front desk to call Conor to let him know she'd arrived. She listened with half an ear as she looked around the fancy foyer of the bougiest apartment building she'd ever seen. She knew Conor was wealthy, but this place was driving home just how loaded he *really* was.

She might have appreciated the beautiful building more if she wasn't so distracted.

Earlier this morning, Luca had called her and Conor to let them know there'd been a theft at the site. The electrical wiring delivered to replace what had been damaged in the fire had been stolen.

Luca was pissed because the wire had only been delivered the day before, and they'd intended to start installing it this morning. Conor had arranged for security cameras to be outfitted in and around the building, but the company he'd hired couldn't do the work until late next week.

Apparently, the theft of copper wasn't an unusual thing, but that didn't make this any less annoying. They were already scrambling to make up lost time because of the fire, and here they were, dealing with yet another setback.

"Yes, sir," the front door attendant said, hanging up the phone. "Mr. Russo is expecting you. Right this way." The man led her to the elevator, pressing the button and standing next to her, waiting for the doors to open. Once they did, he stepped inside with her briefly, just to swipe a card in front of the reader before pressing an unmarked button that was clearly for Conor's place on the top floor.

"Hold the elevator," a deep, familiar voice called out.

"Luca," Harper said as he joined her, a narrow bag in hand, clearly containing his promised wine. "You made it."

Luca grinned. "What else would I be doing on a Monday night?"

"Luca Moretti?" the man asked.

Luca nodded.

"Mr. Russo mentioned you would be visiting as well." He asked Luca for his ID, just as he had hers at the desk. Once satisfied Luca was who he said he was, the man said, "The elevator will take you directly to the penthouse. Enjoy your evening." The man stepped off and the doors slid closed.

"Good timing," she said.

A week had passed since the building had been cleared by the code inspector, and while she had a million things to do to prepare for the opening of the restaurant, she tried to get out of the hotel at least once a day for fresh air.

During her walks around the city, she usually found herself swinging by the construction site and Conor's club, Enigma. Not so much to check on the crew's progress or to discuss business matters with her partner, but because she was very low on friends in Philadelphia—Luca and Conor comprising the entire list—and if she wanted any sort of human interaction, they were it.

Fortunately, neither man seemed to mind her unscheduled visits, though she wasn't sure if that was because they genuinely liked her or because she made a point to always bring food.

"Here. Let me help you with that." Luca reached out, taking the large tote bags away from her, tucking his smaller bag inside one. "My God. It looks like you've brought enough food to feed an army."

"I probably did overbuy. Which is why..." She reached into one of the bags and pulled out a stack of take-out containers. "I bought these as well. You and Conor can divvy up the leftovers."

"You thought of everything. So what are you making us?"

Harper narrowed her eyes and shook her head. "Oh no. Tonight is going to be a joint effort. Those bags hold what the three of us are making *together*."

"I thought..."

"That I had intended to cook for you. But I decided that falls under the category of enabling you, now that I know you and Conor are lazy about mealtimes. I picked a simple recipe you can make for yourself and have plenty of leftovers for a few extra lunches and dinners. Give yourself a break from microwave meals, which are terrible for you, by the way."

Luca pretended to pat his pocket in search of his phone. "Hey. Give me a minute, sunshine. I want to Google the nutritional value of a Quarter Pounder with Cheese," he teased.

"Hush." She laughed as she shoved him on the shoulder, secretly loving that somewhere along the line, Luca had given her a sweet nickname. All he had to do was call her sunshine and all her happy, horny places woke up and did a little jig.

"I should probably warn you," Luca said, as the elevator continued to climb. "Nonna and my aunts have tried for years to teach me to cook. It's never ended well. Apparently, I have a heavy hand when it comes to spices *and* setting the timer. Everything I've ever made has either been burned or burned all the way down."

Harper laughed, curious why his mother hadn't taught him to cook. The more time she spent with Luca and Conor, the more she wanted to know. So far, their conversations had been filled with a lot of polite chitchat or work talk. She was hoping they might progress beyond that tonight.

She'd been delighted when Conor texted the two of them a

couple of days ago to set up a time for dinner. She'd been worried that perhaps he wouldn't follow through on the invitation after she'd added Luca to the guest list. It felt as if the two men were on more stable ground, though Harper sensed some tension still lingered. What she couldn't decide was if it was work tension or sexual tension.

Regardless of Luca and Conor's issues with each other, she planned to put tonight to good use because she had a million get-to-know-you questions she hoped to have answered over the course of the evening. While they were the only people she knew in Philadelphia, she'd learned enough about them to know she wanted to be friends, in addition to colleagues.

"Too much spice isn't going to be a problem. We're making shrimp and grits."

Luca, the charming bastard, put his hand over his heart dramatically, acting like she'd just gifted him a diamond mine. "Harper. I hope you don't think I'm moving too fast, but will you marry me?"

She started to laugh, but the elevator doors had opened halfway through Luca's pretend proposal, revealing Conor, who'd obviously been waiting there to greet her and help with the bags.

"Should I leave the two of you alone?" Conor asked.

"Hang on," Luca said, holding one finger up. "Depending on her answer to my proposal, you might need to get your tux dry-cleaned."

"The answer to both your questions is no," Harper said. "Luca's marriage proposal was simply proving an old adage true. The way to a man's heart is through his stomach."

Luca shrugged. "What can I say? I'm a simple man with simple needs."

Harper stepped off the elevator, and Luca followed her with the bags. The elevator opened directly into Conor's spacious living room. It was clearly a room Conor lived in, versus a show-place. The furniture looked comfortable, though she barely spared it a glance as she scanned the walls. The room contained several floor-to-ceiling bookshelves, all of which were overflowing with books.

So. Many. Books.

"Read much?" Luca was taking in the shelves with the same astonishment. "Damn, man. I think this is more books than we had in our high school library."

Harper started to make a comment about them as well, until something else caught her eye. "Oh wow, Conor. You weren't kidding about the view." She walked over to the large windows that overlooked the city. The sun was just setting, painting the sky with an array of warm colors, muted pinks, reds, yellows, and oranges. "This is beautiful."

"I'll say." Luca stepped behind her to look as well. "The view from my apartment is across the street, where there are more apartments that look just like mine."

"Here." Conor took the bags from Luca. "Let's drop this in the kitchen and then I'll give you a tour of the place."

Harper trailed behind them, the view forgotten, her interest in the kitchen taking precedence.

"Oh my God," she said, drawing in a sharp breath. "I love this room."

Conor's penthouse boasted a state-of-the-art kitchen, complete with restaurant-style range and cooktop, high-efficiency refrigerator, gorgeous ventilation, a workhorse sink, and hands-free faucets.

"It's gorgeous," she gushed as she took in his dedicated task stations. "Please tell me you were kidding about takeout."

Conor shrugged. "This place had been newly renovated when Russo Enterprises bought the building a couple of years ago. Obviously, the previous owners liked to cook. I kept everything the same when I moved in. I'm happy this kitchen will finally be used the way it was intended because it's wasted on me and my delivery-style dining."

"You're killing me, Smalls," she murmured.

"To be perfectly honest, I'm not even sure how some of this stuff works or what it's for," Conor confessed.

Luca laughed, but Harper didn't find a damn thing funny about a kitchen this beautiful going unused.

"I'm going to teach you how to use every single thing in here. I don't care if it takes me weeks, months, years," she claimed.

"Years, huh?" Conor shifted next to her, his expression suddenly very serious. "I need to warn you. I'm a very slow learner. It might take a lot of meals before I get the knack of things."

Luca burst out laughing again, and this time, Harper joined in, smacking Conor's forearm. "You're shameless, both of you. Preying on my kindness and killer cooking skills."

"Did she tell you what she was making, Conor?" Luca asked.

He shook his head.

"Shrimp and grits," Luca said.

Conor's eyes widened. "Now I understand that marriage proposal because I suddenly feel the desire to issue one of my own."

Harper rolled her eyes, secretly delighted by their playful flirting. Not that she was taking it seriously. Conor was obviously interested in Luca, and she had a sneaking suspicion that Luca—the charmer—flirted with every woman he met.

Even better than the flirting, though, was Conor's joke. He was more at ease here, the man actually wearing—gasp—blue jeans. Though to be fair, the dark denim was crisp and looked brand-new, not at all broken in like every single pair she'd seen Luca wearing over the past couple of weeks.

In a fun twist, Luca had traded his jeans tonight for a nice pair of light khaki Chinos.

"Okay. Tour first, please, Conor," she said. "Then the three of us are going to get down to business in this kitchen. We're going to give all these lovely appliances a workout."

Conor gestured back toward the living room. "You've obviously seen this room."

"Have you read all these books?" Luca asked.

Conor shook his head. "Not all but most. I tend to read the books I buy for myself first. Apparently, I have a reputation as a reader because most everyone in my life buys me books as gifts, and not all of them are ones I particularly want to read. I keep meaning to donate a bunch to the library, but I never seem to make time to go through the shelves and purge."

"I can see why. It would be quite an undertaking," Harper pointed out.

Conor sighed. "Yeah, well, I'm going to have to break down sooner rather than later because I'm out of room. Can't cram any more books on these shelves."

"If you want to keep procrastinating, let me know. I can build you more shelves."

Harper couldn't tell if Luca was serious or joking, but Conor looked touched by the offer.

"I might take you up on that," he replied softly. "If you'll follow me," he started down the hallway, "while the kitchen wasn't much of a selling feature for me in terms of buying this place..."

Harper groaned.

"This room sold me in an instant," Conor continued, opening the door.

Luca whistled as Harper's eyes widened when they stepped inside.

"Whoa. I thought I loved your kitchen, but *this* room..." she said.

Conor led them into the largest theater room she'd ever seen. There was enough seating for at least fifteen people on four different stadium-style levels. Every plush leather recliner had its own drink holder and faced a huge TV that covered one whole wall. In the back of the room was a refreshment area, complete with a full-sized refrigerator, popcorn machine, hot dog oven, and an honest-to-God glass cabinet filled with movie-theater-size candy.

"Conor." Luca walked in, looking as awestruck as Harper felt. "Holy shit, man. I'm pretty sure I could live in this room."

"I love movies as much as books," Conor admitted. "Both are great ways to escape real life for a little while."

Harper could sympathize with feeling the need to escape. She'd spent most of her life—from childhood all the way through her twenties—in constant motion, always rushing from one job to the next, always fighting to trim off another pound or three with countless training sessions and starvation diets, juggling her career and culinary classes.

The past couple of weeks—even though she was busy with a myriad of things to prepare for the opening of the restaurant— were the most relaxing of her life.

"Escape sounds nice," she said, realizing that was what cooking had become for her. The ultimate escape.

Luca walked closer to the television. "Jesus. You must feel like you're actually at the arena when you watch hockey games on this. Good resolution?"

"Very sharp," Conor replied. "If Gage was here, my tech nerd brother could rattle off all the specs, tell you how many pixels and crap like that. My brain only holds on to numbers that have dollar signs in front of them."

Luca walked back to Conor, placing a hand on his shoulder. "You never watch sports in here, do you?"

Conor shook his head. "I'm not much of a fan, but I know you and your family are. Gage mentioned joining you at a sports bar a few times." Conor hesitated for a moment, and Harper got the sense he was debating with himself over something. "If you and the guys wanted to come over one day and watch a game here instead of—"

"We accept," Luca interrupted. "What are you doing Sunday?"

Conor rolled his eyes, grinning, assuming Luca was joking. But Harper knew he wasn't.

"Oh. Um… I'm not busy," Conor finally replied, when he realized Luca was serious.

"Hockey playoffs are in full swing, and while the Flyers didn't make the cut—don't get me going about that," Luca grumbled. "My cousin Elio's old team, the Baltimore Stingrays, are on fire this year, and I'd love to see them go all the way."

"Hockey. Sounds great." Conor's tone was better suited for someone making plans to go to the dentist.

"Not a hockey fan?" Harper asked.

"Don't watch it enough to have strong feelings one way or the other," he replied.

"Me either. And I'm not usually one to invite myself places," Harper said, "buuuut if someone was to include me on the Sunday invite, maybe we could form some opinions about hockey together. As an added bonus, we'll have Luca here to explain what's going on."

"I will gladly tutor you, my young padawans, in the ways of the ice," Luca said in a solemn Jedi Master voice, his fingertips pressed together in front of him.

"Plus," Harper added, trying to sweeten the deal, "I make killer appetizers."

Luca's eyes lit up as he glanced at Conor.

"You're invited, Harper," Conor said. "With or without the appetizers."

Luca held up his hands. "Now, now, Conor. Don't be too hasty to decline the apps, man." He looked at Harper. "Because if you were interested in making a big platter of wings, I don't think any of the guys in my family would complain."

Harper saluted. "So noted."

"You should invite your brothers too," he said to Conor.

Conor leaned against one of the recliners and crossed his arms. "If I invite Gage and Matt, Penny and Liza will want to come."

Luca nodded. "Yeah, well, the truth is, once I tell the gang about this room, I think *everyone* is going to want to come."

"So it's now an official boy/girl party?" Harper joked.

Conor didn't reply right away, and Harper wondered if he'd ever invited anyone to escape in this room with him. Something about his demeanor told her that he hadn't.

"Fine," he said at last. "And since it sounds like a pretty extensive guest list, we should probably make a real party of it." He looked at Harper. "Do you think you could help me come up with a menu? I wouldn't expect you to cook it all. I could find someone to cater—"

"I would love to make a menu! And don't you even think about hiring a caterer. I want as much time in that gorgeous kitchen of yours as I can get. What time does the game start?" she asked Luca.

"Three o'clock."

Harper nodded. "You okay if I come around eleven to start cooking?"

"Absolutely," Conor replied. "You can either make a list of the ingredients you'll need and I'll buy them, or you can get it all yourself and I'll reimburse you."

"Sounds like a plan." Harper rubbed her hands together gleefully. Since her arrival in Philadelphia, she'd been cooking for one in a crappy kitchenette. The idea of creating a menu and catering a party sounded like absolute bliss.

Conor continued the tour, showing them his office, guest room, home gym—which Luca spent a lot of time exploring— and formal dining room. He even showed them his bedroom, which took up at least half of the top level of his two-floor penthouse. The huge apartment was perfectly put together, decorated tastefully—though somewhat impersonally—and spotless.

Apart from the well-loved books in the living room and the tidy stacks of papers on his large desk, there was very little else that revealed any part of Conor's personality. There were a few family photos hanging on a wall, all of them of three young boys under the age of ten. Conor said they were of him and his brothers.

Harper couldn't help but notice there were no pictures of his parents, or even recent photos.

Wrapping up the tour, Conor led them back to the kitchen, where Harper began to unpack the groceries. Both men were attentive as she divvied up the duties, explaining what they should do. She gave them assignments based on their self-professed weaknesses—Conor learning how to operate the range, Luca getting a tutorial on spices.

While Conor stood next to the cooktop, whisking the grits with stock, heavy cream, cheddar cheese, and butter, she put Luca in charge of tossing the shrimp in garlic, oregano, and Cajun seasonings. In addition to overseeing the men, Harper sauteed the andouille and vegetables, then cooked the shrimp. She had to slap Luca's hand a few times, as he kept reaching out to steal a piece of sausage or one of the jumbo shrimp.

Once everything was prepared, they carried it to the kitchen table, and Conor poured them each a pint of a local IPA beer he had in the fridge, deciding it fit better with their meal than the wine Luca brought. Both men dug into the food like they'd never eaten before and never would again.

Harper initiated the conversation, asking each man for a rundown on the family members she was likely to meet at Sunday's hockey party. Conor's list was easy, consisting of the two brothers he'd mentioned many times before and their significant others.

When Luca continued rattling off a list of names—brothers, cousins, friends—she was sorry she hadn't taken a few notes, though at least she'd met Gio and Joey through their work at the restaurant.

"Did you realize you were inviting all of Philly when you agreed to this party?" Harper asked Conor, only half kidding.

"Actually, I did. There's no shortage of Morettis, and you should be warned, Luca's given you a scaled-down list, only naming the people coming Sunday. I attended a party a month ago with the entire family. It was...God...*a lot*." Conor feigned a shudder, prompting Luca to punch him on the shoulder playfully, something Harper noticed Luca had been doing whenever the three of them were together. It left her wondering if Conor was right about Luca being straight.

"I didn't hear you complaining when you were shoveling that third plate of Nonna's eggplant parmesan in your face," he teased.

Conor tilted his head. "You counted how many plates I had?"

Luca shrugged good-naturedly, completely unaware of what his admission was doing to Conor, who looked both astonished and pleased that Luca had noticed.

She tapped Conor's shin twice under the table. He glanced at her, shaking his head slightly.

It was nice getting to know these guys, who—while quite different—were both interesting and kind. After a lifetime spent around people who valued her only for her looks or viewed her as the competition, her list of true friends she could genuinely trust was painfully small.

"So tell us about your family, Harper," Luca said as he rose to scoop another portion of shrimp and grits into his bowl.

"Oh, that's simple. It's just me and my mom," she replied.

"No dad in the picture?" Conor took a sip of his beer.

She shook her head. "My parents divorced before I was born, and my dad moved from the East Coast to the West. I didn't hear from him at all for the first sixteen years of my life. Then, that year, he called me out of the blue."

"Why?" Luca asked.

Harper sighed. "I signed my first huge national campaign and my career skyrocketed."

"Shit," Luca growled, and it was apparent she didn't need to spell out the rest. Dad's interest in her was obviously tied to her bank account. Unfortunately, her younger self hadn't figured that out as quickly as Luca had. He'd seemed so genuine when he said he wanted to make up for lost time, wanted the chance to be a father to her.

"Mom tried to warn me, but someone please introduce me to

the teenage girl who listens to her mother," she said sardonically. "He kept coming around for about a year, inviting me out for special dinners but always forgetting his wallet. Asking for a few extra dollars for this and that, always with some excuse about his credit card being stolen and a promise to pay me back. He convinced me to take him to one of my photo shoots in Italy, instead of my mother. Free trip for him, right?

"I finally figured it out when he totaled his car and came to me with a sob story about how he'd lose his job if he couldn't buy another one right away. Mom was in control of my funds, and she put her foot down. I acted like a total asshole to her, something I still feel bad about. When I told him I couldn't get the money for him, he lost his shit and disappeared for a couple of years. He showed back up when I was nineteen, but by then, I was wise to him. Told him to fuck off, and he did. I haven't seen him since."

"I'm sorry," Conor said.

She smiled, reaching out to touch Conor's hand. "Oh no. Don't be. It was a hard lesson to learn, but what doesn't kill you makes you stronger."

"Are you close to your mom?" Luca asked.

"Oh yeah. She's one of my best friends," Harper replied. "She traveled with me a lot when I was younger, and we both loved it. We saw the world, and those first years when my career started to take off were exciting, fun. Mom was a classically trained ballerina, and it had been her dream to dance with the New York City Ballet. She never made it. When I made it big, in some ways, it felt like both of us were achieving a dream."

"So I guess she wasn't happy when you decided to retire from modeling," Conor mused.

"Actually, she was extremely supportive. In a lot of ways, she's the person who set me on this new path, since that first cooking class was a gift from her." This was the second time Harper had skirted around the details surrounding her career switch. The night of the fire she'd done a similar dance, giving them only the tiniest glimpses, while holding back so much of the truth.

"I'm glad to hear that," Luca said. "Glad to know your mom is in your corner."

She could tell he genuinely meant that, so much so that she decided to put herself out there. Harper was interested in getting to know them better. Perhaps the best way to encourage that was to lead by example. There was something about these men that told her she could trust them. Or at least, she hoped she could.

She'd learned a long time ago—starting with her dad—that her trust gauge was faulty. What was also faulty was her ability to stop *offering* her trust anyway. Harper was painfully optimistic, determined to see the best in people. And that was despite the long line of assholes who'd tried to knock that attribute right out of her.

"That cooking class probably saved my life," Harper admitted. "About four years ago, I collapsed after a particularly grueling sixteen-hour shoot."

"Collapsed?" Luca said in alarm.

She quickly lifted her hand. "Sorry. Collapsed sounds way too dramatic. I got light-headed and passed out. Hunger, dehydration, a lack of sleep, and stress are a nasty combination."

"So collapsed *was* the right word," Conor said, sounding almost angry.

"I guess so. After a night in the hospital, the doctor suggested I take some time to recover. Bradley said that wouldn't be possible. I was scheduled to walk the catwalk in Milan during Fashion Week. It was a huge deal, high profile, and we both knew I couldn't miss it."

"Did you go?" Luca asked.

Harper shook her head. "No. Mom put her foot down. First time ever. Typically, she went along with whatever Bradley and I decided in terms of my career, but she swore hearing that I'd collapsed had taken five years off her life. She informed Bradley that I wasn't going anywhere but home to sleep for a week. Ordinarily, I would have fought her, but I literally didn't have the strength that night. Or the will."

"Good for her," Conor said. "So you took some time off?"

She nodded. "Yep. For a whole week, I relaxed. Took the cooking class, watched movies, read a pile of dirty books, and pigged out on takeout and wine with Mom and my best friend, Luna. It was the best time of my life. Luna pointed out that the collapse was my wake-up call, and she told me I'd better listen or she'd kick my ass."

"Luna sounds like a good friend," Conor said.

"Yeah. She is. Though I'll admit, I didn't listen right away. I went back to work, determined to pick up where I'd left off...but things were different. The spark was gone, and while it took me at least six months to admit it, I think I knew deep inside that my modeling career was coming to a close. Just hard to face something like that when modeling is all you've ever known."

Conor reached out and placed his hand on hers. "It was a brave thing to do, Harper. A lot of people wouldn't have the strength to walk away."

That was when Harper realized the *real* appeal of these two men. They looked at her and saw a whole person, not just a face or a body but someone with thoughts and dreams and stories they wanted to hear.

"And it's obvious you made the right decision in terms of your new career path because these shrimp and grits..." Conor finished that sentence not with words but with a long hum of appreciation. "You really need to make sure this is on the menu at the restaurant." Then to prove just how sincere he was, he stood, helping himself to more.

She'd been stressed when she arrived here earlier, annoyed by the robbery and yet another delay. Because now that she knew what she wanted her future to be, she wanted that future—the restaurant—to start right now.

After a few hours with these men, the impatience had faded, reminding her to appreciate where she was. Which was currently right here, in a happy food coma with two of the sexiest guys she'd ever met.

Life was good.

They polished off their second helpings—third for Luca—then cleared the dishes. Harper started to clean up, but Conor shook his head, opening Luca's bottle of wine.

"Leave that. I have a cleaning lady who comes in every other day. She'll take care of it tomorrow," Conor said.

Luca snorted good-naturedly. "A cleaning lady who comes every other day, he says, like it's the most normal thing in the world."

Conor shrugged, grinning shamelessly, and Harper realized this was the most she'd ever seen him smile. She wasn't sure if it was because he was more comfortable in his own home or because they were getting to know each other well enough to start lowering some walls. Whatever the reason, it was nice.

Maybe too nice.

Because tonight, she was struggling to keep the lid on her libido, and it wasn't just Conor's smiles causing the twittering in her stomach or the dampness in her panties. When Luca had tossed a couple ten-pound weights on one of Conor's chest press machines in his gym and done a few lifts, her pussy had clenched tightly enough that she thought she might seriously come simply from the gun show.

"Grab your glasses," Conor said, lifting his and the open bottle of Malbec. "It's more comfortable in the living room."

She and Luca followed Conor from the kitchen, each of them claiming a spot on his cozy sectional couch. Harper was tucked in the corner, while Luca and Conor plopped down on the opposite ends.

"Tonight has been wonderful," she said, leaning back, taking a sip of her wine.

"It has," Luca said. "We should do this again. I'd offer my place for another cooking lesson, but I don't have half the shit in my kitchen Conor does."

"Or we could just keep meeting here," Conor offered. "I don't entertain often. Having the two of you here...it's been nice."

Luca leaned forward. "Maybe we could even make it a weekly thing, considering Harper needs a chance to refine her menu for the restaurant, and we need cooking lessons."

"Seriously?" Harper was excited by the prospect.

Conor stuck his arm out. "Twist it."

Harper laughed as she did what he asked.

"No going back now." Luca puffed out his chest dramatically. "Sort of feel like doing a little bragging myself, now that I have my own personal chef."

"Personal chef, huh?" Harper repeated, liking the sound of that more than she cared to admit. "Sounds a hell of a lot more fun than supermodel."

"So you really don't miss modeling at all?" Conor asked.

Harper shook her head. "I keep thinking I should. And maybe somewhere down the road, I will. But modeling is a very grueling profession, and it was obviously starting to take a toll on my body. I spent a lifetime saying no to things—food, wine, parties, late nights with girlfriends—all because of work commitments. So this Harper." She pointed to herself. "This girl is all about saying yes."

Conor lifted his glass, tapping it against hers. "To saying yes."

"I'll drink to that," Luca added.

She tapped Luca's glass and took a sip from her own. Then she did something she ordinarily would never do. Tonight had been so easy, so comfortable, it felt natural to slip off her heels and tuck her feet beneath her with a happy sigh that both men heard.

"Not sure how you walk around in shoes like that." Luca pointed at her discarded heels. "Look like torture devices to me."

She took another sip of her wine before leaning forward to place her glass on the coffee table. She'd already had two IPAs with dinner, and they'd been considerably strong.

"I've spent a lifetime in heels," Harper replied. "I'm used to them. Though I will admit, there is nothing like those first couple of minutes after I slip my shoes off and rub some feeling back into my feet."

"Criminal." Luca shifted a bit closer to her, putting his own wineglass down.

"What is?"

He bent toward her, surprising her by gripping one of her ankles. "A beautiful woman forced to rub her own feet." Before she realized his intent, Luca had both her feet in his lap, his thumbs pressing firmly on the soles.

Her first thought was that she should pull away. The problem was, it vanished into the ether when he added more pressure to the balls of her feet. After that, her only response to his impromptu foot rub was a blissed-out moan.

The second the sound crossed her lips, her gaze flew over to Conor. She expected him to be bothered, maybe even jealous, but instead, his eyes were locked on where Luca's strong hands slowly and deeply massaged her feet.

"You have some experience with that," Conor said after a minute or two.

Luca, the charming devil, flashed Conor a cocky grin. "It's one of the best moves in my seduction arsenal." Before she could ask if he was trying to seduce her, Luca continued, "Gave my first foot rub right after junior prom. I went with Trina Paulson."

"I remember her," Conor said, his voice gruff and...

Her gaze flew to Luca, wondering if he heard the same thing she had. Because Conor sounded jealous.

Luca studied Conor's face for a moment, and it felt as if there were a shit-ton of emotions flying between the two men.

"She wasn't as accomplished in heels as you are, Harper." Luca broke the silence by returning to his story. "By the time the dance was over, she was seriously limping. When we finally made it back to my car, she broke into tears. If there's one thing that kills me, it's tears, so I took her shoes off and rubbed her feet."

"And you put that in your arsenal because..." Harper prompted playfully.

Luca shrugged. "Well, I don't like to kiss and tell..."

"I love that show," Harper interjected.

Luca chuckled. "Remind me to introduce you to Joey's best friend Miles."

Harper wasn't sure where that comment came from, but he kept talking before she could ask.

"Let's just say my prom night ended in a very traditional way." Luca wiggled his eyebrows.

She spared another glance at Conor, and once again, she was surprised by what she saw...and what she *didn't* see.

The jealousy she'd heard when Luca mentioned Trina's name was now absent. Instead, he was looking at Luca—God, and *her* —with an interest that made Harper's heart skip a beat.

"I never went to prom," she admitted, grasping for something to distract herself from Luca's strong hands, rubbing and caressing her feet, and Conor's hungry look.

"Really?" Luca asked.

"I didn't attend a traditional school. Because I traveled so much, I had a private tutor from the time I was ten, right through to graduation. Not sure I care much about missing most of the drama and angst associated with high school, but I *am* sorry I didn't get to go to prom."

"You would have liked it." Luca's strong thumbs dug deep into the balls of her feet, the part that was the sorest.

"So you got lucky after prom and now you're the foot rub king. And *you* just accused Conor of bragging about his cleaning lady," Harper teased, her giggle quickly turning to a groan when Luca hit a spot...the perfect spot.

She was fighting off some serious issues with arousal when it came to these two men, and rather than do the mature thing and start mentally listing all the reasons why it would be a bad idea to indulge in an affair with one of them, her thoughts took off in the wrong direction as she considered how each of them might be as lovers.

Conor struck her as the type of man to be slow but thorough, the kind of lover who made sure the woman came first—and maybe more than once.

While Luca... God, she'd bet anything he would fuck hard and fast, his passion laced with delicious roughness.

Both ways sounded damn good to her.

And to add insult to injury, her new motto began playing on repeat in her mind, as she hoped one of them might ask her out.

Because this girl...

*This girl says yes!*

## Chapter Six

"**S**hit!" Gio cussed loudly, slamming his hand down on the armrest of the recliner. "They're losing to Toronto, for God's sake!"

The Stingrays were currently getting their asses handed to them in game seven of the quarterfinal.

"It's not looking good," Rafe grumbled. "Two behind with only five minutes left to play."

"They're choking," Joey added. "Always the same fucking thing."

"Jesus H. Christ!" Aldo exclaimed, while Kayden and Miles merely shook their heads in disgust as the Stingrays took a penalty for high-sticking.

"What in the actual motherfuck was *that*?!" Liza yelled at the TV.

"Charming as always, Princess." Matt wrapped his arm around Liza's shoulders. Clearly, Matt wasn't as invested in the outcome of the game as the rest of them.

"Bite me," Liza retorted, not even looking in Matt's direction.

Until he said, "Remember that invitation when we get home."

Luca had to hand it to Matt. He'd found a way to distract Liza from the game.

She grinned, snuggling closer to her boyfriend, prompting Gage to throw his hands up. "Get a room, you two," he groaned.

Matt rolled his eyes. "Sure thing, Gage. Because none of us has gotten annoyed with you stroking and kissing Penny's stomach all damn afternoon."

"Hey," Penny retorted, lifting Gage's hand to place it on her stomach. "I think that's sweet...most of the time," she added after a brief pause.

Penny's baby bump had arrived, and with it, Gage's utter obsession with touching and talking to his future child. It had been cute at first, but when Gage bent down to loudly sing the Canadian National Anthem to Penny's stomach, they'd all begged him to give the child and his—or her—mother a break.

It had been an awesome day. They'd gathered a half hour before game time, loading platters with Harper's appetizers, setting up the first round of beers, and fighting over where to sit. After that, it had been nonstop eating, drinking, bitching, and laughing.

"Why aren't they pulling the fucking goalie?" Kayden asked.

"I bet Elio's not sorry he's not playing in this game," Hazel, Aldo and Kayden's girlfriend, pointed out. She was still relatively new to their group, only moving to Philadelphia from Boston last spring.

"He hated games like this," Liza confided. Elio, her older brother, had played with the Stingrays up until the end of last season, when he'd hung up his skates and moved back home. Within months of retiring from the game, he'd married Gianna, the two of them having a daughter in September.

Elio and Gianna had planned to come today, but their daughter had been up all night with a fever, so they opted to stay home. Elio had sounded exhausted when he'd called Luca earlier this morning to bail.

Keeley perked up from her spot between Gio and Rafe in the

front row, turning to look over the top of her recliner at Hazel. "They were planning to watch it at the inn. I might text Gianna to make sure Elio hasn't thrown anything at the TV."

Elio, Gio, and Rafe were all business partners, the three men opening a "haunted" inn that Elio and Gianna ran. The haunted part of the inn's description sounded scarier than it was, considering the ghosts were believed to be Rafe's grandparents, who were proving to be mischievous matchmakers rather than frightening spirits.

Ordinarily, Luca would have been right in the middle of the bitching and moaning about the Stingrays' shitty playing, but he was struggling to follow the game today, too amused by Conor and Harper's reactions to the utter chaos surrounding them.

Harper had admitted to being an only child, and while Conor hadn't said a lot about his upbringing, Luca had spent enough time with Gage to learn that the Russo household hadn't been overly familiar with things like laughter and fun when the boys were growing up.

"This is insane." Harper leaned over Luca so that Conor could hear her. The noise level was currently off-the-charts as the clock clicked down and everyone kept yelling at the refs, the players, the coaches, the commentators, and whoever else they thought had let them down.

"You're not kidding." Conor did the same lean, so now Luca sat with both of them bent over his lap. He hoped neither of them glanced down because as the game progressed, and they continued to down beers and Harper's endless array of appetizers, Luca found it increasingly difficult to keep his mind on the game and not on the smell of Harper's shampoo.

Or, God help him, Conor's cologne.

Fucking Joey had planted a seed when he'd expressed his opinion on Conor's sexuality. After three weeks of thinking about it, and spending time with Harper and Conor, he'd finally given up the internal battle and admitted to himself that he was attracted to *both* of his current clients. Like, off-the-charts attracted.

Today had been a true test of his willpower every time Harper grabbed his arm when someone scored...when Conor reached into the bowl on Luca's lap to steal a handful of chips...as they took turns leaning in to whisper their questions about the game into his ears.

Luca had spent years watching his siblings with their partners. Enough that he'd come to realize he likely wouldn't be satisfied in a relationship with just one person. He figured the reason he'd been resistant to admit that truth before now was because he'd been suffering a long streak of bad dates and zero sex. How could he hope to find *two* people who made his heart race when he couldn't even find one?

He grinned as Harper and Conor joined in the countdown to the end of the game with the rest of his friends and family.

"Ten, nine, eight!"

"Goddammit! Shoot the fucking puck," Aldo yelled, using every angry Italian gesture in his repertoire, while Hazel and Kayden rolled their eyes at their boyfriend's over-the-top fury.

Meanwhile, Gio and Rafe had appeared to accept the defeat with a bit more grace, the two men tickling Keeley over some disparaging remark she'd made about the Rays, demanding she take back whatever it was she'd said while she giggled and tried to fight them off.

Since that post-fire walk-through of the restaurant, followed by donuts, Luca had seen Conor and Harper every single day, the three of them meeting for an after-work drink to discuss the renovations. Initially, that was exactly what they'd talked about. But given how little they'd discussed work this past week, talking about everything else under the sun, it was obvious they were using the construction as an excuse to get together.

The more time Luca spent with Harper and Conor, the more he started believing the relationships Gio and Aldo had might not be such an unachievable goal for himself.

Luca's dick twitched when Conor's arm brushed against his. *God.*

"Three, two, one!"

The buzzer sounded, and just like that, the Stingrays' stellar season came to an end.

"Damn," Luca muttered. "Well, that sucked."

"Sorry your team lost." Harper bumped her shoulder against his.

"Did you have fun at least?" Luca asked.

His family was extremely important to him. So much so, he could never be in a relationship with someone who couldn't accept them. He'd broken up with a long-term girlfriend once because she began refusing to attend family events, claiming all the noise gave her a headache. When he assured her that he was fine attending alone, she'd doubled down, constantly putting him in the position of having to choose between his family or her.

He'd stupidly picked her a few times, missing a couple birthday parties and a Fourth of July picnic, before he figured out he had a hell of a lot more fun with his family than he did with her. Since then, getting along with his family was high on his list of what he was looking for in a relationship.

"Are you kidding?" Harper replied. "Who could sit in a room with these people and *not* have fun?"

Luca smiled, feeling like a million bucks.

"It occurs to me I haven't been using this room to its full potential any more than the kitchen, keeping it to myself when it was made for a lot of people," Conor mused. "Do you think everyone would want to come back for the finals, even if the Stingrays aren't in it?"

"Jesus, man. I think that's a given." Luca placed his hand on Conor's shoulder. "You'll be lucky if they don't camp out here until then."

The three of them laughed. Harper hadn't lied about her lack of knowledge regarding hockey. He thought Conor *had* exaggerated, until the man confessed to watching hours of YouTube videos of game highlights in preparation for this party.

Luca had teased him for being a nerd, doing homework, while reassuring him that he hadn't needed to study just to watch hockey with the gang.

Conor stood when everyone else rose and started to tidy the room.

The Morettis partied hard, but when the fun was over, they always stuck around to deal with the mess. With so many hands at work, the theater room was put back to rights quickly. Liza, Keeley, and Hazel had headed to the kitchen to help Harper pack away the leftover food. She'd made a ton after listening to Luca talk about the spreads his aunts and Nonna put out at family gatherings.

Luca placed an empty wings platter on the counter, while Conor followed him with the chip and dip bowls.

"I clearly overestimated the food." Harper spun around the room, looking at how much was left.

Luca stepped next to her, wrapping his arm around her waist. "If Elio had shown up like he was supposed to, you wouldn't have had enough," he joked.

She grinned. "Well, those leftover containers I bought for shrimp-and-grits night are still here, since you and Conor plowed through all of that in one sitting."

Conor pulled the containers out of a cabinet, encouraging Liza, Hazel, and Keeley to fill them with leftovers to take home.

Soon, everyone began to leave, one couple or throuple at a time, until only Luca, Conor, and Harper remained.

"What an incredible afternoon," Conor said, smiling widely.

"You're one hell of a host," Luca said.

"You really are." Harper stretched up on tiptoe to give Conor a quick kiss on the cheek. "Thank you so much for including me. Now..." she said. "Do you guys have plans for the rest of the evening? Because if you don't, I was hoping we could have another drink or two and chill for a while. I have soooo many questions about everyone who was here."

Luca was thrilled she wanted to know more.

Conor walked to the fridge. "I don't have any plans for the evening. Beer?" he asked before pointing to the counter. "Or red wine."

"Wine," Harper said. At the same time Luca said, "Beer."

Conor chuckled as he pulled a beer out of the refrigerator and tossed it to Luca. Then he opened the wine and grabbed two glasses. "Back to our spots on the couch?"

They walked to the living room, and they did indeed claim the same seats they'd taken a week earlier, though Luca noted that this time, there was less distance between them. Harper still sat in the corner seat, but he and Conor had shifted away from the ends of the couch, sitting sideways in the middle of their sides of the sectional, facing her and each other.

"So let's have it," Luca said to Harper. "What are your questions?"

"Gio and Rafe," she started. "They're with each other *and* Keeley?"

Luca nodded. "Yeah. They are. Same with Kayden, Aldo, and Hazel."

"And that works?" she asked.

"You just spent the last four hours with them. What do you think?" Luca asked with a grin.

"They look very happy," Conor said. "I'll admit, I've always wondered how they make it work, but it's clear they do."

"I think it's awesome," Harper admitted.

Thank God, Luca thought, grateful that Conor and Harper seemed accepting of the threesome concept. Then he did an internal eye roll, aware he was getting carried away, putting the cart before the horse, imagining the three of them in a relationship that hadn't even reached the first square on the game board. While they'd spent a lot of time with each other this week, what they'd been doing was far from dating.

Hell, none of them had even kissed.

"Do you think the throuple-ing is some sort of genetic thing with your family?" Harper asked with a twinkle in her eye.

Luca suspected she was joking, but he shook his head, taking the question seriously. "I don't think it's genetics as much as experience. We watched my sister, Layla, fall for her guys, Finn and Miguel. When you see something like that, see firsthand how well it can work, it sort of opens your eyes to more possibilities than you realized were there. Then Gio and Rafe both fell for Keeley— they'd been best friends forever, and they didn't want to lose each other fighting over a woman. So..."

Harper took a sip of wine. "They decided to share."

"Yep. To be honest, at first, it was just that. The two of them sharing Keeley. Then Rafe and Gio's physical relationship with each other grew from that."

"So when you say they shared at first, it wasn't taking turns, one man one night, the other the next, kind of thing?" Conor asked.

"Nope." Luca was thrilled they were asking so many questions and happy to have a chance to hopefully shed a positive light on the kind of relationship he was hoping to embark on himself.

Gio had talked to Luca a lot at the beginning of his relationship with Keeley and Rafe, talking out his concerns about pushing Rafe away, if he asked for more in the bedroom. Luca was glad his twin had taken the leap and that it had worked out because he'd never seen his brother so happy.

"Ah. Three bodies in the bed. Kinky." Harper wiggled her eyebrows.

"Did the same thing happen with Kayden and Aldo?" Conor asked.

Luca took a sip of his beer. "No. Those guys had been in a semi-relationship, off and on for years. But when Hazel showed up in Philly, Aldo said it was like the piece they'd been missing was suddenly there. All they had to do was convince her to take a chance on both of them."

"You Morettis sure are lucky in love," Conor observed.

"I wouldn't say the Russos are lacking in that luck. Gage and Matt look very happy," Luca observed.

Conor didn't reply to that immediately. "Yeah. They are."

There was something about Conor's tone that captured Luca's attention. "You hoping for some of that luck?"

Conor hesitated—long enough that Luca started to worry about his response.

"I don't know," he finally admitted. "I'm not sure I am."

Harper frowned. "Why not?"

It became instantly clear that Conor wasn't comfortable with this subject. Then again, Luca realized the man seemed reluctant to talk about himself most of the time.

"Not the settling-down type." Conor was trying to joke himself out of the conversation.

"Ah." Harper helped him make his escape. "So you're a love 'em and leave 'em guy."

Conor chuckled. "Yeah. Something like that."

Luca grimaced, hating that Conor felt like he couldn't open up to them. Harper had given him the bye...but Luca couldn't let it go.

He lifted his beer bottle, leaning forward to tap it against Conor's wineglass. "You're a good guy, Conor. And I think you're selling yourself short by dismissing the idea of a relationship and love."

Conor held his gaze, a deep frown line cutting a groove between his eyes. Rather than reply, he just shrugged.

Luca wasn't sure what part was hard for Conor—the compliment or the idea. "You and I are pretty much the last bachelors standing in our families. It's hard being on the outside looking in. I'm happy for my brothers and cousins, but..."

"*You* wouldn't mind a bit of that luck," Conor finished for him.

"Not at all."

"Me either," Harper admitted.

"No long-lost loves?" Luca asked, somewhat surprised. He was on social media enough to know there were plenty of stories about Harper dating some famous rock icon or Hollywood movie star or billionaire.

Harper stared at her wine glass for a moment, and he got the impression she was going to follow Conor's example and shrug off the question.

He tried to tell himself to ease up. Just because he had a clear view of where he hoped things between the three of them might progress, didn't mean these two weren't still blind to the possibility. Conor was too much of a professional, so he'd resist having an affair with his business partner and his contractor.

As for Harper...

"Love doesn't seem to be my strong suit," she answered at last. "I always pick the wrong guy."

Luca resisted the urge to fist pump the air. Once again, Harper was putting herself out there. Maybe if she kept sharing, eventually Conor would feel comfortable doing the same.

"Always?" Conor asked.

Harper blew out a slow breath, then gave them both a rueful grin. "I lost my virginity to a popular modeling agent I was familiar with—not mine," she hastened to add. "I was eighteen, he was forty."

"Damn."

"Yeah. We snuck around, hooking up in various cities for the better part of six months."

"Why did it end?" Conor asked.

"My manager, Bradley, found out about it and lost his shit, told me the guy was married, something my 'boyfriend'," she air-quoted the word, "failed to mention to me."

"You didn't know he was married?"

"He said he'd gotten a divorce. Turns out that was a lie. He was hoping to entice me to drop Bradley and sign with him."

Luca scoffed. "What a douche."

"That he was."

Conor grabbed the wine bottle, topping up their glasses. "That must have hurt."

She nodded. "Unfortunately, that wasn't the worst relationship. I dated Fulton Tevin for almost a year."

Fulton had burst onto the rock scene about a decade ago, but Luca wasn't a fan of his music. Felt like the guy screamed more than he sang.

"He was fairly new, still trying to make a name for himself. Not the mega star he is now," Harper explained. "After a couple weeks on a shoot in Paris, I returned to the States and drove straight to Fulton's apartment in Brooklyn. I had a key, which I thought meant something. I walked into the middle of a freaking orgy. Fulton was stoned out of his mind. He invited me to join them. When I called him every name in the book, broke things off, and threw his key at him, he acted like I was pissed off over nothing. He seemed to think I knew the score."

"The score?" Luca scowled.

"Apparently, Fulton was of the opinion our relationship was a marketing ploy. He imagined us being some sort of super couple. He even tried to give us one of those stupid connected names like Brangelina."

"I'm afraid to ask..." Luca prompted.

She rolled her eyes. "Harton. He liked it because if you changed one letter it spelled hard-on. Should have realized what a douchebag he was when he suggested it and made that joke."

"Was that true? About the marketing ploy?" Conor asked.

"If it was, it came from Fulton's camp because he didn't let me and Bradley in on the scheme."

"Fulton was the one who benefited from going out with you, not the other way around," Conor pointed out. "You made his career. He didn't do a damn thing for yours."

Harper touched Conor's hand. "Thanks for saying that. I wouldn't mind, but the asshole sent me dick pics for months after. He would not give it up."

"You didn't block him?" Luca asked, aghast.

"Of course I did. Two seconds after the first one arrived with a text "reminding" me of what I was missing out on. When he figured out I'd blocked him, he started using other people's phones. Finally, I just changed my number. Every now and then, he mentions me in an interview, claiming I'm the one who got away and that he's going to win me back one day. I like to refer to my Fulton days as my period of low self-esteem because seriously...how could I not realize what an idiot he was."

"You're telling the truth? He's not still bothering you?" Luca was ready to track down the rock star and teach him a lesson in how to treat a woman.

"I blocked him on everything. If he's still trying, I don't know, so it's all cool."

Luca wasn't sure he agreed, but he let it go.

"Please tell me Fulton was the worst," Conor said.

"Nope. I was just warming up with those first two stories." Harper was putting up a good front, attempting to take some of the darkest moments of her life and make light of them, but he could tell she'd been genuinely hurt by the assholes she'd dated.

"Not sure we want to know," Conor muttered.

"This is the last one, I promise. I dated Ashtyn Lewis."

Luca figured that made sense. Ashtyn was heir to the Lewis high-fashion house, who produced Siren's Smile. The guy was a billionaire a few times over. "Okay—let's have it. Why did that relationship end?"

Harper sighed. "I walked into his home office one afternoon and found him bent over his desk, getting fucked by one of the gardeners on his estate. Turned out, he not only wanted me to serve as his arm candy in public but also as a beard."

"Jesus." Conor raked a hand through his hair.

Harper laughed it off, leaning forward to put her wine glass on the coffee table. "God, you should probably cut me off. Obviously, I've had too much to drink. I can't believe I just told you all of that."

"Why not?" Conor asked.

"I don't exactly come out of those stories sounding so good. Constantly falling for guys who were using me. You would think I'd have learned my lesson the first time without having to reinforce it."

"What lesson do you think you should have learned?" Luca asked.

Harper shrugged. "My mom says I have a bit of a Pollyanna personality. I'm too trusting for my own good."

Luca frowned. "There's nothing wrong with having a positive attitude, sunshine. You're open and giving. Those aren't negative attributes."

"They were the assholes, Harper," Conor said, scowling. "Preying on a beautiful woman with a big heart."

"Don't let a few bad apples stop you from being yourself," Luca added. "And I'm glad you told us because you've got *us* now. We've got your back. You can share secrets with us without fear of judgment."

Conor glanced at Luca, that frown still in place. Maybe he didn't like Luca making promises for both of them.

Luca wasn't sure why he'd used *we* instead of *I*, but he wasn't sorry. It felt right. Besides, his personality was the equivalent to a bull in a china shop, which meant he tended to bulldoze straight through situations until he got his way. If that meant he had to drag Conor along until he started walking on his own, then so be it.

Harper was pleased by their supportive comments. "I'm glad we're becoming friends."

"Friends," Conor murmured quietly, almost as if he was trying the word on for size.

Luca wasn't sure if it was the alcohol or her openness or the fact they'd been in each other's faces for two weeks solid, but he was starting to feel as close to Conor and Harper as he was the lifelong friends who'd just left. They saw and spoke through text every single day, Harper and Conor making daily visits to the construction site, in addition to the happy hours.

At first, Luca thought perhaps they were keeping tabs on his work, but lately, he got the sense they were coming because they liked hanging out with him for a little while. God knew those visits were the best parts of *his* day.

Conor typically stopped by first thing in the morning, armed with two large coffees. Like Luca, Conor drank it black and strong enough to wield its own hammer. He and Conor would drink coffee, discuss the day's plan or the weather or gossip about their newly combined families, then Conor would say goodbye and head to his office at Enigma.

Harper's chosen time of day to visit was lunchtime, and she always came toting something delicious she'd made that morning, or sometimes with takeout from a local restaurant. She'd spent most of her time this week in Conor's kitchen while he was at work, experimenting with recipes she hoped to include on the menu for her restaurant—something he and Conor were benefitting from as her official taste-testers.

The one thing none of them had broached since the night of the fire was his and Conor's fight. While the tension between them was much less, Luca got a sense it still wasn't completely gone.

Maybe it was time to try to clear that hurdle once and for all.

"I think we've become friends, Conor, but you tell me. I thought we were on our way to a friendship once before, and you ghosted me. What happened between us in high school?" Luca asked. "One day, we're palling around in class, working on a Spanish assignment together, and the next, you just disappeared."

"You really don't know what happened?" Conor asked, and Luca watched as Harper shifted, slowly leaning back on the couch, attempting to make herself invisible, giving them space to hash this out.

Luca shook his head. "No. I don't."

"The library." It was clear Conor thought that response was enough. But it wasn't.

"Say more."

Conor sighed. "I... I thought you were going to kiss me."

He heard Harper's soft intake of breath, but Luca didn't let it distract him. This conversation had been a long time coming, and he wanted to understand what he'd done wrong.

Luca let his mind drift back, let himself play it through. A light went on. "We were standing in the stacks."

"I can't believe I'm saying this. But I had a crush on you back then. *No.*" Conor shook his head. "It was more than that. I misread everything between us. I thought all that clowning around in class, passing notes, roughhousing...I thought we were flirting with each other. It meant something different to me than it did to you. It meant *more*. So much more, that you were my first love...and you didn't even know it."

Joey had been right—and Luca hated his younger self for not realizing. Especially when he let the rest of that scene in the library play out. He'd just started dating Trina, and she'd come to find him. He remembered turning away from Conor and kissing *her*.

"I'm sorry, Conor."

"It's not your fault, Luca," Conor said. "I never told you."

"Why didn't you?" he asked.

"A lot of stupid reasons that made sense when I was fifteen. I'd never kissed a guy—or a girl, for that matter, so it's not like I was brimming with confidence. When I saw you with Trina, well...the jealousy was real. I got really pissed, and then really sad, and then..." Conor rubbed his chest. Something Luca had seen him do more than a few times these past three weeks. He wondered if it was a nervous habit. "I panicked."

"Panicked?" Luca could understand the first two emotions, but the last one didn't fit.

"I was afraid maybe you'd been leading me on, playing a game with me."

"I would never—"

Conor held up his hand, cut him off. "I know you wouldn't do that, Luca. *Now.* But you know how it was with our families. So many years of hurt and distrust. After getting to know your relatives, I have a feeling that was where the emotions ended for you, but in my house...my father and grandfather didn't just distrust the Morettis, they hated them with a passion."

Luca's dad, nonno, and uncles had spent more than their fair share of time complaining about the Russos and all the shit they'd pulled over the years, and Tony really, REALLY hadn't liked Matt, but hate wasn't a word his family threw around lightly.

What would it have been like to grow up with a dad who spewed such an angry emotion all the time?

Luca could feel Harper's gaze traveling between them, but she hadn't attempted to join the conversation, letting them discuss this on their own.

Luca was suddenly seeing Conor in a different light, and he realized how lukewarm his attraction toward the man had been until this moment, when he felt a strong, almost overpowering pull he was helpless to fight. "It couldn't have been easy for you, surrounded by all that hate. I can understand you getting swept up in it."

Conor gave him a funny look. "I've never hated you, Luca. I couldn't if I tried. But when you kissed Trina, I discovered I had my own Russo voice, talking in the back of my head, telling me you'd set me up and that you were going to tell everyone at school I was gay. I was terrified it would get back to my dad."

"Jesus," Luca whispered, hating he'd unwittingly caused Conor so much pain. "Conor," he started to apologize, but Conor waved it away.

"None of that was your fault. I saw what I hoped for, not what was there, and when it fell apart, I let the lessons my father taught me about the Morettis interpret the situation in the worst possible way."

"Even so," Luca murmured.

Conor looked away from him, and when he spoke again, it felt as if he was simply saying his thoughts aloud. "My dad wasn't the most tolerant of people. If he'd found out I was bi—"

"You're bi? Not gay?" Harper broke her silence. The fact she was surprised more about him being bisexual rather than gay told Luca that she and Conor had shared things with each other he hadn't been privy to. He was surprised to discover how much that bothered him. He wanted to know all their secrets, be a part of every conversation, be there for all of it.

Everything.

Conor nodded. "Yeah. I've always been attracted to guys and girls. My first sexual experience was with a girl in college. We dated for a while. She was cute, and I really liked her. When that ended, I hooked up with a guy from my business law class."

Luca ran his hand over his beard. "It's killing me that you went through all that because of me. I wouldn't want to be near me either."

Conor grimaced. "I was terrified and pissed, so I tried to put as much distance between us as I could. I switched seats in Spanish class, asked our teacher to switch groups."

Luca saw a way to try to lighten the mood. "I guess that's better than what *I* thought," he said with a small grin.

"What did you think?" Conor asked curiously.

Luca didn't hold back his smile, leaning forward, needing to be closer to Conor. "I thought it was because I was crap at Spanish."

Conor's eyes crinkled at the corners with light lines as he laughed. "Well, you *were* pretty shit at it. So..." Conor shrugged. "Silver linings, I guess."

The three of them cracked up, and when the laughter faded away, they sat quietly, simply looking at each other, and Luca felt every bit of strain that had existed between them for years completely fade away.

"I guess it's true what they say," Luca said after a moment or two.

"What's that?" Harper asked softly.

"With age comes wisdom. Because I definitely kissed the wrong person that day in the library."

Conor drew in an audible breath, his brow creasing. "What are you saying?"

Luca shifted forward until his leg was flush against Harper's, crooking his finger. Conor responded, moving toward him until the two of them sandwiched her between them. "I've never kissed a man."

"You haven't?" Conor murmured.

Luca shook his head in response. "I didn't get to be *your* first, but maybe you could be mine."

"I should—" Harper whispered.

"Don't move," Luca demanded. At the same time Conor said, "Stay."

Conor's gaze slipped to his lips, just like they had that day in the library. Luca could see it all so clearly now.

God, he'd been an idiot all those years ago. He swiped his tongue along his lower lip, closing the distance even more...until no space remained.

Conor's lips were warm, soft, and a hell of a lot less timid than Luca might have expected. It was as if too many years of pent-up need bubbled to the surface, and it erupted like lava from a volcano. For a split second, their lips merely touched, and then— it was fucking fireworks.

Conor gripped Luca's shirt, fisting the material, as Luca tilted his head, pushing his lips against his harder, driving the kiss further. Luca snaked one of his hands around Conor's neck, gripping his nape tightly, his other landing on his thigh, squeezing.

For several minutes, they fought for dominance, a battle of lips, tongue, and teeth, and breath hot enough to singe. Luca was the first to shift away, to catch his breath, because even as Conor's kiss blew his fucking mind, he was ultra-aware there was someone else there...watching them.

And he had to know, had to see...

Luca's gaze drifted from Conor's flushed cheeks to Harper's. She had leaned forward, her eyes locked on them, her warm breath tickling Luca's face.

"Holy shit. That was so hot," Harper whispered.

Luca didn't bother to hold back his grin at her words.

Conor twisted slowly to look at her, and with both of their gazes on her, it seemed as if she came to her senses. "I'm sorry. I shouldn't be..." She glanced around the room, and Luca could tell she was thinking about leaving.

"Don't," he said, his tone sharper than he'd intended.

Harper didn't respond. Instead, she looked at Conor, and it felt as if she wasn't going to listen to Luca if Conor didn't agree.

"I already told you. Stay." Conor grasped her hand. He lifted it, kissed her knuckles, and Harper offered no resistance. They crowded together, a tight, close circle of three.

Conor bent toward Harper and gave her the softest, gentlest of kisses, and Luca swore he felt the impact of it as strongly as the rough kiss he and Conor had just shared. The moment Conor and Harper parted, Luca was there.

Unlike Conor, he couldn't hold back because the second his lips touched hers, he knew.

God.

He knew.

It was magic, hot, and hungry. She tasted spicy and sweet—barbeque sauce and wine. His new favorite flavor.

Harper pulled away slightly, her lips a mere inch from Luca's as the three of them shared the same space, the same air.

"What's going on?" she whispered.

"I think you know," Luca said.

"I...don't." The look in her eyes told him she knew as well as he did those words were a lie.

Conor shook his head, looking as if he was coming out of a trance, when he shifted away from them on the couch. Luca knew the second he heard the other man sigh heavily, he wasn't going to like what came next.

Conor bent forward, his elbows on his knees, his posture one of defeat. "This can't happen."

The only thing keeping Luca from losing it was the fact it

sounded as if Conor had had to fight to pull those three words out.

"It would be irresponsible," Harper added, though her comment sounded more like a question than a statement. "We're working together," she added, as if that somehow solidified it.

"Exactly," Conor said, rubbing his chest, suddenly looking very uncomfortable. Luca hated seeing him retreat, but he also knew Rome wasn't built in a day.

Harper needed more time to get to know them, to realize that her trust in them wouldn't be misplaced, wouldn't be betrayed.

Her vow to say yes to things that made her happy was certainly something Luca could work with. Because he planned to make her—*and* Conor—very happy.

They'd hit square one.

At last.

Luca wanted to tell them that, wanted to protest their denials and reassure them that not only could this thing between them happen, it was going to—irresponsible or not.

Like Joey, he'd just planted the seed.

Now he needed to give it time, let it take root.

All he had to do was keep watering it.

# Chapter Seven

Harper closed the lid on the picnic basket she'd pulled out of storage a couple of days earlier. She was struggling to believe she'd been in Philadelphia six whole weeks. They say time flies when you're having fun, and that certainly wasn't a lie. Summer was right around the corner and with its imminent arrival, those perfect days had appeared when the sun was shining, the sky was blue, a gentle breeze was blowing, and it wasn't too hot or too cold.

When the weather app forecasted a lovely seventy-degree weekend filled with bright sunshine, all she could think about was getting out of the hotel and soaking up as much of the fresh outdoor air as she could.

It had been three weeks since she'd stolen those too brief, too wonderful kisses from Luca and Conor. Every part of that night felt like a dream, and sometimes she had to convince herself it had actually happened.

She'd spent many nights since then alone in her bed, rewriting the ending, taking out the part where Conor said it couldn't happen and she'd foolishly agreed. In her new, revised version, they'd taken those amazing kisses and expanded on them in the bedroom. Harper had burned through too many batteries, giving her vibrator a workout as she fantasized about sex with Luca and Conor.

Two men.

Just the thought of that kind of complication should have her running for the hills, but Luca had been right when he'd said seeing that kind of relationship played out through others was eye-opening. She'd had the opportunity to spend more time with Luca's family and friends. And seeing the threesomes together, and how happy they were, had her longing for something she never would have considered a possibility.

Since the afternoon of the hockey party, Harper had been invited to a couple of happy hours with Liza, Keeley, Hazel, and Penny, who'd all been at the party, plus their girlfriends, Gianna and Jess. It wasn't until she was surrounded by the group of friendly, open women that she realized just how much she missed having her best friend Luna around.

In addition to the girl time, Conor—true to his word—had hosted three more hockey nights in the buildup to the finals. She'd finally met Elio, the hockey star, and Penny's doctor brother, Rhys. Luca had truly been blessed with a large, loving family, and he was very generous when it came to sharing them with Harper, who'd always been very light on relatives.

Best of all, she'd spent all day last Saturday and Sunday with Luca's nonna, the dear woman sharing the secrets to making her eggplant parmesan and homemade pasta with her. Harper had learned more in two days from the elderly woman about cooking Italian cuisine than she had in weeks on the subject in culinary school. Nonna, as she demanded Harper call her, had invited her to the family's annual Fourth of July picnic, something she couldn't wait to attend, as it would include the entire Moretti family. She knew it would be a blast...if only she wasn't swimming in a sea of hormones, thanks to Luca's continued flirting and sexual innuendoes.

Conor insisted that not only was Luca working for them, but she and Conor had signed contracts that ensured they'd be business partners for the foreseeable future. There was too much at stake, should things fall apart. And while he'd held true to his assertion that it would be utterly irresponsible for the three of them to begin an affair, Luca didn't seem to be taking heed.

And unfortunately, her libido was proving to be every bit as powerful as her common sense. It didn't help that she'd adopted that new "yes to happiness" motto. Because she didn't doubt for a moment that saying yes to sex with Luca and Conor would make her very, very happy.

They now had set dinner nights, the three of them dining together a couple times a week. In addition to that, their group text thread—which she had named *Two Guys and a Girl*—was never silent, and they had established a standing movie night at Conor's place every Friday as well.

All of it ridiculously, annoyingly platonic...with the exception of Luca's flirting.

Part of her suspected she would have caved, seeking more kisses, more *everything*, if not for Conor. While they *were* spending a lot of time together, he'd retreated emotionally, once more becoming that serious guy who was less open, less willing to smile. She'd always gotten the sense he subscribed to an all-work, no-play lifestyle, and he was proving that true. Spending longer hours at his office, joining them for dinner, then making excuses to cut the evening short when the ever-growing sexual tension between them became too much.

A few times, she and Luca had dined alone when Conor played the "I'm busy" card. Sometimes she thought he was genuinely trying to push them away, but then the next time they were together, he'd be more chill, and his efforts to stay away felt almost half-hearted.

Up until now, she'd been following Conor's lead. But today, she'd woken up and felt different. Felt more like she wanted to skirt the line—like Luca. He hadn't initiated any more kisses, but damn if he wasn't finding other ways to close the distance between them, to tempt her. The sexy man could push her buttons with the simplest of touches. With anyone else, a polite hand on the small of her back as they walked down the sidewalk or gently brushing her hair out of her face or leaning close to whisper something into her ear during a movie would seem completely innocent. Yet, when Luca did it, her nipples budded, her panties grew damp, and she'd wind up spending an hour with her toys, trying to masturbate the man out of her thoughts.

And it wasn't just Harper that he was treating to those tempting touches. Sharing his first kiss with Conor must've spun the arrow on Luca's dial...because it no longer just pointed at women. Conor was on the receiving end of Luca's sexual teasing as well.

Last night, immediately after a meal shared at Conor's penthouse, he'd claimed he still had hours of work left to do. Luca stood from the table, crossing to stand behind him and placing strong hands on Conor's shoulders to "massage out the kinks."

Watching Conor and Luca together was as hot as Luca's hands on her *own* body. She reacted to Luca massaging his shoulders as if *she* was the one being caressed. As if Luca—a master electrician—was slowly and methodically rewiring her sexual system, and she was *not* mad about it.

She pushed those thoughts out of her mind, trying to remind herself again that they'd all agreed it wouldn't be wise—or at least she and Conor had. She couldn't recall Luca saying much of anything.

She didn't expect that decision to stick, but at least it allowed her to pretend she was being an intelligent, mature adult for another hour or two.

At least the restaurant curse seemed to have lifted. Since the fire and the theft, things had been fairly smooth sailing, and Luca was going above and beyond, making sure completion of the project wasn't delayed too much.

Glancing around the kitchenette, she tried to make sure she hadn't forgotten anything. She was surprising Luca and Conor with a picnic, hoping she could entice them to knock off a little bit early. The construction crew worked half days on Saturdays, and for the last two in a row, Conor had begun working with them.

Luca had convinced the buttoned-up businessman to let him teach him some practical carpentry skills so that he could build his own bookshelves. She and Luca had both expected the idea to be turned down flat, but it turned out, Conor loved wielding a hammer, claiming it helped him work out some of his anxiety. She wasn't sure that was true because she noticed he rubbed his chest whenever he was tense—and unfortunately, she'd seen him do it too much the past couple of weeks.

According to Luca, Conor was a quick study. So quick, in fact, that Joey had convinced him to help him put up the drywall in the kitchen. Real progress was starting to be made on the restaurant, the place taking shape and looking better than she ever could have imagined.

Even more exciting was the fact that work was underway on her future apartment as well. Another one of the Moretti Brothers' crews had finished a job, so Luca scheduled them to start renovating the two floors above the restaurant. They were still in the gutting stage, but Harper didn't care. Things were moving forward, and if all went to plan, she could actually be in her new home before summer ended.

Satisfied she had everything she needed, she grabbed her purse, just about to throw her cellphone inside when it started to ring. Glancing at the screen, she smiled when Bradley's name popped up.

"Hi, Bradley. This is a surprise." She hadn't talked to her manager since the night of the fire. The silence hadn't been intentional. She'd considered calling him several times, but something had always come up before she managed to dial the number.

"Hello, Harper. Have I caught you at a bad time?"

"No. Not at all. I'm so glad you called."

"I wanted to see how you're settling in," he said.

She and Bradley had started working together when she was

fifteen, and she and her mom signed on with his new agency. He'd impressed Mom with his can-do attitude, and while other, more reputable agencies had tried to sign her, she and her mom had decided to take a chance on Bradley.

Working together for fourteen years naturally led to a closeness, though she wouldn't call him one of her best friends. They got along great, worked well together, and for over a decade, their goals were completely the same—to turn her into a supermodel. And they'd been successful.

Unfortunately, their relationship was still a bit fractured—at least in Harper's mind—because of the way Bradley reacted three years ago, when she'd told him she was quitting. He'd cajoled, pleaded, cried, and cursed, but in the end, she wasn't swayed. When it became clear that she wasn't going to change her mind, he finally relented. The last six months, he'd been very supportive.

"It's fantastic, Bradley. I love Philadelphia."

"And the restaurant? Everything good there?" he asked.

"Yeah. Absolutely."

Bradley cleared his throat. "I ran into your mom a few weeks ago, and she said something about a fire?"

"There was a small fire, but that happened early in the renovations. You can't even tell now. The place is really starting to come together."

"I'm happy to hear that. I was worried when she mentioned it. You've been so determined to open this restaurant. I don't want anything to stand in your way."

"Aw, thanks, that's so sweet of you to say. How are things with you?" Harper silently hoped Bradley would have good news to share about the agency. She was aware she'd left him high and dry when she retired. Bradley represented other models, but for too many years, he'd stuffed all his eggs in one basket—hers. The agency had acquired a reputation as being the Harper firm, with all the big contracts, campaigns, and opportunities going to her.

He'd always referred to her as his lightning strike, and there was no denying over the years, he'd tried to make it hit again, but without much luck.

"Things are fine. We're in a growing phase, obviously, but I've just signed two new models who remind me of young Harper Bransons."

She smiled. "That's wonderful. You'll have to text me their names. I'll follow their socials. Share some of their work."

"That would be really nice of you. I'll send the names on. So have you set a date for the grand opening? I'm hoping I'll be able to score a table at the hottest restaurant in Philly," Bradley joked.

"You absolutely will, and we're still on track for a midsummer opening. Not putting anything in stone just yet because you know how it is with construction. A lot of times we're at the mercy of when we can get materials. As for the actual renovations though, the restaurant is amazing!" she said excitedly. "They laid the floor in the main dining area and it's absolutely stunning. The counters and appliances are going to be installed in the kitchen next week, and Luca has a crew working upstairs to start renovations on my apartment."

"Luca?"

"Luca Moretti. He's my contractor," she replied.

"Oh, that's right. I recall you being excited about your business partner hiring some prestigious construction firm. Sounds like it's working out."

"It is. Luca is so talented. I swear there's nothing he can't do, from electrical work, to plumbing, to construction. Conor's worked with countless construction crew on other projects, but he swears this is the smoothest one, primarily because of Luca."

"You and Conor are working well together?" Bradley asked. "I still can't understand why you thought you needed a business partner. I'm worried you might be bringing future trouble on yourself if the two of you don't see eye to eye on everything. The restaurant should have just been yours. You had more than enough money to open it on your own."

"Money wasn't the issue. Conor owns and operates two

restaurants as well as a nightclub. It was his experience within the food industry and his brilliant brain that I needed. He's been right there with me, every step of the way, guiding me so that I don't make any missteps."

"Well, I hope it stays that way."

"I'm not worried," she lied. Because she was definitely treading a very thin line and one misstep would damage her relationship with Conor. Introducing sex was the ultimate in stupidity, but her body was winning the battle over her brain these days.

"It sounds like you're working with good people," Bradley said. "That takes a load off my mind. You're a kind, trusting person, Harper. I never want to see anyone take advantage of you."

"Luca and Conor would never do that. They're the best. They're really great guys, easy to be with."

"Be with or work with?"

"Oh, well...both, I guess."

Bradley fell silent for a moment. "Harper, are you dating one of these men? Because I'm not sure entering a relationship with someone you're working with, especially your business partner—"

"I'm not," Harper interjected. "The three of us hang outside of work sometimes, but that's just because they're the only people I know in Philly. Or they were," she added, recalling the happy hour she'd just shared with the girls.

"Were?"

"I've made friends with some of Luca's relatives, went to happy hour with a bunch of women the night before last. It was a lot of fun."

"Well, it sounds like you really are settling in fine." Bradley sounded a bit grumpy, and she worried perhaps things weren't as great at the agency as he'd alluded.

"I am," Harper insisted. "In fact, I'm just on my way out to meet Luca and Conor. The crew only works half days on Saturdays, so we're going on a picnic."

"You're living it up these days," he joked.

"I'm not going to lie, I love the slower pace of life."

Bradley scoffed. "I know you very well, Harper Branson. I give you another month before you're climbing the walls, bored out of your mind. You're too much of a go-getter to spend your time on happy hours and picnics."

That had been true of the old Harper, but this new version was relaxed and laid-back. "I'm simply taking advantage of the downtime before the restaurant opens because then I'll be all go go go again."

"Well, I won't keep you any longer. Just wanted to touch base and make sure you haven't forgotten me," he teased.

Harper laughed. "Never. Text me the names of the new models, and as soon as I have a date for the grand opening, I'll let you know."

"Perfect. Talk to you soon," Bradley said.

"Goodbye." Harper tossed her phone in her purse and grabbed the picnic basket before heading out, trying to still the butterflies in her stomach that appeared whenever she was about to see her guys.

Her guys?

She grinned, and then thought a very dangerous word.

*Please.*

* * *

Luca was the first to spot Harper when she walked into the restaurant, handing whatever tool he was using to the man next to him and asking him to take over.

"This is a surprise. Didn't think I'd see you until tonight." Luca hugged her, their usual greeting these days. He was such a big teddy bear, and she loved the way he engulfed her in his arms, lifting her off her feet a few inches every time, making her laugh... and horny.

"Summer is coming," she said, in her deepest, most dramatic *Game of Thrones* voice. "And I think that calls for a picnic." She lifted the basket. "I was hoping I could encourage you and Conor to pack it in a little early and walk to Franklin Square with me."

"You had me at picnic." Luca looked around until he spotted Conor. The building was buzzing with activity, at least ten men all working at the moment. "Hey, Conor," he called out.

Conor smiled when he saw her, taking off the tool belt strapped around his waist and placing it on the ground. Harper couldn't believe the difference a couple weeks could make. Mr. Bespoke Suits was nowhere to be seen on the weekends, this Conor decked out in jeans and a light blue cotton T-shirt. He brushed sawdust off his hands as he approached. While Luca hugged hello, Conor's greeting came in the form of a brief kiss on the cheek. "What are you doing here? I thought we weren't going to see you until later."

Last night, after the movie ended, Luca suggested they take advantage of the warm weekend weather by doing something outdoors. As such, the three of them had made plans to go roller skating in Dilworth Park. It had actually been Conor's idea, when he confessed he'd never been skating but had always wanted to try.

"The skating is still on," she reassured them. "I was just hoping to entice you out into the sunshine a little earlier. I was going stir crazy in that hotel room."

Luca pointed to the basket. "She's packed us a picnic."

While Luca looked pleased whenever she brought food, Conor's expression always seemed equal parts touched and surprised, as if he couldn't believe someone was doing something for him. Which made her even more curious about the man.

One of the subjects Conor was decidedly closemouthed about was his parents. Apart from the little bit he'd shared the night they all kissed, he was quite adept at changing the subject whenever it turned to his family, or—now that she thought about it—himself.

"That was very thoughtful of you." He took the basket from her.

"So what do you say? Wanna blow off work early?" she asked.

Both men nodded.

"Let me tell Joey we're heading out. He can oversee things until quitting time, then lock up." Luca walked over to his brother, leaving her alone with Conor.

A couple of men glanced their direction, or probably it was more accurate to say *her* direction. She noted, with some pleasure, the number of looks she received whenever she showed up here was going down. It was what Harper longed for. She was no stranger to people staring at her, paparazzi flashing cameras in her face, or fans approaching for autographs or selfies. But as she became a more permanent fixture in Philadelphia, with a day-to-day routine that didn't vary too much, she was seeing the same people, who were starting to view her as just Harper rather than the supermodel or Siren's Smile. It was nice.

Luca rejoined them. "Okay, we're all good, although Joey says you owe him one of those Reuben's you made us for lunch last week as payment for him doing, and I quote," he made air quotes, "'Luca's job for him.'"

"I accept the debt." Harper tried hard not to reveal how pleased she was when Conor reached for her hand and Luca wrapped his arm around her waist, as the three of them headed out together.

Yeah, professional schmofessional.

She wanted them.

Period.

* * *

"All I'm saying is," Luca said, as he unlocked the door to the restaurant a few hours later, "we didn't establish a time limit on me collecting."

The picnic had been a blast as the three of them chowed down on turkey, apple, and brie sandwiches and caprese salad before venturing over to take a spin on the carousel. Then Luca had challenged them both to a game of mini golf, proclaiming the losers had to honor any request the winner made of them.

Conor had argued about the prize, saying it was too open-ended. However, Luca—the persuasive bastard—ultimately convinced them to take the bet. And then the shark had soundly trounced them.

Conor hadn't taken the loss well, attempting to pay off his debt right away so it could be forgotten. "The assumption was you'd make your request immediately."

Luca shook his head. "That should have been stated up front. Because I'm not sure what request I want to make just yet."

"He's going to drag this out and torture us with it for ages, isn't he?" Harper asked, laughing.

Conor crossed his arms. "I think we can bank on that."

After leaving Franklin Square, they'd walked to the restaurant together because Luca and Conor's cars were parked here. Conor had offered to give her a ride back to the hotel so she could change before tonight's outing.

Harper wasn't sure that she'd ever wanted to spend so much time with two people. She would have expected the three of them to get sick of each other at some point, but that day didn't seem to be approaching anytime soon. They always had a good time, and as soon as one get-together ended, they were already planning the next.

"Today was great," she said. "Thanks for indulging my picnic craving."

"You're the one who fed us...again." Conor placed the empty picnic basket on the floor. "We should be thanking *you*."

"Prior to moving here, I could probably count on one hand the number of weekends I didn't work, with fingers left over. You guys always make the weekends so much fun. And the weeknights. And lunchtime," she added with a laugh.

Luca reached out, tugging her toward him. She expected him to give her a hug, so she was shocked when he broke the rules, pulling her chest flush against his, their faces close. "You're easy to be with, sunshine. Spending time with you," he glanced over her shoulder to where Conor stood behind her, "and Conor has become my favorite thing to do."

Then he backed his words up with a hot kiss that was soooo not responsible.

Yes! This was what Harper had been hoping for. She was tired of denying herself what she wanted. A lifetime of dieting had been child's play compared to abstaining from kissing Luca and Conor.

She behaved equally irresponsibly when she wrapped her arms around his neck, building on his passionate kiss by adding her tongue to the mix. Luca's hands gripped her waist tightly, as if he was afraid she'd come to her senses at any moment and pull away.

"Luca," she breathed, her lips still touching his.

One of his hands left her waist, and it wasn't until she felt Conor's chest brush against her back that she realized Luca had beckoned him forward.

"I thought we agreed—" Conor started, though he sounded a hell of a lot less convinced this was a bad idea than he had three weeks earlier.

"I never agreed," Luca interjected.

Harper considered that, then realized he was right. While she and Conor had determined it would be a mistake, Luca had been quiet. Never uttering a word.

Conor released a long, slow sigh, and she held her breath, waiting for his continued refusal.

Before he could say anything, another sound captured her attention. It sounded like rain, which was impossible because it was still a beautiful, sunny day outside.

"Is that water?" she asked, when she realized Luca had taken a step back, hearing the same thing she was.

"Yeah." Luca looked around the room, then toward the ceiling. "It sounds like it's coming from upstairs."

Harper was sorry she'd pointed it out when Luca and Conor both stepped away, Luca turning and walking toward the kitchen.

There were going to be two entrances to her apartment, the original one at the front of the building, accessed from the street, and the new one Luca and his crew had just finished putting in a few days ago that was off the kitchen. Luca hadn't liked the idea of Harper having to go outside late at night after closing the restaurant to get into her apartment, so he'd created a safer inside entrance.

That was the one he was walking to now, she and Conor in his wake. They climbed the stairs, following the sound of running water until they reached what had been the bathroom in one of the former apartments. The room was one of the few that hadn't been gutted yet.

"What the fuck?" Luca said as they spotted water gliding across the hallway floor. He quickly ran into the bathroom and crossed the small space, splashing and almost slipping in his rush to turn off the water. The bathtub was filled to the brim, overflowing onto the floor.

"Why is the water running?" Conor asked as they looked around. There was at least an inch of water on the bathroom floor, flowing out into the hallway.

"I don't know." Luca reached down into the tub, his arm causing a waterfall as more water splashed onto the floor. "Fuck. Someone plugged the drain with cement!"

"On purpose?" Harper was aware it was a stupid question the second she asked it.

"It looks like," Luca replied, frowning. "No one was supposed to be here again until Monday morning. Do you know how much damage this could have done? It would have been worse than the fire."

The second he said the word fire, he and Conor exchanged a look.

"This has to stop," Conor murmured, pulling his phone out of his pocket, tapping on the screen.

"Checking the cameras?" Luca asked.

Conor nodded, clicking several times. "Yeah. Need to give it a second to load up."

Luca rung out the bottom of his T-shirt, which was now dripping with water. "There's no way these things aren't connected. We assumed the space heater had been brought in by a squatter because there hadn't been any other logical answer. Copper gets stolen from construction sites way too often. But this? This was done deliberately."

The idea that someone would purposely try to destroy what they were building was hard for Harper to wrap her head around. "But who? And why?"

Luca shrugged.

"Someone on your crew?" Conor pointed out what was the most obvious answer, though not one Luca seemed willing to accept.

He shook his head. "I can't believe that. I've worked with most of the guys on quite a few projects. Hell, I hired every single one of them myself." Luca stepped around them, out of the bathroom, walking down the hallway and checking every room along the way.

Conor and Harper watched—until he stopped.

"Son of a bitch," he muttered, then he turned toward them and cocked his head, gesturing for them to come take a look.

"What is it?" Conor asked.

"There's a broken sill, window looks like it's been pried open with a crowbar," Luca replied as he walked across the room to look outside.

"Someone gained access from the fire escape," Conor observed, stepping next to Luca.

"It's broad daylight," Harper said.

"Yeah, but I've had construction workers crawling all over this place for weeks. Not sure a guy with a crowbar would send up any alarms these days."

"Goddammit," Conor cursed.

"What's wrong?" Luca asked as he and Harper flanked him, looking over Conor's shoulders.

"The position of the camera is wrong. I can't see this part of the building at all. Whoever did it was smart enough to figure out the weak point in our security."

Luca sighed, then repeated Conor's sentiment. "Goddammit!"

"I'm going to call the security company, get more cameras. And I know we were waiting until most of the construction was done to set up the alarm system, but I vote we do it now." Conor was clearly upset.

"Agreed. Given the amount of water in the room, I'd say it hasn't been running more than an hour or so." Luca lowered the window, studying the frame. "The latch is broken. I'm going to run downstairs and grab a hammer. Nail this shut so no one else gets in. Might go ahead and nail shut any others that aren't in view of the cameras."

Conor glanced her direction, concern in his gaze. "You okay, Harper?"

She started to nod, then stopped. "You really think someone is trying to sabotage our restaurant?"

Luca ran a hand through his hair. "I don't know, but this broken window means our pool of suspects has grown beyond that of my crew. Anyone could have climbed that fire escape and broken in."

"Do you think it's possible someone is doing this to harm your company...or mine?" Conor was looking at Luca.

"That's a possibility. We've won more bids than we've lost lately. I guess we could be stepping on toes without realizing it. You have any enemies?" Luca asked.

Conor grimaced. "I could probably come up with a few or twenty, if I thought about it. Matt and I have acquired a bit of a reputation for being cutthroat when it comes to real estate acquisition. I suppose there's a chance we've pissed off the wrong person."

Neither man asked *her*. Harper considered it as if they had, wondering if there was anyone out there who might want to hurt her. Six months ago, she might have suspected Bradley, but he'd been supportive—mostly—since finally accepting her decision to retire. Fulton came to mind, but he didn't seem to hate her. It was more like he was mildly obsessed with her. Besides them, the only other person who was probably pissed off at her was her dad. But that didn't track because she hadn't heard from him in a decade.

"The fact we caught this when we did..." Conor rubbed his chest as he studied the broken windowsill.

Luca ran his hand over his beard. "We were lucky in that regard. The damage would have been a hell of a lot worse if the water had run all weekend. Jesus, I don't even want to think about how bad that would have been. Let me call Joey, get him to come back—with a mop—so we can clean up the water. In the meantime, I'll get that hammer."

He headed downstairs as she and Conor looked around the room, frustration rife on both their faces. Conor walked over and placed his arm around her shoulders.

"Never a dull moment," he murmured as he embraced her, his attempt at a teasing tone making her feel better almost instantly.

She looped her arm around his back, nestling close. "True. Let's just hope all the crap ends here. My mom said bad things always come in threes. Fire, robbery, flood. We've officially hit that limit."

Luca stood in the doorway, hammer in hand, listening to their conversation.

Conor, bless him, found a way to lighten the moment. "As long as we don't hit the plague-of-locusts stage, I'm cool."

She and Luca chuckled at his joke.

Crossing over to them, Luca leaned in until his lips were next to her ear. "You know, three isn't *always* a bad thing," he murmured, loud enough that both she and Conor heard.

Then, because he was shameless and sexy and wonderful, he gave her a quick, hard kiss before swatting Conor on the ass.

Oh yeah...their luck was changing.

# Chapter Eight

Conor stepped out of the back of the limousine as Luca left his apartment building, dressed in his tuxedo. Actually, he was wearing Matt's tuxedo.

Luca had shown up at Enigma late Wednesday afternoon, ready to claim his reward for winning mini golf.

His demand?

A prom for Harper.

Conor had half-heartedly attempted to talk Luca out of it, knowing that way lie disaster, but in the end, he relented. One, because he'd made the bet, and secondly, because it was a very thoughtful idea.

So while it was the most irresponsible thing they could do, Conor had gone along with it, his ability to remain aloof when it came to Harper and Luca all but gone.

Besides, if he'd been serious about being responsible, he wouldn't be dining with the two of them three times a week. He wouldn't be wielding a hammer every Saturday as Luca taught him the ins and outs of construction work. He wouldn't be participating in the Wednesday lunches with Luca and his buddies. He wouldn't be grocery shopping with Harper on

Monday nights as she continued building her menu for the restaurant, while creating dinner masterpieces for him and Luca. He wouldn't have taken up running with her on Sunday mornings.

He also wouldn't have established a daily coffee break with Luca every morning at eight. Well, it was a break for Luca. He and the construction crew reported to the worksite by six a.m., while Conor enjoyed bankers' hours, not heading into the office until nine.

He hadn't intended to make coffee a daily thing. Originally, he'd stopped by one morning on a whim, armed with two cups of java, just to check on the crew's progress. They'd drunk the coffee, chatted amicably...then Luca had flashed him that charming grin and joked, "See you tomorrow?"

Damn if Conor hadn't taken the bait, showing up the next day, and the next and the next, until suddenly the two of them had a standing coffee date.

So really, when placed next to all of *that*...what would a little prom hurt?

He did an internal eye roll.

He was fucked.

When the crew had clocked out at noon today, since it was Saturday, he and Luca had remained behind, putting their plans into action. They were going all out. In addition to Luca's decorations—somehow, he'd managed to get his hands on an honest-to-God disco ball—and the special playlist Conor had spent the better part of the last two days putting together on Spotify, Luca had asked his nonna and aunt Berta to prepare the "pre-prom" dinner.

Work had been completed on the main dining room of the restaurant just yesterday, the crew now focusing their time and energy on the large kitchen and Harper's apartment upstairs.

Most of the permanent components of the dining area were in place, including the recessed ambient light fixtures, the gorgeous accent lighting that emphasized the private, built-in booths along one wall, and the long, mahogany counter that would serve as the bar and a place for patrons to sit while waiting for tables. Still to come were the tables, curtains for the front windows, as well as the mirrored shelves for behind the bar, but those final touches were a couple of weeks out as the crew focused their energy on the kitchen.

However, enough of the room had been completed for their plans for this evening. They'd set one of the private booths for their meal, complete with a white tablecloth, three place settings of Nonna's special china, and a single tapered candle. Nonna and Aunt Berta—as they'd insisted Conor call them—had shown up late this afternoon while he and Luca were decorating to deliver the dishes and food, currently warming in the restaurant's kitchen. The two women had walked around the room, oohing and ahhing over everything they'd done, even as they subtly tweaked their work.

While Conor owned his own tuxedo, he'd borrowed his brother Matt's for Luca, both men conveniently the same size.

"You clean up good," he said as Luca approached.

Luca paused to admire the stretch limo Conor had secured for the evening. "Damn, man. Harper is going to flip out when we pick her up in this."

Their "prom date" didn't have a clue what they'd planned. They'd simply informed her they had a surprise for her and that she should dress in her fanciest dress.

Luca hopped into the back of the car, Conor following him and closing the door. They were picking Harper up at the hotel, then taking a driving tour of the city, while drinking the champagne Conor had on ice. From there, it was on to the restaurant for dinner and dancing under Luca's disco ball.

"Did you rent this limo, or is this your Sunday car?" Luca liked teasing Conor about his money.

Conor scoffed. "Please. The limo belongs to Russo Enterprises. My preferred Sunday car is the Aston Martin," he replied in the snootiest tone he could fake, while pretending to wipe invisible dust from the lapel of his jacket.

Luca narrowed his eyes. "Yeah. I want to believe you're kidding, but I'm not gonna lie...I might have a doubt or two."

Conor chuckled but didn't confirm or deny. Since clearing the air about high school, it felt as if he and Luca had done a reboot, their friendship picking up where it had left off in Spanish class. Luca was an easygoing guy, fun to be around, and he never failed to make Conor laugh.

The same held true for Harper.

For a guy who'd laughed precious little in his life, he appreciated being able to spend so much time with them.

It was impossible to deny that he was attracted to both, so strongly drawn to both, that everything he prided himself on—his self-control, his stoicism, his ability to make intelligent decisions without being blinded by emotion—was gone.

Cupid's arrow had struck him in the ass. Twice.

Which was absolutely fucking terrifying.

The night of his first kiss with Luca, Conor had woken up in the middle of the night in the throes of a major panic attack. He'd spent close to an hour shivering in cold sweat, fighting for every single breath, his usual methods for regaining control failing.

For a couple days after, he'd been determined to get his life back on track, retreating into his permanent patterns—work, home, sleep, repeat.

He'd failed miserably.

Because Harper and Luca refused to leave him alone.

Conor hadn't known how to fend them off because he had no experience with such persistence. Growing up, no one noticed or cared when Conor slipped away to his room. He kept his office at Enigma rather than the Russo Enterprises' building because there were only a few employees at the club during the day—and they knew not to bother him—so he was guaranteed solitude there.

He lived alone, dined alone, slept alone, worked alone. No one had ever questioned it because they assumed that was what he preferred.

Luca and Harper were the only people to ever challenge him, constantly finding ways to draw him out...draw him closer.

Giving in to his attraction to them was a huge mistake, one that would lead to heartbreak in the end. Regardless, he seemed destined to break the Russo code.

Because he was going to be weak.

Because he was going to fail.

He hated the idea of hurting Harper and Luca, of dimming their light with his dark shadows, but his ability to do the right thing was on shaky foundation at best.

Especially when Luca reached over and gripped his knee, giving it a squeeze. "You look great, man. You've got that whole sexy James Bond thing going on right now."

Conor laughed, his cock twitched, and before he could recite all the reasons why he shouldn't do this—again—he pressed a quick kiss to Luca's lips. "Thanks."

Luca regarded him, his expression equal parts surprise and pleasure.

As they pulled up in front of Harper's hotel, they stepped out of the limo. There was a distinct spring in Conor's step. Despite his objections, he'd secretly been looking forward to tonight since Luca made the suggestion.

And now, Conor felt lighter. Probably because, with that quick kiss in the limo, he'd decided to loosen his grip on the reins.

Just for tonight, he lied to himself.

"Good evening, Mr. Russo," the woman at the front desk said as he approached.

"Hello, Jenna. I need a keycard to the executive floor."

"Yes, sir."

Conor had given Harper an executive suite on the top floor of the hotel, the floor only accessible with a special keycard. Also on that floor was a large conference room with an amazing view of the city. Conor preferred to hold his meetings here rather than at the Russo Enterprises' building, so he was a familiar face with the hotel staff.

He and Luca entered the elevator, and Conor swiped the card before pushing the button for Harper's floor. Luca fussed with his jacket before running a finger under his collar, tilting his neck uncomfortably. Unlike Conor, the sexy construction worker wasn't used to ties—bow or neck. Luca tugged harder, and Conor swatted his hand away, turning to adjust it.

"Stop messing with it."

Luca sighed. "I'm not used to wearing monkey suits, let alone owning one. It was nice of your brother to loan this to me."

"You and Matt both have abnormally broad shoulders and arms," Conor teased.

Luca laughed. "They're called triceps and biceps, and we found them at the gym. If you spent a little more time using your fancy weights versus flipping pages in that living room-slash-library of yours, you might find some too."

Conor snorted, the sound cut short when Luca reached up to return the favor, fixing his bow tie. His breath caught when Luca's hands slid into the lapels of his jacket, closing around them to draw him near.

"Thanks for agreeing to help me put this together." Luca's face was so close Conor could feel the heat of his breath, smell the mintiness of his toothpaste.

"You're welcome." Conor fought the overpowering desire to close the distance between them, to steal another kiss. A real kiss. The one in the limo had been nothing more than a tease. Nothing like the first one they'd shared.

As Conor wrestled over whether to go for another kiss, Luca made the decision for him, using his grip on the jacket to pull him forward. It was hard for Conor to believe Luca had never engaged in an affair with another man. There's wasn't a trace of hesitance or reticence in his touch. And his kisses...

Jesus.

Conor's dick woke up and took notice.

When he released Conor, Luca grinned and gave him a wink.

"Never considered kissing James Bond before tonight."

Luca admitted last weekend that he'd never agreed to keep things between the three of them platonic. Then he'd backed up that assertion by kissing Harper. Had they not been interrupted by the damn water leaking above them, Conor knew without a doubt, he would have allowed himself to be drawn in. He'd tried to convince himself he'd been saved by that overflowing tub, but he could see now all it had done was delay the inevitable.

Regardless...his conscience wasn't completely down for the count just yet.

*Russos aren't weak.*

*Russos don't fail.*

God, he hated that fucking voice in his head, but he couldn't deny it would be wrong to give in to this simply because he was too weak to do the smart thing.

"Luca, about tonight. I'm not sure—"

The elevator doors slid open, Luca stepping off without giving Conor a chance to finish what he wanted to say. Conor followed when he took off in the direction of Harper's suite.

"Luca." Conor placed his hand on the other man's forearm when they reached her door, trying once more.

Luca knocked, then faced him. "Just roll with this, Conor. Trust me to get us there."

Conor frowned, confused. "Get us where?"

Luca raised one eyebrow, giving him a look that said they both knew *exactly* where this was headed, but before Luca could call him on it, the door opened—and they fell silent.

No.

Silent was the wrong word.

He was awestruck, and a quick glance Luca's direction told him that he was too.

Harper had followed their instructions, the beautiful woman

standing before them in a shimmery, off-the-shoulder evening gown that appeared black at first, until Harper turned slightly, revealing that the dress was a rich, deep emerald green. The skirt had a scandalously long slit that revealed most of Harper's right leg, ending at her upper thigh. The bodice dipped in the front, giving Conor a generous glimpse of the top halves of her breasts. The waistline nipped in to create the most perfect hourglass shape he'd ever seen. She'd paired the dress with black heels adorned with sparkling jewels.

Harper had left her hair down, the thick blonde waves flowing over her shoulders and back, framing her gorgeous face. Normally, Harper's makeup was minimal, the woman rarely doing more than swiping on some mascara and lip gloss and calling it good enough.

Tonight, while her natural beauty still shone through, she'd taken special pains, doing that look women referred to as smoky eye, her lips a shimmery red that drew his attention to how plump and full and utterly kissable they were.

Her eyes lit up when she saw them in their tuxedos, those perfect lips parting slightly with a quick intake of surprise. That initial response morphed quickly, as he and Luca were graced with what the world referred to as Harper's siren smile.

God knew it was calling to him. Conor was fully prepared to throw himself on the rocks for this woman.

"Wow," Harper breathed. "You guys look... Wow."

Luca reached for Harper's hand, lifting it to kiss. "You're the most beautiful woman I've ever seen, sunshine."

Conor nodded, struggling for a moment to speak. "Beautiful isn't a strong enough word," he finally managed to say.

Harper blushed at their compliments, then reached out to a table by the door to grab her clutch. "So, are you going to tell me what this surprise is now?" She stepped out into the hallway and closed the door behind her.

Luca shook his head. "Nope."

The question from Harper and that response from Luca had

been playing on repeat ever since Thursday night at dinner, when they'd issued the invitation. Harper was, apparently, no fan of surprises. She'd texted, called, and nagged, and Conor had been grateful they'd only had to survive two days of her constant inquisition.

When they stepped out of the hotel and Harper spotted the limo, she stumbled slightly. "That's for us?"

Conor placed his hand on the small of her back, propelling her toward the car. He was aware they were drawing a bit of attention as several phones were suddenly pointed their direction. While Harper was becoming more of a familiar face around Philadelphia, she still turned heads every time she went out in public. It wasn't unusual for her to sign autographs or pose for several selfies as they pushed their cart through the grocery store. That kind of scrutiny would have driven Conor mad, but Harper handled it with good grace, always smiling, never rude. It was no wonder people loved her, viewed her as the girl next door. There truly wasn't a mean bone in her body.

They climbed into the limo together, Harper laughing as Conor popped the cork on the champagne bottle, pouring them each a glass. The three of them were sitting together on the backseat, Harper nestled between him and Luca.

"To surprises." Luca lifted his glass.

Harper narrowed her eyes, pretending his toast annoyed her, but she still tapped her glass against theirs and drank.

Conor was amazed by how comfortable he was with these two people. He'd always struggled with establishing close relationships. Most of his younger years were spent with his brothers as his constant companions and playmates. Dad was a private, judgmental man, who believed children should be seen, not heard. Between his temper and Mom's wavering mental health, he'd never felt comfortable inviting friends over to his house.

Then, after he started having panic attacks, he retreated even more into himself, terrified someone might witness him falling apart. After so many years on his own, he figured he was probably socially stunted, but none of that was apparent when he was with Luca and Harper.

With them...he fit.

The chauffeur had been given directions to take them on a scenic drive of the city, mainly because Harper's hotel was only a few minutes away from the restaurant and he wanted to ensure they had time to drink their champagne and enjoy the ride.

They'd just polished off their second glasses when they pulled up in front of the restaurant.

Harper frowned. She'd stopped by just this morning armed with their Saturday coffee and donuts—yet another set routine established over the past few weeks.

"My surprise is the restaurant? Did you finish something?"

Conor could hear the confusion in her tone. Probably because she knew they were weeks away from completing the kitchen and the apartment above.

He shook his head, stepping out of the limo when the chauffeur opened the door before reaching back to help her.

Harper took his hand, joining him on the curb. He didn't release it. When Luca emerged from the limo, he grasped the other.

"Ready?" Luca was clearly excited to reveal what they'd done.

Conor unlocked the front door, hitting the light switch—the one Luca had rewired just for tonight, to turn everything on at the same time.

Harper's eyes widened as the disco ball began spinning, and the soft accent lights beside their booth and countless strings of twinkle lights turned on. Those lights, plus some dim recessed lighting behind the bar, allowed them to create the perfect atmosphere for their prom.

Luca had even gone so far as to recruit Liza and Keeley to create a banner that he'd hung on the wall, revealing their prom theme. Because of time constraints for decorating, he'd opted for "Night Under the Stars," something they'd managed to create simply enough by stringing all the twinkling lights around the room.

"Oh my God!" Harper released their hands, walking farther into the room, spinning around to take it all in. As she did so, Luca strolled over to their booth, lighting the candle, while Conor headed to the bar, turning on the instrumental music he'd selected for during dinner.

He'd called Liza for suggestions, and she'd told him to simply download the soundtrack to *Bridgerton*, which he'd never heard before but had to admit was quite beautiful. The orchestral strands of "Wrecking Ball" began playing.

When he turned around, he caught sight of Harper wiping her eyes.

"Harper," he said, walking over to her at the same time as Luca.

"You made me a prom." Her voice was thick with unshed tears.

Luca smiled, pulling her into his arms for a hug. "We wanted to do something nice for you. You've been feeding us gourmet meals for weeks."

Harper stepped into Luca's embrace. A second later, one of his arms snaked out, and Conor found himself being tugged into the hug.

The three of them stood there, swaying slowly to the music.

"Actually," Luca said, the first one finding the strength to pull away. "The dancing starts after our pre-prom dinner."

"You cooked?" Harper asked with just enough shock—and perhaps terror—that Conor was torn between laughing and taking offense.

Of course, the terror was justified, so when Luca shot her an "are you kidding" look, the three of them cracked up.

"Hell no," Luca replied. "I recruited Nonna and Aunt Berta because, well, you heard me say we wanted to do something *nice* for you, right?"

Harper grinned. "This is perfect. So incredibly perfect."

Her words warmed Conor's heart, and he was so grateful to be a part of this, that Luca had thought to include him. He only wished he'd thought of it himself.

"Why don't you go take a seat," Conor said to Harper, "while Luca and I go grab the food?"

Heading to the kitchen, Luca walked straight to the warming pans, but Conor stopped him with a hand on his forearm.

Luca turned to face him. "Everything alright?"

"Thank you," Conor said. "For thinking of tonight, for asking me to help. This is..." He couldn't put into words how much this night meant not just to Harper but to him as well.

Luca gave him a quizzical look. "Conor, man. Tonight was *never* happening without you. You're a part of this."

His throat closed as those words sank in.

He was a part of this, of them, of something...incredible.

Luca studied his face intently—so intently that Conor didn't need to say anything. Luca grinned. "You finally ready to accept it?"

Conor nodded, his throat clogged by so many emotions—Jesus, *positive* emotions—that he couldn't speak.

"Good. Now let's go woo our girl. If it was any woman except Harper, I'd suggest we skip dinner and go straight to the dancing, but you and I both know the best way to win Harper's heart is—"

"To feed her," Conor interjected, the two of them laughing as they grabbed the plates piled with chicken parmesan, lasagna, green beans, as well as the basket overflowing with homemade crusty bread.

Dinner was the perfect blend of fun and intimacy. They had chosen the booth because it was a circular one, nestled into a corner, and Harper clearly sensed the switch in their dynamic as every "just friends" wall came crashing down.

At one point, Harper dipped her bread into the olive oil, seasoned with herbs, lifting it to give Luca a bite. He accepted it from her fingers, sucking them in along with the food.

It was the sexiest thing Conor had ever seen.

Then Luca cut off a bite of his chicken parmesan, lifting his fork to Conor—who'd selected lasagna for himself—and encouraged him to try it.

Conor leaned forward, allowing Luca to feed him, and any hope he'd had of keeping his hard-on at bay was lost for good.

Not that Harper was helping the situation. Her hand found its way to his thigh, slowly gliding upward. One glance across the table told him she was giving Luca the same sexy caress. He hissed at the same time Harper's hand grazed Conor's cock, discovering the tent he'd pitched in his tuxedo pants.

Harper huffed out a soft breath—half laugh, half moan—then she pulled her hands away, both of them scowling, already missing her touch.

"Just making sure I'm not the only one about to spontaneously combust," she said, grinning shamelessly.

"Too much more of this and I'm not sure I'm going to be able to dance." Luca reached down to adjust his pants.

"It's prom," Conor said. "We have to dance."

Reaching for his phone, he changed the music, selecting the song he wanted to play for their first dance.

Harper smiled when he stood and held his hand out to her. "May I have this dance?"

She nodded, and Conor drew her into the center of the room, directly under the disco ball. She started to clasp one of his hands, placing the other on his shoulder, but he shook his head, drawing her hands to his shoulders before placing his on her waist in true high school dancing style, the two of them slowly swaying.

"If memory serves...this is how the teenagers dance."

"Never would have pegged you for a country music fan," she said.

Conor tilted his head toward Luca, who remained in the booth, watching them. He had fired up a romantic country song, Blake Shelton's "Nobody But You."

"Blame his cousin, Liza," Conor replied. "She and I spent an entire Sunday at Gage and Penny's house, painting the nursery a few weeks ago."

"You, not Matt?" Luca rose from the booth.

"He got called away on business and asked me to help Liza. I'm ninety-nine percent sure he scheduled that unavoidable meeting in New York on purpose to get out of painting."

Luca chuckled. "No doubt Liza bombarded you with country music the entire time."

Conor nodded. "Yep."

Luca stood next to them for a second or two. "I was going to wait my turn, but I like this song. *Our* song," he declared.

Conor sucked in a long, slow breath as Luca moved to stand directly behind Harper, placing his hands below Conor's, more on her hips than her waist, joining them in the dance.

Two sways later, Luca had closed the distance, shifting until his chest was pressed against Harper's back. Then he pushed a little harder, not stopping until her breasts brushed against Conor.

They were close enough now that they shared the same air, and Conor recalled those first kisses in his living room, how close they'd been, how much he'd liked sharing his personal space with them.

At the time, Conor had thought himself so smart for pulling away, putting space between them, thinking professionalism was more important than...this.

He'd been a damn fool.

Because if this was weak, he never wanted to be strong again.

For most of his life, he'd avoided situations that might cause him stress, convincing himself he was better off alone rather than dragging someone down with him. He'd grown up in a house with mental illness. He'd felt the pain, the uncertainty, the fear. His mother's depression, her dark days, had terrified him when he'd been young. Conor had read enough since to know that panic attacks and depression often went hand in hand. He'd decided a long time ago that he didn't have the right to ask someone to live under that same dark cloud, and God help him if he had kids because there was no way in hell he'd subject a child to the things he'd gone through.

But now...there was a part of him, a quiet, optimistic part, that was certain if anyone could help keep his anxiety at bay, it was these two people.

Tonight, that hope was stronger than his willpower. He was so fucking tired of being alone, of making himself invisible.

For the first time in his life, he refused to hide in the shadows.

He felt seen, but more than that, he felt *wanted*.

"This is nice," Conor murmured, wishing time would stop right here.

"It is," Harper whispered, lifting her face, inviting him to kiss her.

He kissed her softly as they continued to dance. Her lips parted, her tongue touching his. Conor's eyes drifted closed, but not before he saw Luca lean forward to place his own kisses to Harper's bare shoulder.

He felt her shudder, heard the rumbling growl of need low in Luca's throat, felt his own body heat rising.

Conor broke the kiss, and Harper twisted in his arms, turning until, now, like before dinner, they were wrapped in a three-way embrace. Luca pressed his lips to Harper's, kissing her with that same hunger Conor had felt from the man during their own kisses.

Then Luca turned toward *him*, gave him the softest of smiles before laying claim to Conor's lips in a kiss so hot, it could render him to ash.

Over and over, they switched partners as he kissed Harper again, then Luca, then watched the two of them. Conor had never been a part of anything more incredible.

They continued moving in time to the music, as Blake sang about the person he couldn't live without.

The lyrics matched Conor's feelings perfectly. Since hearing it for the first time with Liza, he'd played it over and over, always with images of Luca and Harper floating through his mind. Conor was certain he'd never want anyone but them.

Right or wrong.

Just for tonight or for always.

When the song ended, Luca pulled back a bit. "I think we should move this dance to somewhere more private. Preferably somewhere with a bed."

Chapter Nine

Luca wasn't sure how they'd managed to make it from prom to Conor's penthouse in a limo without losing any clothing, especially considering how hot and heavy they'd gotten.

The second they'd climbed into the vehicle after turning off the lights and locking the door of the restaurant, they'd come together in a rush of hands and lips and tongues. They hadn't even cleared the damn dishes off the table; they were in too much of a hurry.

Fortunately, the limo had been parked close.

The ride had passed in the blink of an eye, but that didn't mean they'd been idle. Luca had climbed into the car first, Harper following. She hadn't bothered reclaiming her seat from earlier, instead hiking up the skirt of her dress—thank God for slits—and straddling his hips.

Luca hadn't dry humped since high school, and he'd sure as shit never come from it, but damn if Harper hadn't gotten him close. So close, he'd panicked enough to lift her off his lap and onto Conor's, where she'd taken him on the same ride.

Luca had played out tonight—this night—with Harper and Conor so many times in his head since those first kisses that he'd almost fooled himself into believing it had already happened. He'd never had so many vivid fantasies in his life, never jerked himself off so much, only to grow rock-hard again seconds later.

The chauffeur dropped them off at the private parking garage entrance, off-loading them directly next to the elevator that led to Conor's apartment. They didn't waste the brief ascent, resuming the hot kisses from the limo.

As the elevator doors slid open, they walked into the living room as a singular unit, the three of them a mass of intertwined arms, their lips kissing anything and everything they could reach.

Luca ran his tongue down the side of Harper's neck, stopping only to place a sucking kiss on her shoulder as she and Conor frenched like the plane was going down.

"Bedroom," Luca managed to growl when they paused just inside the penthouse. Either they moved now, or Luca was pulling them down to the floor and fucking them right there.

His demand had the effect of a starter pistol as Conor and Harper broke apart, gasping for breath.

Conor clasped hands with Harper, pierced Luca with a "follow me" look, then headed toward the steps that led to his room upstairs.

Once they were in the bedroom, Conor reached for Harper again.

Luca watched them kiss, his mind going a million miles a minute, every thought leading him back to the same realization.

He was falling in love with them.

Shit, there was no *falling* about it. He'd already taken the tumble. Because he was pretty sure he'd lost his heart to Harper the second she'd flopped down onto that curb, bit into that Quarter Pounder with Cheese, and let loose with a moan so sexy, his dick woke up and took notice.

Luca had always been attracted to witty, fun-loving girls, looks falling much lower on his list of turn-ons. Give him a girl quick with a joke and an infectious laugh and he was a goner.

Considering all the crap Harper had endured in her life—

between her shitty lovers and user dad—he was amazed by her immense positivity and giving nature. She was an amusing storyteller with a self-deprecating sense of humor, especially when it came to her newfound love of food. Luca couldn't remember a time when she hadn't shown up at the construction site, shoving a cookie or donut or cheesesteak sub or potato chips or God only knew what else in her mouth.

She not only had a huge appetite when it came to food but also for life.

Before her arrival, Luca had fallen into a rut, his days playing on repeat, the same daily grind, same weekend activities, same hangouts, same everything. And he hadn't sought to change it because at the heart of it all, he'd started to give up hope.

Hope that he would find the same deep, amazing love that his brothers and sister had found.

Harper had given that hope back to him, reminded him to be grateful for the small things in life, to find pleasure in the simple everyday tasks that he'd forgotten he loved.

He had never felt such an instant, visceral attraction to a woman. And it had fuck-all to do with the fact she was gorgeous, and everything to do with the fact that she was Harper.

As for Conor...well. That first kiss had been eye-opening— and it had only whetted Luca's appetite for more.

While Conor was proving to be a tougher nut to crack, Luca didn't intend to stop trying, because his attraction to the man was off-the-charts intense. During the rare times when Conor let his guard down, he'd revealed himself to be intelligent and insightful and fascinating. The guy was literally a walking encyclopedia, full of all these interesting tidbits, his knowledge seemingly endless. Which made sense when Luca considered all the books the man had read.

Conor's confession about his feelings in high school had rocked Luca to the core, but more than that, it had sparked an awareness deep inside him. Because the more he played back that day in the library over in his mind, the more he considered that near kiss, the more he wondered if he really would have pushed Conor away. They'd been standing very close—*too* close for just friends. And it hadn't occurred to Luca to move back because...he hadn't wanted to.

Luca thought Joey had planted the seed about Conor, but he was starting to believe it was *Conor* who'd dug a hole all those years ago.

Unfortunately, Conor hadn't lowered all his walls, and while Luca felt confident their past had been fixed, there was still something holding the other man back.

Luca shook himself free of those thoughts, his attention refocused to the here and now as Conor shucked off his jacket, tossing it heedlessly to the floor, something Luca would bet a million bucks the tidy man had never done before. He and Harper had started teasing Conor about his fastidiousness—in his home, his office, and his attire. Conor never had a hair out of place.

Except for right now, when the strands were standing on end, thanks to Harper running her fingers through them, gripping handfuls of the dark brown hair in her attempt to keep his lips on hers.

Harper kissed like she ate, voraciously, with a lot of appreciative moaning. Luca could watch these two for the rest of his life and never get tired of the show. He wasn't the type to hold back in the bedroom, his past lovers calling him dominant, even aggressive—though that hadn't been a complaint.

However, Luca was in uncharted territory tonight because he'd never been with a man. He and Conor had only shared a few kisses, most of those tonight, and while he knew what fit where, it wasn't like the two of them had discussed the important shit.

Like top and bottom.

Fuck.

Luca had promised to get them there, but what he *hadn't* done was lay the groundwork. Instead, he'd reverted to character and bulldozed them all into this bedroom together because it was where he'd desperately wanted to be.

So he needed to proceed with caution.

Because this mattered.

Too much.

So much that he didn't want to rush things, didn't want to screw it up. He'd misinterpreted Conor's feelings when they were younger, and he'd unintentionally hurt him. He didn't want to do that again.

Luca didn't realize anyone had noticed his hesitance, too lost in his own thoughts, until he felt Conor's hand on his shoulder.

He shifted until his lips brushed Luca's ear. "We have time. Tonight is for her."

Luca pulled back, looking at Conor's handsome face. They should have always been friends. It had been obvious in high school they were...not exactly kindred spirits but a matched set. Or maybe polar opposites was the better descriptor.

Where Conor was book smarts and the definition of white collar, Luca was the blue-collar guy who'd read one book in his life and used it for every book report from seventh grade to graduation. Luca liked to have a good time and was frequently called the life of the party, while Conor was quieter, more likely to hold up a wall than tear down the roof.

Luca couldn't explain why it worked, but it did. He nodded, shirking off his foolish doubts because he was exactly where he wanted to be.

He cupped Conor's cheeks and kissed him, a long, deep kiss filled with promise. When they parted, their foreheads pressed together. "Soon," he murmured.

Conor stepped away, his breathing heavier. Harper, like Luca, seemed to enjoy the voyeur role as much as the participant one. She stood just to their side, taking in everything. They'd spoken loud enough that she heard every word. There were three people in this relationship, friends and soon-to-be lovers. Luca never wanted any secrets between them.

"Come here." Luca crooked his finger at Harper, whose eyes were heavy-lidded, still drunk on Conor's kisses.

She stepped in front of him, offering no resistance when he placed his hands on her hips, turning her so that they both faced Conor.

"Take off your clothes," he said to Conor, his arms wrapped around Harper's waist. His words were a test—a small one—and the slight pause and narrowing of Conor's eyes before he pulled the knot of his bow tie loose told Luca what he needed to know.

Conor would follow *some* of his commands, but not all.

He slowly slipped the tie from the collar, dropping it on top of the jacket before lifting his fingers once again to unbutton his dress shirt. Conor took his time, drawing it out, perfectly aware of the effect it was having on his audience.

When he shrugged the shirt over his shoulders, and Harper drew in an audible breath, Conor gave them a sexy smirk. Luca's authority had tweaked him, so Conor was getting even by giving them the slowest, hottest striptease in history.

Luca reached down to adjust his pants, the tight material beginning to chafe, given how long his dick had been hard. His erection had made its first appearance the second Conor stepped out of the limo outside Luca's apartment, and it hadn't softened beyond half-mast since. He was approaching the danger zone, aware that it was going to take every ounce of self-control to keep himself from coming in Matt's tuxedo pants if Conor didn't hurry the fuck up.

When Conor reached for the button of his slacks, Luca felt Harper still, aware that neither of them was breathing. The only sound in the room was the hiss of Conor's zipper sliding down. He was moving faster now—halle-fucking-lujah—his haste apparent in the way he toed off his dress shoes, then shoved his pants and boxer briefs down together.

Luca had grown up with three brothers, played countless sports, spent plenty of time in locker rooms. He was no stranger to seeing other men's naked bodies, but he'd never felt an iota of attraction or need or...*whatever the fuck* he was dealing with now.

The best way he could describe it was overwhelming, devastatingly painful desire. He'd never looked at a man through less than straight eyes, never studied the male physique and gotten fucking hard from it, but the image of Conor's thick, hard cock, jutting upward, bouncing against his tight stomach, sent his imagination down some wicked, dirty paths.

Conor was a desk jockey, but there was no denying the past few weeks had changed that, had hardened his body, defined some muscles, now that he was doing manual labor every Saturday, as well as running with Harper.

Conor held their gazes, not shying away from the fact he was the only one naked. He let them look their fill before tilting his head. "You two are good for the soul. No one's ever looked at me like…"

"Like they're going to die if you don't fuck them in the next few minutes?" Harper asked.

Conor snorted. "Yeah. Like that."

Luca appreciated the humor, but he'd be damned if he could join in on the joke. Harper had overestimated how much time they needed. He wasn't counting in minutes, rather in seconds.

Reaching for the tab, he drew down the zipper at the back of Harper's dress. Once it cleared the small of her back, the shimmery material fell loose, gravity taking it straight to the floor. She'd kicked off her heels the second they'd walked into the bedroom, which left her in a black strapless bra and tiny thong.

"Fuck," Conor breathed, his gaze traveling the length of her body.

If there was something that turned Luca on more than anything, it was confidence, and the fact Harper and Conor were both standing there without seeking to cover themselves, comfortable in their own skin, ramped up Luca's desire for them even more. Something he wouldn't have thought possible.

Luca remained behind her, his hands grazing her sides as he looked over her shoulder, treated to a bird's-eye view of her breasts, framed by the lacy bra.

She'd gained weight since moving to Philadelphia. Not a

surprising thing, considering she was determined to make up for too many years of dieting. He was glad because, in his opinion, she'd been rail thin before, and knowing that she'd once collapsed due to overwork and starving herself, he planned to help her understand just how fucking beautiful she was right now. Her body was changing, filling out in all the best ways. She had curves that he couldn't wait to race his lips and hands and tongue over, her tits were larger, her newly rounded ass utterly spankable.

Luca unfastened her bra, dropping it onto the discarded dress, then he knelt behind her, slipping his fingers into the elastic of her thong, pulling it off as well.

Rather than rise immediately, Luca sank his teeth in, nipping one of her ass cheeks until she yelped, then he soothed the red spot with a wet kiss.

Standing, Luca watched as Conor reached out for Harper, clasping hands with her, drawing her over to his bed. Luca teased Conor about his Midas-like wealth, but he was grateful for it now as the two of them sank down on the side of his California king.

"Your turn." Conor tilted his head at him, even though Luca already had the bow tie unknotted.

He quickly shed his jacket and shirt, tossing them over the arm of a chair. He saw their eyes drink in his tattoos.

Harper crooked her finger at him, beckoning him over. He stepped in front of them as they each reached for an arm, running their fingers over his tattoos.

"I love these," Harper whispered.

"Me and Gio got our first ink together when we were sixteen. Had to badger our dad for months to sign the consent form. He finally agreed, but only if we chose small designs that were completely hidden under our shirts."

Conor snorted. "Guess that rule didn't stick."

Luca grinned. "We followed it every time we convinced him to let us go back. After our eighteenth birthdays, though, it was on like Donkey Kong. Gio's got full sleeves on his arms too."

"Totally sexy," Harper said, Conor nodding in agreement.

"There's no way in hell my dad would have ever let me get a tattoo," Conor said.

"The funniest part is, Dad's gone with us the last few times, getting several of his own tats—none of which are fully covered by his shirt."

"Do as I say, not as I do," Conor murmured.

"Yeah. Something like that." Stepping back from the bed after letting them look their fill at his ink, Luca wasted no time stripping off his pants, boxers, socks, and shoes.

"Whoa," Conor said, his gaze slipping down to the tattoos on Luca's thighs. "Fuck me, you're hot."

Luca reveled in their scrutiny, reaching down and fisting his hard cock, loving the way they followed the motion of his hand.

"How does this work?" Harper's face was flushed. She was looking at Luca for guidance, which thrilled him because if there was something Luca had no trouble doing, it was giving orders in the bedroom.

He glanced at Conor. "Kiss her."

Conor didn't need to be told twice. Enveloping Harper in his arms, he kissed her passionately, neither of them breaking apart as Conor pushed her to her back on the mattress, leaning over her.

Luca moved to the other side of the bed. "Climb into the middle. Leave room for me."

Harper and Conor shifted almost as one before resuming the same positions—Harper on her back, Conor hovering over her, caging her beneath him. They continued to kiss as Luca crawled onto the bed, lying down next to them. He'd considered merely watching this time, ready to tell Conor to take her first, but it was impossible to be so close to them without touching.

He ran his hand down Conor's spine, his long stroke ending at his ass, which Luca gripped and squeezed.

Conor lifted his head, the hunger in his eyes almost tangible. "Condoms are in the nightstand drawer behind you," he said to Luca, who was closest.

Twisting and opening the drawer, he grabbed two.

Rising to his knees, Conor reached out for one, but Luca shook his head. While they agreed tonight was for Harper, that didn't mean Luca wasn't going to be hands-off when it came to Conor.

Using his teeth, Luca tore the packet open, then pulled out the condom.

Conor hissed when Luca slid it on him, his palm rolling the rubber down Conor's thick erection with a firm grip.

"So hot," Harper whispered.

Once the condom was in place, Luca released him, planted a hard kiss on Harper's lips, then winked at her.

She gave him a breathy laugh. "I'm going on record right now as saying this is the best thing I've ever said yes to, and I'm pretty sure there's no topping it ever."

Conor grinned. "Better than that Quarter Pounder with Cheese?"

"Oh damn, I forgot about that," Harper joked. "Okay, this is second best."

Luca laughed, ruffling her hair before closing his fist around her long tresses, giving it a tug to see...

Harper's eyes slid closed, her lips parting. "Oh!"

"We haven't touched the tip of the iceberg on the things we're going to do to you, sunshine," Luca purred. "Maybe hold off on determining rank until after."

Conor groaned. "Keep talking like that and this isn't going to last long."

Reaching between them, Luca slid his finger between her legs. She was wet and hot, so ready for what came next. Finding her clit, he stroked it, Harper's hips tilting upward as she sought more. She jerked slightly when Conor joined the game, slipping two fingers inside her as Luca toyed with her clit. They continued to play as she gyrated beneath Conor, her body on sensory overload.

"God. Please! Conor," she whispered, panting. "Come inside me. I need—"

She didn't get the chance to finish, didn't need to as Conor pulled his fingers out, then thrust inside her in one deep, hard push.

Her back arched, and she moaned as Conor began moving in earnest, Luca watching, spellbound.

They shifted together, their movements fluid. It was hard to believe this was their first time because he'd never seen two lovers so in sync, so in tune to each other's needs.

"Jesus!" Conor breathed when Luca slipped his hand between them again. He caressed Harper's clit because he was desperate to be a part of this moment. Watching wasn't enough. It would never be enough.

Three firms strokes later and Harper was there, crying out Conor's name and—God help him—Luca's as she came.

But Conor, the sexy fucker, pounded her through that orgasm, not giving way.

Luca gripped his cock in one hand, stroking himself as he slid his other hand lower, letting his fingers glide over Conor's dick as it slid in and out of Harper.

Conor and Harper both groaned as Luca played with them, alternating between stroking her clit, cupping Conor's balls, while fighting like hell not to erupt into his own fist.

"Fuck," Conor cursed through gritted teeth, glancing up at Luca with a pleading expression. Luca knew exactly what he wanted. While Harper had already come once, Conor wasn't content with that, didn't want to come without her.

Luca released Conor's balls, returning to her clit, stroking it with the same speed and force of Conor's thrusts until she jerked roughly, the next orgasm causing her body to visibly shake. Goddamn, she was gorgeous when she came, her cheeks flushed bright pink, her shiny blonde hair tumbling over the pillow beneath her head, thick, curly eyelashes fluttering over her bright blue eyes.

Conor was right there with her this time, his back arching, his face contorted by the pleasurable pain of his climax.

Luca had never felt more connected to anyone in his life as he did these two people.

And he had a twin, for God's sake.

Time passed slowly as his lovers fought to catch their breath. Then Conor withdrew, dropping to the mattress on the opposite side of Harper.

"Holy shit," Harper said at last.

Luca grinned. "That was the sexiest thing I've ever seen in my life."

Conor sat up, throwing his legs over the side of the bed. "That was... I never... *Jesus*," he mumbled, rising and walking to the bathroom to dispose of the condom.

Luca chuckled. "I think you fucked our brainiac senseless."

Harper giggled with delight. "I can't believe I'm here. With the two of you. Like this."

"It feels good, doesn't it?" Luca asked.

She nodded emphatically. "Sometimes I have to remind myself I've only known you guys a short time. It feels like you've always been in my life. Of course, maybe part of that is because I don't feel like my life—the one I wanted to live—really started until I moved here. So when I look at it that way..."

"We've lived a lifetime together." Conor leaned on the doorframe between the bathroom and the bedroom. He'd washed up, the fringes of his hair wet from where he'd splashed his face with water. He had a washcloth in his hand.

Walking to the bed, he gently tugged at Harper's knee, running the cloth along her slit.

She stared at Conor. "I thought guys only did that in romance novels."

He snorted. "I think you'd be more likely to find Luca in the pages of one of those books than me. Not sure there's a lot of demand for the broody, nerdy, boring businessman types."

"You couldn't be boring if you tried," Harper said.

Luca gripped the back of Conor's neck, placing a kiss on the side of his head. "I think nerds are hot."

Conor rolled his eyes. "Come on, man. Read the room. That was your cue to tell me I'm *not* a nerd."

Harper cracked up, shaking her head at Luca. "Even I didn't fall into that trap."

Only with these two could Luca be sitting buck naked with an erection hard enough to cut glass and still laugh his ass off.

"Come on." Luca rose from the bed and slapped Conor's ass. "Time to get serious again."

"Ooooo. I like when you guys get serious," Harper said, sitting up.

Conor sat on the bed with his back against the headboard. Obviously, he was settling in, expecting to merely watch.

Luca shook his head. "Shift to the middle of the bed, sexy nerd. You're not sitting this one out."

Conor gave him a crooked grin. "What did you have in mind? Because I'm not sure what kind of world-class recovery time you romance novel heroes have, but I might need a few minutes. Or, you know, an hour."

Luca rolled his eyes. "You'll be fine. Lie down, Conor."

Once Conor was in place, Luca placed his hand on Harper's back. "You and Conor are switching positions this time. Climb over him. Hands and knees."

Harper moved quickly, and once again, he felt compelled to bite her very juicy, very gorgeous ass.

She squealed when his teeth sank in and attempted to escape. Luca gripped her hips, holding her in place.

"Is this ass-biting a fetish of yours?" She looked over her shoulder at him, batting those curly lashes.

"If it is, it's a new one inspired by you," he admitted. "I've never bitten a woman's ass before in my life, but damn if I don't want to leave a mark on yours."

"Is this a good or bad time to tell you guys that my sexual experiences so far have been limited to strictly vanilla?" she asked. "Although you probably figured that out on your own, given the descriptions of my past boyfriends—the older, married man, the stoned rock star, and the gay billionaire."

Luca worried perhaps they were pushing her too far, too fast.

But before he could address that concern, she added, "You've seen me eat, so you know firsthand that boring vanilla will never sate my appetite. I'm chocolate, butter pecan, rainbow sherbet, and pistachio, all rolled into one. So I hope you're prepared to indulge every single one of my kinky fantasies."

"Jesus, sunshine. I don't think that will be a problem," Luca replied, as he cupped her breasts.

"Remember you said that," Harper warned. "Because I'm not kidding. My list is extensive and...adventurous."

Luca released her tits, pressing a firm hand between her shoulder blades. "Consider us warned. Now give Conor a kiss but keep that ass in the air. We're about to go on an adventure."

Reaching for the second condom, Luca quickly put it on before caressing Harper's ass and the back of her thighs as she and Conor kissed.

"Is a spanking on your list?" he asked.

Harper lifted her head a few inches, turning to glance at him. "It's at the very top."

And they were off.

Luca smacked her ass lightly, just to see how serious she was. When she wiggled it, silently asking for more, he slapped her harder, until her skin flushed pink.

Harper whimpered but didn't attempt to escape, even as Luca added more strength to his spanking.

"God," Conor groaned. "She loves it. She's soaking wet."

It wasn't until Conor spoke that Luca realized the other man was fingering her.

"More," Harper whispered.

She was the answer to a prayer he never would have been bold enough to pray. Luca started spanking her again, and from the up and down motion of her hips, he could tell she was fucking herself on Conor's fingers.

She flew apart only a minute later, her body shimmering with sweat as she cried out. She went stiff, then limp as she fell fully atop Conor's body.

Luca remained where he was, kneeling between hers and Conor's outstretched legs. He gave her a moment to recover, his gaze locked with Conor's as Harper rested her cheek on his chest. Conor's arms were wrapped around her back, his fingers lightly stroking her.

Luca saw the same wonder, the same "how the fuck did we get so lucky" emotions he felt reflected back to him in Conor's eyes.

He started to fear Harper had fallen asleep, and he was about to come up with a plan B if so because there was no way in hell he could go to sleep without taking care of his erection. The blue balls would kill him.

However, Harper surprised him when she stirred, slowly shifting until she was back on her hands and knees.

The look she flashed him was pure seduction. "What are you waiting for?"

It was all he needed to hear. Luca gripped his cock, guiding it to her opening. He felt Conor's fingers sliding along her slit. He seemed to suffer that same overwhelming need to touch, to be a part of the action.

Once the head of his dick was lodged inside, Luca gripped her hips. "Hold on, sunshine." He slammed inside, straight to the hilt, then held steady for a second before he reared back and began to fuck her in earnest.

She cried out his name, then Conor's, falling from her hands to her elbows, no longer able to support her own weight.

Conor was there, wrapping his hand around the back of her neck, kissing her lips, her cheeks, her forehead, his whispered words weaving their way around all three of them.

"So beautiful. So perfect. God...I never want this to end," Conor repeated, speaking with an openness Luca had never heard from him.

Luca felt those words all the way to the depths of his soul because he felt the same.

Then words didn't matter as he was swept over the edge, into the abyss with Harper, the two of them coming together.

Conor didn't have to worry about the end.

Because Luca had found his forever.

## Chapter Ten

Harper popped a jelly bean into her mouth as she stepped into the cabin and looked around, equal parts impressed and amused by their surroundings. The impressed part was how cozy and homey this little cabin in the woods was. The amusement was solely driven by the horrified look on Conor's face.

"Where's the rest of it?" he asked.

"No worries, city boy. There's no outhouse." Luca, oblivious to Conor's concern, pointed to a closed door toward the back corner. "Bathroom is through there."

Harper tried not to laugh, but the way Conor's frown grew more pronounced was just too damn funny. Her laughter captured the attention of both men.

"I think this is called roughing it," she said to Conor.

His scowl lightened a little when he realized he wasn't doing a very good job of hiding his opinion of the place. "I offered to put us up in a five-star hotel," he pointed out. "In New York City."

Luca scoffed. "There's no way a five-star is going to compete with this. Come here." He led Conor back through the door to stand on the front porch. "Draw in a long, deep breath, man." Luca placed his hand on Conor's shoulder. "Smell that?"

Conor shook his head. "I don't smell anything."

"That's right. You don't. Because what you're not smelling is garbage, smog, and greasy hot dogs floating in tepid water."

"Mmm. Hot dogs," Harper joked.

"Brat." Luca ruffled her hair playfully before turning his attention back to Conor. "What you *are* smelling, my sexy nerd, is fresh, clean mountain air. There's nothing like it."

Conor smirked. "Fine. Odorless air. Got it. But I feel like I need to repeat my original question." He turned, pointing into the cabin. "Where's the rest of it?"

This time, Luca understood and, like her, he was amused. Tilting his head toward Harper, Luca shrugged nonchalantly. "What she said. We're roughing it."

"I love it." Harper walked farther inside, dropping her overnight bag on the floor, as Luca and Conor walked the five steps necessary to travel from the front door to the kitchen, where they put down the bags of groceries.

She popped another jelly bean, wincing at the taste. "Oh fuck."

Luca and Conor turned around quickly, alarmed.

"What's wrong?" Luca asked.

"Blech. I just ate a toasted marshmallow one. Disgusting." She looked at the bag of jelly beans and scowled. "A mixed bag of Jelly Bellys is a goddamn war crime." Then she tossed another jelly bean in her mouth and smiled. "Mmm. Strawberry Daiquiri. All better."

Both men laughed, returning to the groceries as Harper drifted five steps in the opposite direction, to the area designated as the living room. She studied the entire place, which was complete with what she assumed were standard Cabin 101 prerequisites—rough-hewn floorboards, log walls, a handmade quilt on the bed, and a fireplace with a soft bearskin rug in front of it.

Luca noticed her attention was focused on the bed.

"I didn't think you guys would have a problem with us

sharing the one bed, since I made it pretty obvious this was going to be a weekend hookup," Luca said.

Harper snorted. "Like we haven't been doing that practically every night for the past two weeks."

Following their prom night—which seriously ranked at the top of the most thoughtful gestures ever—the three of them had established a routine.

And by routine, she meant they'd regressed right back to their "first love" teen years, texting and talking on the phone all day, counting down every minute until they saw each other again. In the past two weeks, they'd returned to Conor's penthouse seven times for sex, dinner, sex, then sleep.

Seven times!

If Luca had gotten his way, they would have spent all fourteen nights together, but Conor insisted he needed to work some nights, which made sense considering he oversaw the management of a nightclub.

Even so, it had been seven nights of so many orgasms, Harper's clit felt like it had a permanent pulse. Her guys kept her so primed and ready with their sexts and stolen kisses whenever she stopped by their work during the day—because she couldn't wait until quitting time to see them—that she was starting to think a light breeze could make her come.

She'd been delighted when Luca had told them to pack a bag for the weekend this morning as they lay in bed, trying to ignore his early-as-fuck alarm. As a model, she'd pulled some early mornings, but since moving to Philadelphia, she'd become a professional at waking up naturally.

When Luca announced his plan for a weekend escape, Conor had been quick to offer an alternative to the cabin-in-the-woods idea. Obviously, Conor wasn't much of an outdoorsman. She and Luca had laughed their asses off when he pointed out that every horror movie in the world couldn't be wrong when it came to sleeping in a secluded cabin in the middle of the forest. He'd even gone so far as to offer to fly them to New York City in his family's private jet and put them up in a ritzy suite in the middle of Times Square, sweetening the deal with the offer of a spa day and Broadway show.

Luca had been completely unimpressed, so Harper suggested a compromise. They would take Luca's trip this weekend, and Conor's another.

"There's no TV," Conor pointed out as he joined Harper in the living area.

Luca, who'd been putting the groceries in the fridge, turned around and scoffed.

"Now you're *really* reaching for shit to bitch about. There's a TV in every room in your penthouse, including the fucking big screen in the theater room," Luca pointed out. "We haven't turned a single one on in two weeks."

Conor couldn't argue with that, so he didn't bother trying. Instead, he plopped down on the couch, lightly rubbing his chest as he glanced around the small space again, a slight stress line creasing the space between his eyebrows.

Luca had convinced their workaholic lover to take off a few hours early so they could begin their two-hour drive to the Poconos shortly after three. Perhaps it was stress over missing work that had Conor looking slightly on edge. Hopefully once they got settled, he'd start to relax and enjoy himself.

Luca had taken the whole day off—his first break since work had begun on the restaurant—so by the time he'd picked them up, the car was loaded with groceries, wine, beer, a case of water, bait for fishing, and everything else he claimed they would need for the next couple of days.

"I bought some steaks." Luca tossed a pack of meat on the counter. "Thought we could grill these for dinner."

The moment Luca mentioned food, Harper found herself gravitating toward the kitchen, curious about what else he'd packed. She'd done most of the cooking over the past couple of months, Luca and Conor referring to themselves as her "sous chefs," which meant they leaned on the counter, drinking wine or beer, handing her ingredients or stirring the pot while she did the lion's share of the labor.

Before she could peek into the refrigerator, Luca closed it on her, holding it shut.

She frowned, but he didn't give her a chance to complain.

"You've been cooking for us nonstop, Harper. This weekend, we're feeding *you*."

Harper wasn't entirely sure that was the kind gesture he intended. The guy really was a disaster when it came to over-seasoning and overcooking. "I like feeding you," she said, trying not to reveal her concerns.

Luca gave her a quick peck on the cheek. "And believe me, we love you feeding us too. But let us do this for you. One weekend. I swear, sunshine, I bought stuff that even *we* can't screw up."

"Speak for yourself," Conor said from the opposite side of the kitchen counter. "I don't even know what's on the menu."

Luca smirked. "Trust me, Oven Mitt. You can handle it."

Harper laughed at the nickname, one she and Luca had given Conor a few nights earlier when Harper had asked him to pull the pizza from the oven—and he'd reached right in, grabbing the stone with his bare hand.

"Burned the hell out of my hand," Conor grumbled, though he was grinning. "And that was *your* fault, Luca. You were distracting me."

Luca shrugged unapologetically. "Not my fault you've got a sexy ass."

He'd been fondling said ass, his hands shoved in the back pockets of Conor's jeans, when she'd made her ill-timed request.

"So how did you find this place?" Harper asked.

Luca opened a bottle of red wine, pouring a glass for Harper. "It belongs to Uncle Cesar and Aunt Margaret, Liza's parents," he added for clarification, which Harper appreciated, because *damn*, he had a big family.

"They used to bring their kids up here at least once a month year-round," Luca continued.

Conor frowned as he looked around the cabin. "Liza is one of four kids."

Luca chuckled. "Yeah, well, I'm one of five, and we used to come here from time to time too. Uncle Cesar likes to see the place used, so he was always offering it up to the rest of the family on weeks when his brood wasn't coming. When we were kids, Mom and Dad would bring us up here one week each summer. We didn't have a lot of money, so it was the only vacation they could afford."

"Where the hell did you all sleep?" Conor asked.

Luca pointed to the living area. "Sleeping bags on the floor. It was great."

"It *sounds* great." Harper carried her wine to the kitchen table, sitting down as Luca grabbed a bag of frozen fries from the freezer. He wiggled his eyebrows at her, so she responded in kind by rolling her eyes, then sticking her finger down her throat in true "gag" style, especially since she'd spent one night teaching them how to make homemade fries. "Lazy," she mouthed.

He chuckled as he placed them on a cookie sheet, sliding them into the oven before handing Conor a bowl and a knife, pointing out the salad fixings. Harper loved to cook, but there was something very sexy about watching these guys work in the kitchen. "I always wanted a brother or a sister," she admitted.

"I have a couple of brothers I'm willing to off-load for cheap," Conor said, though Harper knew it was a joke, given the affection in his tone whenever he mentioned Matt or Gage.

"There's nothing like a big family," Luca said. "Those summers here were magic. We fished and swam in the lake, hiked all over the place, told scary stories around the firepit, played hide-and-seek in the woods. One summer, when Layla was in kindergarten, we thought we'd lost her for good. Spent nearly an hour searching the area for her before we worked up the nerve to tell Mom and Dad we couldn't find her. Mom laughed and said Layla had come inside because she was tired, so she'd put her down for a nap. Didn't have a clue we'd been playing a game or were freaking out. Those weeks were some of the best times of my life. Then..."

"Then?" Conor prodded.

"We stopped coming after we moved to Baltimore. I was in fourth grade. My dad had started a new job and couldn't get a lot of time off. Then Mom got sick...and for a couple years, we didn't go anywhere except to the hospital."

Harper had learned Luca's mother passed away from cancer, but it was the one subject he seemed reluctant to talk about.

"How old were you?" she asked.

Luca put a skillet on the stove and started heating some oil. "When she got sick? Twelve. I was fourteen when she died. Ovarian cancer."

"I'm sorry," Harper said quietly.

"Funny how it feels like it happened so long ago and yesterday at the same time," Luca said.

"I get that," Conor replied softly.

Luca placed his hand on Conor's shoulder. "You lost your mom when you were pretty young too."

Conor nodded. "Nineteen."

Harper waited for him to say more, perhaps tell them how she died, but he remained silent, and she could tell he was uncomfortable with the subject.

Her heart ached as she thought about these two men, just boys when they'd lost their mothers. She suddenly felt the need to call her own mom.

"It was rough for a couple years after she died," Luca said. "I mean, Dad was struggling, grieving while trying to take care of five heartbroken kids. Nonna and Nonno told him he needed to come home, needed to be with family. That was when Uncle Renzo came up with the idea for Moretti Brothers Restorations. Talked my dad into going into business with him. So we uprooted again, moving from Baltimore back to Philly."

Conor stopped chopping the lettuce, looking at Luca. "That

must have been rough on all of you. So many changes in such a short period of time."

Luca shrugged. "The moving back wasn't so bad. I didn't hate Baltimore, but I hated living so far away from Nonna and Nonno, my cousins. It was just... Coming home didn't feel the same, you know? Without Mom there."

Conor looked as if he understood perfectly.

Harper swallowed hard, a lump forming in her throat.

"The first year back was an adjustment. Gio and I were just starting high school. Tony was a senior." Luca put the steaks on. "That whole school year, we were just going through the motions because nothing felt normal. Dad was working overtime to get the company started, Aunt Berta and Nonna took turns coming to our house to make dinner, both of them doubling down on giving us motherly love. Never been hugged so much in my life," he said grumpily, though the half smile gave him away, told her he didn't mind those hugs at all.

Harper had spent an entire weekend with Nonna, learning to make her eggplant parmesan. Luca had hung out a few hours with them, waiting to "humbly" sample his favorite food. Even now, his grandmother smothered him with hugs and kisses, calling him *patatino*, though why she thought six-foot-five Luca resembled a little potato was anyone's guess.

Luca flipped the meat. "At Tony's graduation party, Dad announced we were taking a family vacation, so a few days later we packed up the van and came here. We fished and swam in the lake, hiked, told scary stories, and for the first time since my mom died, things felt okay. We felt like ourselves, like a family again. This place...it's special to me...and I wanted to show it to both of you. Wanted to tell you why."

"I'm glad you brought us here." Harper rose from her chair and gave him a kiss on the cheek.

Conor moved closer, wrapping his arms around them. "You've convinced me. This is way better than a hotel in New York."

The three of them finished preparing dinner, eating together just as they had countless times over the past couple of months. Harper recalled the first night the three of them had dinner together at the pub, after the fire. Even then, she'd felt this instant connection to them, and it had only continued to grow as they spent more time getting to know each other.

As a model, she'd always felt like she was playing a part, never able to truly be herself. With Conor and Luca, she was the real deal—not holding anything back.

After dinner, they cleaned up, then moved to the living room. Even though it was early summer, it was still chilly in the mountains, so Luca started a fire. Harper quickly stretched her legs out on the bearskin run, and Conor wasted no time sitting down near her.

Luca walked back to the kitchen, returning with an open bottle of wine and three glasses. Pouring a glass for each of them, he dropped down next to Conor.

She sighed. "This is perfect, Luca. So relaxing. Getting away for the weekend was a good idea."

Luca took a sip of his wine. "Thought maybe we could take advantage of the change of scenery, take a break from work," he said, looking at Conor, their resident workaholic.

"Okay," Conor said. "I get it. I've been working too hard."

Luca shoulder-bumped him. "You do realize you're basically the boss, right? You don't have to burn the midnight oil every night."

Conor snorted. "I'll be sure to tell Matt you said that."

"Please do. Because I know for a fact *that* guy's clocking out every day before five."

"Liza snitching on him?" Conor asked.

Luca chuckled. "Bragging is more like it, talking about how he's always waiting for her with a glass of wine when she gets home from work."

Conor shook his head in disbelief. "I have to admit, I'm trying to figure out where my brothers acquired these romantic inclinations. Because they sure as shit didn't learn them from our father."

Harper noticed Conor's slight wince. He really wasn't comfortable talking about his parents. He looked down at his wine glass, reaching up to rub his chest. That action had become a tell, an indication that he was about to pull away—sometimes physically, sometimes by checking out of the conversation.

She didn't want to lose him either way tonight, so she stepped in. "You really think it's only your brothers who are romantic?"

Conor tilted his head, giving her a curious look.

"You threw me a prom," she reminded him. "There's no way Matt's glass of wine after work beats that."

Conor smiled, shrugging off her compliment. "It was Luca's idea."

"Maybe so." She set her glass on the floor before crawling up to him. "But you made that romantic playlist."

Once again, he deflected. "Liza suggested the—"

She placed her finger over his lips, cutting him off. "It was romantic. *You* are romantic." She backed that assertion up with a kiss, not letting up until Conor responded, his tongue stroking her lower lip.

When she pulled away, the clouds that had formed in his eyes had lifted, and he looked relaxed once more.

She gave him a wink. "My work here is done."

Luca laughed, reaching out to ruffle her hair, something that was becoming his habit. It was ridiculously affectionate and endearing...so, of course it made her horny as hell.

Everything these guys did kept her in a constant state of arousal. She'd worry about that if they weren't backing up all those flirty touches and sexual innuendos with orgasms. Lots and lots of orgasms.

Scooting back across the rug, she dropped dramatically to her back, lifting her hands above her head. She cleared her mind completely, living in the moment as she took in everything around her. The wood-beamed walls and ceiling painted orange by the soft flickering light from the fire, the crackle of the logs as they burned, the heat in the room, and the rich red wine, all working together in such a way that she was certain she'd never been this relaxed in her life.

Luca, who was sitting near her head, stroked her hair gently, looking just as at peace as she felt.

Conor scooted down near her feet, his back resting against the end of the couch. He lifted her legs so that her feet were in his lap. His actions reminded her of the foot rub Luca had given her, his claim that it was part of his seduction arsenal.

When Conor dug his thumbs into the soles of her feet, she moaned blissfully.

"Mmm," Luca hummed. "Good call, Conor. Probably best to move things along or our girl is going to fall asleep right here in front of the fire."

"You think a relaxing foot rub will stop that?" she asked.

"Luca knows I don't plan to stop at the feet." Conor tightened his grip on her arches, then shifted, his massage traveling from her feet, to her ankles, to her calves, rubbing her muscles with firm squeezes and deep caresses.

She was wearing loose-legged capris, so his touch was unhindered until he reached her knees. Bending forward, he unfastened her pants, pulling them and her panties down, tossing them over his shoulder.

After two weeks of sex-a-palooza, they'd become quite unrestrained, none of them feeling the need to ask permission, none of them hesitating when it came to getting the others out of their clothes.

"Take off your shirt," Luca said to Conor, his tone filled with that gruff demand she found so incredibly sexy.

So far, Conor had let Luca take the lead in their bedroom games, seemingly content to go along for the ride. Tonight was no different. Conor reached for the hem of his T-shirt, pulling it over his head before reaching out for her again, his hands shifting from her knees to her inner thighs, his touch softer, almost tickling.

Not to be outdone, he also decided to even the playing field. "Take off *your* shirt," he said to Luca, even though his eyes were glued to her legs.

Luca grinned, then did that ridiculously hot move guys have where they reach back, grip the neck of their T-shirt, and pull it off with one hand. Once he was shirtless, Luca moved to her side, closer to Conor. Bending forward, he placed a kiss on Conor's shoulder, and they exchanged a look—a hungry look—as Harper lay still.

The sexual tension between the men sparked so hot, they didn't need the fire anymore. Even though they'd slept together seven more times since prom, their sexual routines followed a predictable pattern. One where the guys kissed and touched each other, but only fucked her.

She'd been a witness to Luca's first male-on-male kiss, so obviously he was new to everything as far as sex with a man. She understood their desire to take things slow.

But there was slow...

And then there was slooooow.

Luca grasped the back of Conor's neck, pulling him forward for a wet kiss, one so rough, Harper suspected one or both might have bruised lips come morning. It went on for ages, but she didn't mind.

Watching them only drove her own needs higher.

"Ohhhh," she breathed, reaching down to touch her throbbing clit, to fill her too-empty pussy. She was desperate for more. Wanted dinner with her show, and she didn't mind taking care of her own needs if it meant Luca and Conor would keep kissing, keep touching, and maybe...more.

That plan failed spectacularly because even though they were still kissing, her actions didn't go unnoticed. She was just about to hit the jackpot when Luca's hand shot out, grabbing her wrist to halt her.

Conor chuckled, a darker, dirtier sound than she'd ever heard from him. "Bad girl."

Holy.

*Fuck.*

She might have expected Luca to say something like that; her tatted, blue-collar lover had proven himself to be a master when it came to dirty talk.

But hearing those two words from Conor?

It took every ounce of her self-restraint not to fan herself.

"No touching." Luca lifted her hands and placed them on the rug by her head. "That's ours. *Only* ours. You gave it to us, and you can't take it back."

"Luca," she said—okay, whined.

He hit her with a stern look that told her she wasn't going to win this argument. "Leave your hands there, or we'll find something to tie them up with. And if you make us do that, I promise you won't come for hours, not until we've taught you exactly who this pretty pussy belongs to."

He backed up that promise—he probably meant is as a threat, but damn, come on—by firmly cupping her pussy, giving her slit only the barest of strokes before releasing her again.

She groaned, half tempted to disobey him. But she knew he wasn't lying, and while the idea of Conor and Luca edging her for hours sounded wicked and wonderful, it also sounded fucking painful because her little kitty needed to come.

Now.

So she'd play by the rules and get her orgasm sooner rather than later. One day in the future, when she'd had her fill of orgasms from them—maybe thirty or forty years from now—they could revisit the edging idea.

Luca ran his hand over her head, brushing a strand of hair from her face, before turning back to Conor. She expected them to start kissing again, but Conor clearly had other ideas.

"Take off your pants, Luca," he demanded, his tone laced with a hint of imperiousness she'd never heard from Conor before.

Luca narrowed his eyes, and she wondered—hoped—that she was about to witness an alpha male battle, because how hot would that be? She sensed only the slightest tug-of-war between them as Conor had thus far acceded to Luca's commands without issuing too many of his own.

The idea that that might change...

She likened Conor and Luca to two male lions fighting over the pride. Maybe she should suggest they wrestle it out. Naked, of course.

She was disappointed when Luca, who hesitated only a moment, rose to his knees, unhooking his belt and unfastening his jeans. Rising, he slid them off completely.

Conor reached out as soon as Luca was naked, taking his cock in his fist, stroking it with a firm, confident grip that had Luca panting within seconds.

So far, Harper had taken the submissive role in all their sexual explorations because she liked it, liked the way Luca took control. Her past lovers hadn't been anything to write home about, all of them unimaginative in the bedroom. She hadn't lied about her inexperience because all she'd indulged in during the past twenty-nine years was missionary and doggie style.

Boring.

Although she understood now that it wasn't the positions, but the lovers who'd made sex so dull. Because, in truth, she, Conor, and Luca hadn't engaged in much more than that these past two weeks either. The three of them still excited by simply exploring, caressing, and kissing every nook and cranny until they fell on each other in a mad dash of explosive passion.

With Luca and Conor, it didn't feel like "just missionary and doggie style." It felt fucking amazing and exciting.

Tonight, however, she wanted more from them...and *for* them.

She sat up slowly. Luca shot her a warning look, but she shook her head, reaching out to run her fingers down his arm, then Conor's.

She followed those touches with kisses. Conor started to envelop her in his embrace, to pull her into that perfect circle of three they'd created, but she shoved away, moving until she was just out of their reach, sitting on the edge of the rug.

"Harper—" Conor started.

"Shhh. It's my turn," she murmured.

"What's that mean?" Luca asked.

She tilted her head, hoping she wasn't making a misstep here, hoping that both men wanted to take their relationship to the next level. Neither of them was making the first move, so perhaps it was time to give them a little shove in the right direction.

Harper gestured to Conor's hand, still gripping Luca's dick. "Use your mouth instead," she whispered.

Luca jerked slightly, the action catching Conor's attention. They looked at each other, and it felt as if they were engaging in some deep, meaningful conversation, all without saying a word.

"You want that?" Conor asked in a gravelly voice.

Luca nodded just once. "More than I can say."

Conor released a slow breath, then gave them one of those too-infrequent grins. He tilted his head toward the couch. "Go sit there."

Luca moved over to the couch, perching on one end, his legs outstretched, making room for Conor, who followed.

Kneeling between Luca's legs, Conor resumed his previous grip, stroking him a few times before bending forward to take the head of Luca's cock in his mouth.

Harper and Luca gasped at the same time.

"Come here, sunshine," Luca said gruffly, moaning at the end as Conor slid farther down his dick.

She stood, pulling off her own shirt and bra, her eyes locked on Conor's mouth on Luca.

Luca patted the couch next to him, but she shook her head, walking over to sink down next to Conor on the floor.

"The view is better down here," she said.

Luca chuckled, but only for a second, the sound cut off by a groan. Her gaze flew to where Conor had reached between Luca's legs to cup his balls.

Releasing Luca with a pop, Conor shifted slightly, making room for her. "If you stay down here, I'm going to put you to work."

She laughed breathlessly. "You say that like it's a threat."

Conor grasped her hand, pulling it between Luca's legs, using his own to hold it as he encouraged to cup his balls the same way he had. Then he grasped her forefinger, guiding it lower, pushing it against a spot that had Luca pounding his fist on the couch cushion, his back arching.

"You two will be the death of me," he said through gritted teeth.

"Perineum," Conor murmured in her ear. "Just call it the guy's G-spot. Keep rubbing it."

She followed his directions as he lowered his head once again, taking Luca deep into his mouth. Neither man was small, their dicks quite impressive, skirting the line between the top range of normal and OMG-that's-huge. Not that Luca's girth was holding Conor back.

Harper continued stroking the spot Conor had shown her, loving that her intelligent, straitlaced guy had called it by the anatomically correct name instead of just saying it was the taint.

Conor showed no mercy for Luca, taking him all the way to the back of his throat in the next rough thrust. His nose brushed Luca's stomach, as Luca's body grew slick with perspiration.

"I don't think...I can hold off...too...much..." Luca reached out, taking a handful of Harper's hair in his hand, his grip tightening to a stinging pain that sent an electrical zap straight from her scalp to her pussy. He'd discovered her love of hair-pulling right out of the gate, and the clever bastard had used it effectively ever since. The fact that even now, as he was on the verge of his own climax, he was thinking of her, of ensuring she was a part of this, sank deep under her skin, finding its way into her heart until a word popped out.

Love.

She was falling in love.

With both of them.

That wasn't an emotion she had a lot of experience with. She'd thought herself in love before, but when she looked back on those shitty relationships, she realized it was just another way supermodel Harper had been playing a part, taking on the role of devoted girlfriend because she thought that was what she was supposed to be.

She knew without a shadow of a doubt that she'd never been in love until now, and the sheer impact of that knowledge left her blinking rapidly to hold back her happy tears, determined not to distract her men from the incredible moment they were sharing, not just with each other but with her as well.

Harper moved back, wanting a better view of their faces. "Finish it," she whispered into Conor's ear, and he moaned around Luca's cock, wasting no time doing exactly that.

Luca didn't last another thirty seconds, his eyes clenched in a pleasure that looked like it hurt, his body going stiff for just a moment before turning boneless.

Conor swallowed, giving Luca one last stroke before lifting his head, looking a bit like a man possessed. Without missing a beat, he pushed Harper to her back on the bearskin rug, caging her beneath him. The blow job had turned him on as much as her, his cock thicker, harder than she'd ever seen it.

She opened her legs and lifted them, using her ankles and calves to pull him toward her. The head of his dick brushed her pussy. She was so ready, she was surprised when he froze.

"Condom," he murmured.

She knew he wasn't wearing one. She didn't care. "I get the birth control shot."

The look Conor gave her was one of pure wonder, and from the corner of her eye, she saw Luca leaning forward, his gaze locked on them.

Conor thrust inside her in one long, deep push—and then he took her with a hunger and a passion she couldn't believe existed.

Luca joined them on the floor, kneeling next to them, his

hand cupping one of her breasts, teasing and pinching the nipple, finding a way to give her a tiny bit of pain that lit up of every nerve ending in her body. She came far too quickly, taking Conor with her, the two of them riding the wave all the way to the shore together.

When she opened her eyes, she saw both men—*her* men—looking down at her.

It was on the tip of her tongue to tell them she loved them; the feeling so strong she felt as if she could explode from the pressure of it.

And though she saw that same emotion reflected in Luca's eyes, it was Conor's gaze that kept her silent.

Because while she was ready to say the words, there was something sad, something distant in his eyes that told her Conor wasn't ready to hear them.

*Chapter Eleven*

Luca stretched but made no move to leave the bed. He'd never literally spent an entire day in bed, but it was starting to look like that was all he, Harper, and Conor were going to manage today.

Of course, he wasn't complaining about that. Right now, his lovers—his boyfriend and girlfriend, as he was starting to think of them—were dozing next to him, Harper's head pillowed on Conor's chest, her bare ass pressed against Luca's thigh.

Life was good.

Really fucking good.

Luca grinned to himself as he recalled Conor's blow job last night.

Jesus. He loved blow jobs, always a big fan, but there was something about getting one from a guy, from someone with a working knowledge of the equipment, that took it to the next level.

Not that Harper hadn't added her own fuel to the fire, following Conor's directions, finding extra ways to ensure he blew his load quicker than he ever had before.

He'd tried all his standard mind games, trying to distract

himself so he could hold out, but not a single one of them worked.

After Conor had taken Harper on the floor, the three of them had made their way to the shower, where they'd blown through every drop of hot water in the cabin, scrubbing each other's backs and fronts and...

Once they finally made it to the bed, Luca decided he'd wanted to repay the favor, wanted to see if he could drive Conor out of his mind with his mouth.

If he lived to be a thousand, Luca was certain nothing—NOTHING—would top the feeling of Conor's dick sliding in and out of his mouth, combined with the image of Harper's back arching, her hips writhing, her ass bouncing in front of Luca. Conor had demanded that she kneel over his face so the sexy man could treat her to the same thing he was receiving from Luca.

Harper and Conor had come at the same time, both panting, groaning, cursing as their orgasms rumbled through them. Luca swallowed every drop of Conor's come, painfully aware that he had wasted too many years as a straight guy.

They'd woken up several times throughout the night, having sex like it was their last day on the planet. While he and Conor had moved their play forward with the blow jobs, they still hadn't broached the subject of fucking each other yet.

Luca had given it a lot of thought, considering himself in both roles—top and bottom. He was willing to try both, but if he was being honest with himself, he already knew he was going to prefer top, going to love fucking Conor's ass.

They'd ventured out of bed briefly this morning, but that was only because they'd worked up quite an appetite. Between the three of them, they'd managed to rustle a big platter of bacon, scrambled eggs, and toast, all of which they fed each other in bed, before falling onto each other for more sex, more orgasms, more...everything.

After that, they'd fallen back to sleep, napping the afternoon away. Luca reached for his phone, surprised to discover it was just after three.

Placing his phone back on the nightstand, he felt Harper stir.

Twisting, he wrapped his arm around her, caging her in place, while he stroked his fingers along Conor's bare chest, waking the other man as well.

"What time is it?" Conor asked gruffly, clearing his throat.

"Three," Luca answered.

Conor seemed surprised. "I don't think I've ever spent an entire day in bed...without being sick."

Harper grinned. "Me either. I love it."

"So do I." Luca placed a kiss on Harper's shoulder, none of them making any move to get up. "Guess at some point, I should start making dinner."

"What's on the menu?" Harper asked. "I can help."

Luca hummed. "Nope. No need. Nonna made us homemade lasagna. It's in the fridge. All I have to do is heat it and bake some garlic bread."

"Sounds delicious." Conor glanced around the room.

"What are you looking for?" Harper asked.

"My cell," Conor replied. "I feel like the thing is usually glued to my hand. It's just occurring to me I haven't looked at it since we got here. Didn't even charge it last night."

"It's nice to unplug once in a while," Harper observed. "I don't know where mine is either."

They both looked over at Luca, and he gave them a guilty grin, since his was right beside him. "Oops."

Conor rolled his eyes, while Harper laughed. "You were the one who said we were taking a break from work," she reminded him.

"I know. All I did was send Joey and Gio a quick text, making sure everything is okay at the restaurant. No more *accidents*," he said, making it clear he didn't think anything that happened had been an accident.

"Still no idea who might be doing the sabotage?" Harper asked them.

Conor sighed. "I've been giving it a lot of thought, wondering if the vandalism might have something to do with the Eddingtons."

Harper pushed up onto her elbows, resting on her stomach with her back arched, so she could see him and Conor at the same time without having to keep turning her head. "I don't know who that is."

"Richard Eddington is a prominent businessman in Philadelphia and up and down the East Coast. Patricia's his socialite daughter." Luca tilted his head, confused. "Why would they want to harm one of *your* businesses, Conor? I thought their beef was with Matt and Liza."

"I'm not sure they would. Patricia had set her sights on Matt, shortly before he and Liza became a couple," Conor explained to Harper. "She didn't take his rejection well, so she dug up some..." Conor paused.

Luca scowled. "She dug up a bunch of shit involving Matt and my uncle Renzo. I was with Tony and Liza the day we confronted him about the gambling markers he'd bought."

Harper's eyes widened. "Matt bought gambling markers? That belonged to your uncle?"

Luca nodded, while Conor grimaced, forced to confess, "Matt planned to use the markers to drive Renzo and Moretti Brothers Restorations into bankruptcy."

"You guys don't mess around when it comes to family feuds, do you?" she said.

Luca laughed, and even Conor grinned as he shook his head. "I guess we don't. Anyway, I was supposed to open a restaurant in one of the Eddington hotels. We'd been in talks for several months. Sage has been successful, so—"

"That's an understatement," Harper interjected. "Sage is *the* premiere restaurant in Philadelphia. It's got two Michelin stars, for God's sake. Why do you think I was so thrilled when you agreed to a partnership with me?"

Conor was clearly pleased by her compliment, proud of his restaurants. In addition to the upscale Sage, he also owned Chives, a comfy American-style restaurant.

Conor continued his explanation. "Richard wanted me to open a Sage Too in one of his casinos in Atlantic City, wanted to capitalize on the name and success of the first. I'd seriously been considering entering into business with him before all the stuff went down with Patricia and Matt. After that..."

"You pulled out?" Luca asked.

"Yes. Told him I wasn't interested in a partnership with him." Conor looked at Harper. "I think he misinterpreted that as I wasn't interested in *any* partnerships, unaware that you and I were already working together. A few weeks later, we did that interview with the local reporter where we discussed opening our restaurant together. Richard called me, pissed as shit that I'd formed a partnership with *you*, while I'd bailed on one with him. He made a bunch of empty threats until I got fed up and hung up on him. Maybe he's seeking revenge."

Harper pushed herself up until she was sitting crossed-legged between them. "You really think the Eddingtons would try to destroy Harper's Dining Room?"

Conor shrugged. "I've since discovered from Matt that Richard is struggling to hold on to his position within the Eddington Group due to a string of poor business decisions. The board of directors want him out, so losing what he'd obviously considered a feather in his cap must've stung."

"Even so," Luca mused. "Was he pissed enough to set a fire? To try to flood the place?"

Conor have Luca a half smile. "You think like a Moretti."

Luca narrowed his eyes. "You say that like it's a bad thing."

"It's not," he said. "But in my world... Well, let's just say while I haven't torched a building—mine or anyone else's," he added, alluding to Luca's accusations the night of the fire, "I may have done other morally gray things to destroy my competition."

Luca shot him a look that the other man interpreted correctly.

Conor put his arms up, his hands under his head, drawing Luca's attention to his bare, sexy chest. "Yes, Luca. When it comes to business, Russos are still assholes. Those attributes didn't die out with my father and grandfather."

"Fine," Luca conceded. "So the Eddingtons are on our list of suspects."

"We have a list?" Harper asked.

"We do now," Luca joked.

"I'm suffering from the wrong emotion again," she admitted.

"What do you mean?" Conor asked.

She pushed her hair over her shoulder. "I told you the night of the fire I was happy. And now, even though we're discussing serious shit, I can't stop thinking about how much fun I'm having."

"Fun, huh?" Luca latched onto that word, hating that he'd dampened their relaxing weekend with talk of work and sabotage and enemies. "Seems to me we haven't scratched the surface on all the fun we could be having. Which reminds me…"

"Yes?" Harper leaned forward, eager for him to continue.

Luca knew exactly how to put them back on the right track. "You said you had a list of kinky fantasies, sunshine. Tell us one. Let us make it come true."

Harper, honest to God, blushed, which told Luca not only did she know what fantasy she wanted, but he sure as shit wanted to do it.

Conor ran the back of his fingers down her cheek. "Are you blushing?"

Harper covered her cheeks with her hands. "No. Don't be silly."

"Tell us what you want." Luca pulled one of her hands away from her face, sucking two of her fingers into his mouth.

Her eyelids went heavy, her nipples growing taut.

It spoke to their level of comfort that the three of them had been lying in bed, having this conversation completely naked, and it hadn't felt a bit uncomfortable.

"I..." She pursed her lips in such a way that Luca suspected she was trying to think of a different fantasy, too embarrassed to ask for what she really wanted.

Luca tightened his grip, squeezing her hand. "Say it, sunshine. It's us. There's no judgment here."

She tugged her hand away, wrapping her arms around her waist. "Okay, but if you decide I'm a freak after I say this, just remember that judgment-free zone comment."

Conor smiled, sat up, and kissed her cheek. "Sounds like it's going to be a good one."

The longer they were together, the more glimpses Luca got of the real Conor. While there were still miles to go in their relationship, Luca was ready to put in the time if it meant he'd get to see more of who Conor really was inside, instead of the buttoned-up stoic he presented to the rest of the world.

With them, he seemed more willing to lower his guard at times. His smiles came more frequently, and the sarcastic son of a bitch had one hell of a sense of humor when he let go.

"Since we're in the woods," she started.

Luca grinned. "I love it already."

Harper lightly slapped his upper arm. "I...well... How wrong would it be to admit that I've always gotten turned on by the idea of being chased through the woods by a stranger? Or, in this case, two strangers? Two strangers who take me captive and have their wicked way with me."

Luca froze for a second—not because he was horrified but because it felt as if Harper and her sexy fantasies had been ripped from his brain, crafted from his own dreams.

This woman had been made for him.

A quick glance in Conor's direction had him revising that last thought.

She'd been made just for *them*.

Luca was glad the sheet was covering him from the waist down, otherwise, his lovers would be treated to an eyeful of his now rock-hard cock.

"Your safe word is cheeseburger," Luca said, his tone deeper. "Because if we're doing this, it's going to be legit. So let's spell it out. I'm assuming you don't want gentle or romantic."

Harper shook her head. "Rough," she whispered. "I want it rough. I want to fight back."

"Fuck," Conor growled. "Yeah."

Luca rose from the bed, walking over to Harper's overnight bag. Rifling through it, he tossed her a T-shirt and a pair of shorts. "Put those on."

"No bra or panties?" She looked down at her limited wardrobe.

Luca gave her a dangerous grin. "Sure, I can add those to the pile...if you don't mind us ripping them off you."

"This is fine." She slid off the bed to toss on the shorts and shirt. Walking to the living room, she retrieved the socks and sneakers she'd taken off last night when they'd settled in front of the fire.

He and Conor remained by the bed, neither of them dressing while she laced up her shoes, then rose from the couch.

"Now what?" She was suddenly looking equal parts excited and nervous.

"Now," Luca said, his arms crossed against his bare chest, his erection bobbing against his stomach. "You run."

"Run?" Her gaze traveled to the front door of the cabin.

Conor picked up his smartwatch, strapping it onto his wrist. "We'll give you a five-minute head start."

Harper didn't move until Luca barked, "Run!" Loudly.

She spun and darted for the door, leaving it open behind her in her haste to make it to the tree line.

Luca bent down, sliding on a pair of jeans, Conor doing the same. They perched on opposite ends of the bed to put on their own tennis shoes.

"We're really doing this?" Conor asked. "Chasing her down, pretending to be strangers, claiming her in the woods?"

"Don't you want to?"

Conor sucked in a deep breath. "Maybe a little bit *too* much."

Luca circled the bed, slapping him on the shoulder. "Time?"

Conor looked at his watch once more. "It's been four minutes."

Luca walked to a large chest by the front door, rummaging around until he pulled out an old jump rope. "Let's go capture our girl."

Conor was hot on his heels as they sprinted through the front door, leaping over the three steps that led off the porch. They ran side by side until they reached the edge of the woods, then Luca put his hand out, gesturing for Conor to stop.

The two of them were quiet as they listened, chuckling at how loud Harper was being. God help the woman if she ever truly had to escape an assailant. Luca made a mental note to start giving Harper some self-defense lessons.

Luca pointed in the direction of a loud crash, followed by cursing.

"Let's split up. Circle around, box her in," Luca suggested.

Conor nodded, jogging—much more quietly—through the woods to the right. Luca took off at the same pace toward the left. Harper must have realized her five minutes was up because she was quieter now. Perhaps that initial mad dash had been her attempt to put some distance between her and the cabin.

He walked at a brisk pace, careful to keep his footsteps as silent as possible, despite the abundance of sticks and leaves in the underbrush. He'd been trudging forward steadily, searching the area around him for ten minutes before he saw movement out of the corner of his eye. Stepping behind a large tree trunk, he peered around it, watching as Harper emerged from behind another tree about thirty yards away.

She clearly hadn't seen him because as she surveyed the woods around her, she chose her direction...walking right toward him.

She was only about ten feet away when a noise behind her captured both of their attention. Conor appeared, waving to Harper, who sprinted forward, intent on making him chase her.

Unbeknownst to her, she was racing right into their trap.

Luca stepped from behind the tree just as she was about to pass, reaching out to grab her around the middle.

"Got you."

Harper flew forward over his forearm as he twisted her, pulling her back against his chest.

"No!" she screamed, clawing at his skin.

He didn't give way. If she wanted to fight, he'd give her a fight. She had the safe word to protect her.

Luca kept hold of her with one arm banded around her waist. With the second, he pushed on the nape of her neck, forcing her forward.

The awkward position of being bent in half made it harder for her to fight, but that didn't mean she'd given up. Their girl was twisting and wiggling, cursing and scratching like a wildcat. Luca suspected if she could get her teeth near any of his body parts, she'd sink them in and draw blood. He was tempted to offer his arm for just such a bite. He wanted her to mark him, to leave him with a physical reminder of this moment.

Conor stepped in front of him, his feet slipping into Harper's downcast view. Her neck craned as she tried to look up, but Luca's grip on her nape was unrelenting.

Her fight had started to wane for a second, but with Conor there, she struggled with renewed energy and determination.

Conor grasped a large handful of her hair, closing his fist around it. "Stop fighting, woman," he warned, using a rough, sexy voice Luca had never heard from the man.

Conor pushed her head back down, forcing her gaze to the ground before winking at Luca.

She wanted strangers. That was what she was going to get.

"Get the rope." Luca's words caused Harper to still for a moment. She was panting loudly, the exertion wearing her out.

He could feel the thudding of her heart against his arm, but he wasn't sure if it was the running or the excitement of what was happening that had it racing so quickly.

Conor released his grip on her hair, reaching around to pull the jump rope from the back pocket of Luca's jeans, where he'd stashed it.

"I think this girl needs to be taught a lesson." Luca laced his words with as much menace as he could. No easy task when he was fighting like the devil not to smile because he was so fucking happy. He backed up his threat with a hard smack on her ass, half hitting the material of her shorts, the rest landing on the soft skin of her thigh.

Harper gasped, either in shock or pain—maybe both. He liked the sound, so he struck her again. Then again.

Conor and Harper engaged in a mini skirmish as he tried to grab her wrists, while she fought hard to pull them from his grip. In the end, Conor won, dragging both of her arms behind her back. Showing off knotting skills that would make a Boy Scout proud, he secured her arms, then looped the remaining rope around her body, securing it in the back so that it looked like he'd created reins.

Once she was tied up and still bent at the waist, Conor reclaimed his grip on her hair, kneeling in front of her. "You were trespassing where you don't belong, Goldilocks. You didn't really think you could escape us, did you?"

Harper decided to change tactics. "Please let me go! I won't tell anyone about this. I was just taking a quiet walk in the woods. I wasn't hurting anyone. *Please.*"

Conor chuckled darkly. "Poor little rabbit. We caught you in our snare. You know what that means?"

She shook her head, though Conor made the movement difficult by tightening his grip.

"It means you're *ours* now. And we're never letting you go," he taunted. Or at least, Luca suspected that was his intent. The threat had a different effect on Luca, who liked the idea of never letting them go.

Forever was a word that crossed through his mind more and more these days.

Luca reached around her waist, unbuttoning and unzipping her shorts, dragging them over her hips as she tried to kick out. She failed to hit either of them due to the awkwardness of being bent over.

"Let me go!" she yelled.

Luca leaned over her body until his lips grazed her ear. "Safe word?" he whispered.

She laughed. "No fucking way."

Satisfied, he stood up, staring at Conor, who held her hair in one hand, the makeshift leash/rein in the other.

Luca reached down, sliding his fingers along her drenched slit. "You *are* a bad girl," he taunted. "You didn't want to get away from us at all, did you?"

He lifted his fingers, showing Conor how wet they were. Luca expected him to smile—didn't anticipate the look of naked hunger on the other man's face.

Conor reached out, grabbing Luca's hand, sucking Harper's juices off his fingers.

When Conor released him, the heat in his gaze almost singed.

"Fuck her with your fingers until she comes," Conor demanded. Somewhere along the line, he'd taken the lead in this game.

And Luca was here for it.

He drove two fingers inside Harper without preamble, his rough thrusts pushing her forward until the top of her head pressed against Conor's stomach. Luca took her hard, giving her exactly what she'd asked for in the cabin. She didn't want gentle. She wanted to be taken, used, claimed, and she'd found just the two men to give her that and more.

Her pussy clenched after a dozen or so thrusts. She groaned in pleasurable pain as she came, crying out when Luca refused to relent, slamming his fingers in and out, drawing out every single twitch and spasm until she went limp over his arm.

"Still with us, baby girl?" Conor asked.

Harper whimpered.

His voice was almost cruel when he spoke again. "You came without our permission. That's the last time you ever do that, or we'll be forced to punish you."

Harper trembled in Luca's arms, but it certainly wasn't fear fueling the reaction.

Conor used the hand in her hair to lift her head. "Do you hear me?"

She nodded, but he narrowed his eyes.

"Don't make me repeat my question, Goldilocks."

"I hear you," she said breathlessly, adding the word "sir" when one of Conor's brows rose, letting her know he wanted more from her.

Looking satisfied, Conor loosened his grip on her hair. "We're not done with you. Before today is over, you're going to understand exactly what it means to be our captive."

Harper was breathing heavily, gasping for air. "Please," she said again, though this time it was clear she wasn't begging for freedom.

Conor tossed Luca the extra length of rope so he could unzip his jeans and pull out his cock.

Luca and Harper sucked in a deep breath, in unison, when Conor stroked his dick from root to tip several times before releasing it so he could cup Harper's cheek. Then he resumed his grip on her hair, holding her head back, forcing her face upward toward him.

"You're going to be good and take this in your mouth, aren't you, baby girl? Show us how sweet you can be," Conor cooed.

Luca groaned over Conor's nickname for her, noticing the impact it had on Harper as she squeezed her thighs together.

She was nodding rapidly. "I'll be good. I swear."

Conor drew his hand along the side of her face, not stopping until he was cupping her chin. "Open up," he demanded.

Harper's lips parted without hesitance, and Conor worked the head of his dick inside, slowly but relentlessly, feeding her more with each return.

Luca heard her gag once, aware at least half of Conor's cock was buried in her mouth. He stopped there, holding her hair tightly as he looked up at Luca.

Conor looked like a man possessed, a dark, dangerous stranger—and it was sexy as shit. "Fuck her while she sucks me. If she's a good baby girl, when we get her back to our cabin, we'll switch places and do it again. Either way, Goldilocks is going to be fucked raw before the night is over."

"Jesus. Christ," Luca whispered. He'd always prided himself on his dirty talk, but Conor just blew everything he'd ever said out of the goddamn water.

Harper whimpered again, her mouth still stretched around Conor's dick.

He looked down at her. "You want that, don't you, dirty girl? Want us to own you, keep you, use you."

Harper managed just one short nod of her head.

After that...words weren't necessary.

Conor used his grip on Harper's hair to drag her on and off his cock, as Luca pulled out his own dick, slamming to the hilt, setting free his own desires to conquer and claim.

Harper started to shake in earnest, her climax hovering right there. But she was holding it back. Waiting.

Luca exchanged a look with Conor, who gave him a slight smirk.

"Come for us, baby girl," Conor growled.

Harper's second orgasm struck fast and hard, and Luca fought like the devil not to let her take him with her.

Conor took her mouth with a passion and a need he hadn't revealed before.

The next time Harper came, Conor was right there with her.

"Swallow every drop, baby girl. Show me how much you want it. Want *me*."

Harper did as he said, her pussy clenching around Luca's cock so tight, he saw stars. Resistance was impossible as Luca came hard, jabbing inside her with one, two, three more thrusts, until there was nothing left.

Harper released Conor's cock, her breathing ragged.

With firm hands on her shoulders, Conor pulled her upright, wrapping his arms around her, even as she remained bound.

"Did you like that?" he murmured, his lips brushing the top of her head.

"So much," Harper confessed. "Fuck me, *too* much."

Pleased with her answer, Conor cupped her jaw. "Good. Because we're not finished."

Harper lifted her head, blinking rapidly. "We're not?"

Conor shook his head. "No. We owe you a punishment, baby girl. Because you did *not* have permission to come that last time."

Luca hadn't thought anything except a three-hour nap would make his well-used dick revive.

He was wrong.

## Chapter Twelve

Conor sighed, feeling more relaxed than ever. He'd been truly horrified when he'd first walked into this cabin Friday evening, stressed out about the idea of sharing such tight quarters. When he realized the place had a large open floor plan, with only the bathroom available if he needed to escape, he'd been seriously tempted to steal Luca's car and drive off the mountain to get away.

His concerns had been for naught because Harper and Luca had a way of pulling Conor out of his head that worked. Despite frequently trying to keep his distance, they continued to drag him back in, and damned if they weren't a delicious enough distraction to keep the bad thoughts and feelings at bay. Every night with Harper and Luca was better than the night before.

While the pessimist who never completely stopped whispering in his ear kept saying that this couldn't last, Conor was getting better at ignoring him.

Luca walked over from the kitchen, setting Harper's glass of wine on the coffee table, while handing Conor one of the IPAs he'd popped the tops off of for the two of them.

Harper thanked Luca for the wine, though she didn't reach

for it. She was lying on the bearskin rug, facing the fire, her head resting on Conor's lap.

He ran his fingers through her long blonde hair, certain he'd never felt anything so soft. Luca plopped down next to Conor, sitting so close their shoulders were touching. He gave Conor a grin and the two of them shared a quick, affectionate kiss.

Fifteen-year-old Conor could hardly believe he was here with Luca.

Hell, thirty-three-year-old Conor was struggling too. Especially with Harper added into the mix. He'd never imagined anything like this for himself.

And while that damn voice kept reminding him not to get too comfortable, Conor refused to listen. He was going to soak up every drop of this happiness, going to hang on to it for as long as he could.

"Do we have to go back to Philly tomorrow?" Harper mused, staring at the fire. "I vote we quit our jobs, sell all our belongings, and live out the rest of our days here in this cabin as legit mountain folk."

"It does feel like we're a million miles away from reality," Conor agreed. "No stress, no responsibilities, no daily grind."

"The mountain people lifestyle sounds damn good to me," Luca added. "Wouldn't be a bad future at all." Luca reached down to draw his fingers along Harper's cheek.

She smiled but didn't move, her gaze fixed on the flames. "It wouldn't. Though I have to confess, when I dreamed about my future self, there was only one guy in my bed."

"Shame on your lack of imagination," Luca chastised.

She giggled when Luca tickled her. "Thank God I met you guys so you could show me the error of my ways."

Conor didn't enter the conversation, uncomfortable talking about the future.

He took a swig of beer, but choked on it when Luca said, "So...are we going to talk about that guy in the woods?"

Harper sat up, patting Conor on the back. The damn beer had gone down the wrong hole.

Luca grinned at him without a hint of remorse, perfectly aware it was his question that caused him to choke.

Conor finally managed to stop coughing, glaring at him.

Not that it did a bit of good.

"I'm going to repeat my question," the shameless tatted hottie said. "So you might want to put the beer down."

Conor felt his cheeks flush.

"I totally think we should talk about *that guy*," Harper said enthusiastically.

"What guy?" Conor asked coyly, painfully aware what they were talking about.

When Harper shared her fantasy with them, it had blown the lid off something Conor had always kept carefully locked away. The idea of chasing her through the woods, a predator in search of his prey, had been too heady to resist. When he and Luca first left the cabin, Conor had told himself he would keep the game simple, a vanilla version of her chase request.

Then he'd seen her struggling in Luca's arms, watched her fight in earnest, and there had been no chance of him holding his dormant inner alpha at bay.

Harper and Luca knew Conor liked to read, and they'd even spent one evening perusing his bookshelves, the three of them discussing many of the books they'd found there. What they'd never seen were the racier titles in the reading app on his phone.

Conor enjoyed steamy stories, finding them hotter than watching porn.

"You know exactly what guy," Harper insisted. "That growly, gruff, hot-as-fuck man who knew all the right things to say. I swear to God, I think I could have come just from the words coming out of your mouth."

Conor chuckled and shook his head. "Trying to decide if I should be annoyed that you and Luca have both pigeonholed me into the uptight, stuffy businessman role."

Luca reached out, taking Conor's hand in his. "There's not a damn thing uptight or stuffy about you, and we both know it."

Harper nodded in agreement.

"Though it's clear you've been holding out on us," Luca continued. "You've been letting me call the shots in the bedroom, which I'll admit I enjoy. But it's suddenly become obvious that I'm better suited to be your assistant coach, letting *you* call the plays."

Conor laughed. "It's always sports with you, isn't it?"

"Absolutely. So I'm passing the ball off to *that guy*."

*That guy.*

Conor had sure as fuck liked being *that guy*.

"You gonna take the lead?" Harper asked.

Hell yeah, he was.

"You liked what we did in the woods?" Conor asked, not because he needed clarification. Harper had done nothing but talk about how she thought she was going to die from what she was calling her "greatest orgasm ever."

He asked because he wanted more information.

Luca and Harper nodded emphatically.

Conor looked at Harper. "Which part turned you on? Being our captive or being our baby girl?"

Harper, the shameless minx, gave him a saucy grin. "I have to choose?"

He chuckled. "No. You don't have to choose. Do you remember your safe word?"

She nodded. "Cheeseburger."

Game on.

Conor rose from the floor, then turned his attention to Luca, schooling his features. "Did we give our baby girl permission to put on clothes?" he asked in a deep, menacing voice. "Because Goldilocks doesn't get to hide her body from us."

Luca got into the spirit of the game immediately. Standing and crossing his arms, he gave Harper a stern frown. "Get undressed."

Harper's hands were at the hem of her T-shirt before he finished his request. She whipped it, her bra, comfy lounge pants, and panties off in record time, until she was standing in front of them naked.

Harper never tried to shield her body from them, confident in her curves and in her ability to seduce them.

She gave them a wink, but they didn't take the bait. Didn't break character.

"We never punished her for coming without permission earlier, did we?" Conor asked Luca.

"No, we did not." Luca was following his lead, adopting the same threatening tone, the same stance. Not that it was provoking a bit of fear in their "captive."

She was grinning at them like they were Santa, the Tooth Fairy, and the Easter Bunny all rolled into one.

"Take off your clothes, Luca. Then lie down on the bearskin rug, on your back. I think we need to teach our baby girl exactly what it means to be owned."

Harper's eyelids grew heavy. She really did like this fantasy. Her nipples were tight, just begging for him to pinch them, bite them, suck them until she cried for mercy.

Luca followed Conor's instructions, stripping off, then lying down.

Conor reached for Harper's upper arm, giving it a little squeeze. He added enough pressure that she resisted, tried to pull away. Her actions had the desired effect because it put Harper in the right frame of mind. This wasn't a game of flirting back and forth. It was a role-play of her fantasy—and his—and he wanted it to feel real. It had in the woods, and God knew it wasn't just Harper who'd enjoyed her best orgasm.

"Straddle Luca's hips." Conor guided her into position, following her down to the floor.

Luca's dick was thick and hard, bumping against his stomach. He hissed when Conor grasped it, giving it a couple of firm strokes before guiding it to Harper's pussy. Neither of his lovers had expected him to move things along quite so quickly.

Or at least…that was what they thought.

The second Luca was lodged deep, he started lifting his hips as Harper set off, intent on taking a ride.

"Hold still," Conor barked loudly, taking them both by surprise. "I didn't give you permission to move," he said to Harper, gripping the nape of her neck, making sure she understood that he was completely in charge of her every movement.

Harper looked at him, licking her lips. Their faces were close, so she was obviously anticipating a kiss. That wasn't part of this game.

"All you're going to do is keep Luca's dick warm inside that tight little pussy of yours, baby girl. Nothing else. Do you understand?"

She nodded.

He raised one eyebrow, waiting.

"Yes."

He waited again.

Her eyes widened and her nostrils flared. "Yes, sir," she whispered.

Conor had never heard two more powerful words, spoken with such undeniable need.

Luca murmured a curse under his breath, as swept away by the moment as Conor and Harper.

"Now—bend over."

Conor didn't give her a chance to obey. He put a strong hand on her upper back and pushed her into the position he wanted. Her breasts were pressed tightly against Luca's sexy, tattooed chest, her soft thighs straddling Luca's thick, muscular legs. They were a study in contrasts, Harper's pale, unblemished skin against Luca's darker ink, her smaller frame almost swallowed in Luca's large build.

Conor was sorely tempted to grab his phone and snap a picture, aware he'd never seen anything more beautiful.

He took a step away until he stood where he could see Luca's thick cock stretching their beautiful captive. Kneeling, he ran his finger around where they were joined. Harper was wet and hot. He hadn't questioned that this was turning her on, but if he had, the proof was right there in front of him.

Harper and Luca both gasped in unison when Conor ran his finger around the place where they were connected again, before exploring more. Harper's slit, Luca's balls. Harper moaned and then...she did exactly as he'd expected. She tilted her hips, desperate for friction.

Conor lifted his hand and slapped her ass, hard, the white skin instantly going pink.

"Ahh!" she gasped in shock and pain.

"I told you not to move," he said, his voice gruffer now as his own arousal grew.

Harper didn't offer any apology.

Nope. She did something even better.

She tilted her hips again.

And with that, the beast was set free.

Conor spanked her a dozen more times, not holding back. He'd expected Harper to groan...not Luca.

Glancing down, Conor realized Luca's jaw was clamped tight.

"You're killing me, man. Her pussy clenches down on me every time you spank her."

"So good!" Harper said, panting.

Conor didn't reply to that. Instead, he continued spanking her, loving the chorus of moans and groans from his lovers.

Harper was starting to anticipate his swats, her ass rising to meet him, which meant Luca's cock was gliding in and out a few tiny inches each time.

Conor paused when she jerked.

Glancing around her body, he realized Luca had begun to stroke her clit.

"She's close, Conor," Luca said breathlessly.

Conor bent down, placing his lips next to her ear. "You want to come, baby girl."

Harper nodded.

"What's the magic word?" he asked.

"Please," she cried out. "God, please!"

Conor spanked her again as Luca continued rubbing her clit. Within seconds, she was there, her body writhing as her climax rumbled through her.

Conor rubbed her ass as she lay still on Luca's chest. Luca had wrapped his arms around her midsection, cuddling her close... until Conor shook his head.

This wasn't over.

Hell, they were just getting started.

Conor grabbed a handful of Harper's hair, closing his fist around it as she hissed.

"We're not done."

Harper's gaze caught his, and even though she was thoroughly wrung out, she gave him a sexy smile. "Good."

"Sit up on your haunches. Keep Luca's dick tucked inside that pretty pussy."

Harper did as he demanded, pausing once she was in position, recalling she was only supposed to do what he told her to do.

Rising, he took a step or two away, slowly removing his own clothing as his lovers watched. Once he was naked, he stepped back to Harper, the head of his rock-hard dick hitting his stomach. Harper looked at it as he moved closer, not stopping until his cock was mere inches from her mouth.

She ran her tongue over her lower lip, wetting it.

Conor cupped her cheeks, forced her to look at him. "You're going to ride Luca's dick while I fuck your mouth."

"Yes," she pleaded.

His expression was stern when he clarified, "This isn't going to be a blow job, baby girl. I'm going to use your mouth the same way Luca is using your pussy." He tapped under her chin. "I'm not going to come in your mouth."

She frowned, and it looked like she wanted to protest.

He placed his thumb against her lips, applying pressure. "Once Luca has filled you up, it'll be my turn. You're going to spend the rest of the night with our come sliding down those sexy inner thighs of yours."

"Jesus," Luca growled, his tone matching Harper's aroused face.

"Please," she said sweetly. "Please, sir. I want that."

She was a fucking miracle.

"So do I," Luca added.

They both were.

After that, words weren't necessary. Luca's fingers dug into Harper's hips as together, they set the pace, Harper rising and falling on his cock, faster and harder with each return.

At the same time, Conor held her face in his hands, his cock slamming into her mouth. She gagged the first couple of times the head brushed the back of her throat, but she learned how to relax quickly, able to take even more of him.

He'd told her he didn't want to come in her mouth, and he meant it.

Mercifully, Harper came in less than five minutes, taking Luca with her. They both grunted, the sounds those of a pleasure so good, it hurt.

Once their climaxes had passed, Conor pulled his cock out of her mouth. Shifting, he knelt over Luca's legs, lifting Harper's ass in the air.

She didn't—or perhaps *couldn't*—lift her head, so it remained on Luca's shoulder as Conor slammed inside her with the same force Luca had just used.

She cried out his name, her pussy quivering around him, still sensitive from her first two orgasms. Regardless, she was far from passive, her body matching his, thrust for glorious thrust.

He came inside her, aware that she hadn't. Harper's eyes were closed, her body exhausted. Typically, he always made sure his lovers came before him, but he knew they'd already pushed her to the brink.

Withdrawing, Conor twisted until he was sitting next to their sated bodies, still connected from head to toe on the plush rug.

They remained there, the silence continuing for several minutes, but it wasn't awkward. More like they were all taking the time to let things soak in. Because...Jesus.

That was the hottest sexual experience of his life.

Luca was the first to speak. "Holy fuck, Conor. That guy..."

Conor grinned tiredly as Luca continued to refer to this side of him as *that guy*.

"That guy rocks my fucking world," Luca said, his voice husky with exhaustion.

"Mine too," Harper whispered, even as she continued to use Luca's shoulder as a pillow, her eyes still closed.

"Not too rough?" Conor forced himself to ask, worried perhaps he'd taken things too far.

Luca and Harper didn't answer that with words, chuckling instead.

"As soon as I recover," Harper said, "I think we need to make a list of other role-playing games."

Conor grinned tiredly. "Sounds like a plan."

As a unit, they helped each other up from the floor, moving to the bathroom where they took a long, steamy shower, scrubbing each other while working out all the kinks. From there, they moved to the bed, Harper climbing into the middle as she had every night, he and Luca taking opposite sides.

Sleep was coming to claim Conor quickly, so he was surprised when Luca spoke.

"Probably should have warned you, my cousins Elio and Bruno both got their wives pregnant in this bed," he whispered.

Harper giggled quietly. "Oh hush. Don't send stuff like that out into the universe."

Conor lay with his eyes closed, maintaining his slow, steady breathing. He felt the mattress shift and could tell from the sound of Luca's voice that he'd turned to face Harper...or them.

When he spoke, Luca was still whispering. "You don't want kids?"

Conor heard a soft kiss. He imagined Luca placing one on Harper's shoulder. Luca was always kissing their shoulders or necks, ruffling Harper's hair, lightly punching Conor on the arm. He'd never been with such a physically affectionate lover. Sometimes it seemed Luca couldn't stop himself from touching them.

"Oh," Harper said, more breath than sound. "I didn't mean that. Of course I do."

"How many?" Luca asked.

Conor's breath staggered, but he quickly regained control.

*In and out.*

*In and out.*

Harper continued, speaking so softly, Conor was struggling to hear her over the thudding beat of his heart pulsing in his ears.

"I always wanted a sibling, so there's no way I'd have an only child. Always pictured myself with two or three," she added. "I'd love to have a boy and a girl, have the experience of raising a son and a daughter."

"I hope you get that. FYI," Luca started in a humorous tone. "My mom had to try four times for that daughter. And to add insult to injury, she got *two* boys on the third attempt."

Harper let out a breathy laugh as Conor lay there, considering his own mother. Had her third attempt been for a daughter?

He'd never thought about that before. His father was of an old-school mindset, with so much arrogance he likened himself to royalty, constantly boasting to his cigar-and-brandy buddies that he'd gotten his heir and his spare. Conor was never mentioned in that sentiment, and he'd always wondered why. Shouldn't his dad have said "heir and spares"? Was he his mother's last-ditch attempt at having a daughter?

"How about you?" Harper whispered to Luca. It was clear his

lovers assumed he'd fallen asleep, so they were speaking quietly. "You want kids?"

"Hell yeah. Same as you, actually. A boy and a girl."

"No big family with five kids?" she asked.

"I love big families. Honestly, I really hope I have twins. There's nothing like that bond."

"Sounds wonderful." Harper shifted, rolling to her side away from Conor, and it fell quiet again.

He didn't think they were purposely leaving him out of this conversation. In fact, if he chose, he knew he could join in, sharing his own dream for a future family.

He didn't.

Couldn't.

Because that wasn't a dream he'd ever allowed himself.

Probably because his parents hadn't exactly been the model when it came to happy marriages. And as far as child-rearing, Dad had been borderline abusive.

Conor reconsidered the borderline descriptor. His father *had been* an abusive asshole. Mom, on the other hand, when she was lucid, was amazing, loving, and attentive.

No. The real reason why he'd never considered marriage and families was because of the ticking time bomb in his head. He'd read countless articles over the years about anxiety attacks and depression frequently going together. Conor wasn't sure when Mom's depression had begun, didn't know if she'd suffered anxiety attacks before the true darkness set in. Depression wasn't a topic for discussion in his childhood home.

When Mom had one of her "spells," as Dad called it, he told them to leave her alone and be quiet. The one time Gage asked what was wrong with her, Dad had backhanded him, insisting there was *nothing* wrong with her.

*Russos aren't weak.*

*Russos don't fail.*

*Russos aren't gay.*

And they sure as shit aren't mentally ill.

After that, neither he nor his brothers talked about Mom's depression again. Not with Dad. Not with her. Not even with each other.

Conor had wished countless times over the years he'd asked her questions about her disease, gotten at least some frame of understanding. Did it run in the family? Did she have anxiety attacks? When did the depression set it?

He was pulled from his thoughts when Luca broke the silence once more. "Looks like we wore our boyfriend out."

Harper giggled. "*We* wore *him* out?"

They shared a quiet laugh, then a kiss, and this time when they fell silent, it stayed that way. He heard their breathing slow as sleep claimed them.

Conor sighed, aware he wouldn't be getting much rest tonight.

Too hung up on a new word.

Boyfriend.

* * *

Conor sat in the passenger side of Luca's truck as the Philadelphia skyline emerged. He rubbed his eyes wearily. After the whispered baby conversation, Luca and Harper had fallen fast asleep, completely ignorant of what their conversation had done to Conor.

He'd lain there next to them on his back, silently staring at a tiny spot on the ceiling, playing the three-three-three game—identifying three objects, three sounds, slowly moving three body parts. His panic attacks typically started in the middle of the night, when all the worries were somehow amplified in the darkness, in the silence.

His subconscious was not a friend, always lurking and working in the background, until it decided to wake him up from a sound sleep and sucker punch him straight into an anxiety attack.

Conor knew the only reason he was able to keep an attack at bay last night was because he'd remained awake and vigilant, employing every coping mechanism he'd ever learned. He was an expert on goddamn coping techniques.

"I'll drop you off first, Conor, then you, Harper." Luca looked in the rearview mirror at Harper, who was sitting in the backseat. "I need to do my Sunday check at the construction site, then run home for some clean clothes. After that, we can all meet back up at—"

"That sounds like a lot of running around, Luca," Conor interjected. "I think maybe we should take a night apart. I've got a shit-ton of work to catch up on from missing half a day on Friday, and you admitted yesterday you've got a mountain of laundry to tackle."

Luca looked like he wanted to argue, so Conor persisted.

"I'm going to be stuck at my computer until at least midnight," he lied.

Luca sighed. "Okay. I know you're right. I should be an adult and do the fucking laundry, but I'm going on the record right now as saying the idea of spending the night alone in my cold bed *sucks*."

"Seconded." Harper raised her hand like they were in some board meeting.

Luca grimaced. "But it's critical mass as far as boxers go, so unless I plan to go commando at work tomorrow—"

"I vote for that." Harper raised her hand again, and despite his exhaustion, Conor couldn't help but chuckle.

At least until Luca said, "So I'll see you tomorrow morning for our coffee break."

Conor shook his head. "I'm afraid I can't. I've got an early meeting."

Luca had been watching the road, but the next time he spoke, he glanced over at Conor. "Then dinner tomorrow night. I was thinking maybe we should try that new rest—"

"Sorry. I'm out for dinner too. There have been some staffing concerns at Enigma, and I need to get a handle on them." Conor cleared his throat, every additional lie getting harder to tell. He needed to put the brakes on this thing before…

There was no *before*, because it was already too late. Conor had let things between the three of them go too far.

He was in love with them.

He ran a hand through his hair, staring out the passenger window, relieved when he realized they were turning onto his street, his building right there. Only a few more minutes and he could make good on his escape.

No one spoke until Luca pulled into the parking garage next to Conor's private elevator.

"Tuesday then." Luca put the car in park, staring Conor down.

"It's kind of a busy week," he started. "I really need to check my schedule before we make plans."

Luca shook his head. "No. You're not doing this again. Conor, you don't have to run away from us. We can take things slow, get to know each other as lovers. There's no race to the end, so you can take as much time as you need to get where I am. To fully understand what this is between us."

It was on the tip of Conor's tongue to ask Luca just where he was, but he didn't.

Because, one, he didn't want to hear the answer, and two, he already knew. Luca was a Moretti—stubborn, passionate, and so fucking sure of himself. All but declaring his feelings aloud, ready to lay down exactly what he thought this was with a confidence that staggered Conor.

He wasn't even that confident about what toppings he wanted on his sandwiches.

"Don't cut me out again, okay? Please?" Luca asked…with a sincerity that pierced Conor's heart.

It was the first time he realized how much he'd hurt Luca by walking away from their friendship back in high school. All these years, he'd thought Luca hadn't even noticed or cared.

He swallowed hard, fighting to dislodge the lump in his throat. In the end, he didn't bother replying, simply giving them both a short, jerky nod.

Harper got out of the backseat, grabbing his weekend bag to hand to him. She gave him a lingering kiss before flashing that siren's smile. "Miss you already," she said softly.

Conor forced the edges of his lips up, trying to return her smile, even as his insides began to crack apart.

Harper got into the front seat, she and Luca waving goodbye as they drove away.

Trudging into his apartment, Conor dropped his phone and keys on the table next to the elevator. He should probably take a second to unpack his charger, as the battery was dead, but he was too damn tired.

He didn't even bother climbing the stairs because Luca was right, sleeping alone sucked. As he walked into his living room, he scrubbed his eyes with the palm of his hands, trying to ward off the coming headache. Stress was a bitch who wouldn't be denied her pound of flesh. He may have managed to maintain control last night, but there was no holding her at bay today.

Dropping onto the couch, he grabbed a throw blanket and closed his eyes, hoping he would make it through the night unscathed.

Those hopes were dashed when, several hours later, he woke up in the throes of an anxiety attack.

And it was a doozy.

*Chapter Thirteen*

Harper climbed into the front seat of Luca's truck after dropping off Conor. The two of them waved at their... well...Luca had dubbed him their boyfriend, and Harper had to admit that sounded just fine to her.

She waited until they exited the parking garage and made it back to the street before she spoke.

"That felt weird, right?" Harper had noticed a difference in Conor the moment they woke up this morning.

For one thing, instead of being in bed with her and Luca, Conor had been sitting across the room, reading a book on the couch. She watched him for several minutes, lazing in bed without revealing she was awake so she could revel in her happiness. Eventually, she realized he hadn't turned the page, not once. He was looking at it, but he sure as hell wasn't reading it. She thought perhaps that meant he was too blown away by the weekend to concentrate on anything other than their relationship and the most incredible sex ever.

That idea was immediately dismissed when she sat up and said, "Good morning."

Conor's gaze hadn't been that of a lover reliving an amazing night. There were too many shadows in his expression, and the dark circles under his eyes told her his sleep hadn't been as peaceful as hers.

Luca sighed. "Yeah. It was weird."

"Did we miss something? Because as far as weekend trips went, that was the best one ever for me."

Luca grinned as he reached across the console to squeeze her thigh. "Me too. I'm not sure what changed."

"He was sure as shit all in last night. That guy…" Harper said wistfully, using the nickname they'd given Conor's seriously alpha side.

"That guy *was* all in last night, but Conor was definitely lukewarm today." Luca rubbed his beard, and she could see he was as bothered by Conor's about-face as she was. "Of course, if we're being honest with ourselves, he's been hot and cold ever since we shared those first kisses on his couch."

"At first, I thought it was because he was determined to stand firm on the professional stance, but since prom…I'd hoped he'd turned the corner on that. Maybe he's having regrets? Or second thoughts?" Harper prayed that wasn't true because she would hate to think Conor was sorry about a single second that they'd spent together.

"I don't think it has anything to do with being professional."

Harper wasn't sure what to make of that. "What do you think it is then?" She recalled Luca asking—almost begging—Conor not to walk away from this a few minutes ago. Was there some part of their history she was missing?

"Do you think it's the threesome concept he's struggling with?" she asked.

Luca shook his head. "No. I don't. I mean, I realize it's unusual—in most families," he added with a grin. "But, Harper, you've been there for all of it. Does it feel like he struggles when the three of us are together in bed?"

"Not a bit," she said immediately. Then she considered the rest of the time. "I would say his struggles are more with himself than with us, but don't ask me why. It's just a feeling I have."

"I'd say you're right. Conor's very closemouthed about himself, especially when it comes to the past. I keep hoping he'll open up to us, but—"

"I wish the same thing," she interjected. "Do you know how his mom died?"

Harper had been moved by Luca's memories of his own mother, but apart from telling them that he was nineteen when he lost his mom, Conor had remained frustratingly silent on the subject.

Luca glanced her direction, and she could tell he *did* know. "Yeah. I know. I was waiting for Conor to tell us about her himself. I've become pretty good friends with his brother, Gage, over the past year or so. We were drinking one night, and the subject of moms came up. Conor's mother committed suicide."

Harper gasped, her heart breaking. "I was thinking maybe an illness or car accident. I never thought..."

"I can see why he'd be reluctant to talk about it, but even so, we've gotten close these past couple of months. I've shared things with the two of you I've only shared with my brothers."

"Same for me," Harper admitted. "With the exception of Luna, I've never told anyone about my fiasco-ridden love life." She leaned back against the headrest. "You know him better than me, so—"

Luca cut her off. "No. I don't. While Conor and I were friends once—many, many years ago—the truth is, we were basically strangers starting over when Moretti Brothers landed the renovation job. Before we started working together, I can count on one hand the number of times I've seen Conor since high school, and our interactions were always minimal. The usual 'how are you?' followed by 'fine' conversation."

Harper bit her lower lip as she chewed over that information, then she smiled. She could tell her abrupt mood change confused Luca.

"What's that smile about?" he asked.

She turned to look at him. "The three of us are less than two months into this friendship and two weeks into the sex. The words 'impatient much?' just flashed in my head."

Luca laughed. "Excellent point. I don't know about you, but I'm getting majorly carried away and I'm not even trying to stop myself."

Harper loved how honest Luca was about his feelings. The man shot straight from the hip, and she knew without a doubt he wasn't playing games, wasn't trying to gaslight her. It was refreshing to be with someone so willing to put himself out there. "I feel the same way. But it's obvious Conor doesn't move at the speed of light like we do."

"So we're going to have to give him time," Luca said, clearly no fan of the suggestion even though it was his.

"Ugh. I hate the idea of staying away from the two of you," she grumbled.

Luca winked at her. "I said time, sunshine. Not distance."

She laughed. As they approached her hotel, real life crept back in and with it, her responsibilities. "It is with a heavy heart that I must report I can't do lunch with you tomorrow."

"That's right. You're starting interviews for the line cooks. That's exciting."

"You have no idea. Oh, hey! I still have those empanadas I made for the weekend and then stupidly left here. There are more than enough for you and Joey and probably a few other guys on the crew for lunch tomorrow." She'd intended to surprise Luca and Conor with the empanadas as car treats for their road trip. They were thirty minutes out of the city before she recalled she'd left them in the fridge. "Want to park real quick and run up to grab them?"

"Hell yeah. I'm not saying no to empanadas."

He pulled into the hotel parking lot and the two of them walked in the front entrance, hand in hand. It was a gorgeous hotel, complete with a fancy restaurant and a huge bar just off the lobby. They were halfway to the elevator when Harper heard a familiar voice calling her name.

She turned, her eyes wide with surprise as Bradley rose from one of the lobby couches, placing an empty cocktail glass on the side table.

"Bradley."

Her former manager walked up to them, offering her a warm, friendly hug that lingered for a moment, telling her how much he'd missed her. Hugs hadn't figured into their relationship in the past, so she was touched by the gesture.

"You're a sight for sore eyes," Bradley said as soon as they parted. He glanced over at Luca, with genuine curiosity. He'd no doubt spotted them holding hands.

"Bradley Renner, this is Luca Moretti," she said, doing the introductions. "Luca, this is my former manager."

"And you're the contractor," Bradley said. She was surprised he'd remembered that. She'd only mentioned Luca a couple of times, and Bradley was notorious for only listening with half an ear to things that didn't involve or interest him.

"Nice to meet you," Luca said, extending his hand.

The two men shook hands.

"What are you doing here?" Harper asked.

Bradley placed his hands in the pockets of his suit jacket. "I had some business in Philadelphia, so I thought I'd stop by and catch up with my favorite model. When I realized you weren't here, I decided to have a drink and wait for a bit. I was just about to leave when you walked in."

"Great timing then. I'm about to grab something from my suite for Luca before he heads home. Want to join us? I have a bottle of red wine up there."

"That sounds perfect."

Harper took her purse off her arm, rummaging for the keycard for the elevator. She really needed to put the damn thing in a dedicated pocket or something because she was no stranger to this digging nightmare every time she stepped into the elevator.

"Here." Luca flashed his keycard. Conor had gotten a card for

Luca so he didn't have to wait for the front desk to call for permission to allow him up.

Luca tapped the card against the reader, then pushed the button to her floor.

Bradley gave her a knowing look before glancing over to Luca. So it appeared part of their catching up would include questions about her love life. Not that she was going to go into any of the details about that with her former manager.

By the time they reached her door, Harper had located the key to her suite. She opened it and invited both men in. Luca followed her to the kitchenette, where she reached into the refrigerator to pull out the large to-go container of empanadas.

Luca's phone pinged. He pulled it out of his pocket and glanced at the screen. "That's Joey. He's at the restaurant for our walk-through. Wants to know when I'm getting there." Luca fired off a response, then placed his phone on the counter next to hers so he could open the lid on the empanadas. Lifting the container to his nose, he closed his eyes as he inhaled. "Harper, I swear to God, your cooking is as good as my nonna's."

She smiled. "Wow. Best compliment ever."

He grabbed his phone, shoved it in the back pocket of his jeans, then walked to the door. "It was nice to meet you, Bradley. You two have a good time catching up, and I'll see you tomorrow night, Harper?"

She gave him a quick kiss before closing the door behind Luca as he took his leave.

"So," Bradley said. "That was the contractor."

Harper laughed. "How about a glass of wine?"

"Nice deflection. And yes, please."

Harper opened the bottle of wine, pouring them both a glass and taking them to the living room area. Bradley claimed the couch, while she took the oversized chair on the opposite side of the coffee table.

"You look happy," he said after taking a sip.

"I'm very happy."

"You're gaining weight."

She had expected that to be the first thing he'd said after hello, so she was impressed by his restraint. "Yep. I sure am. I've spent the couple months refining recipes I plan to include on the menu at Harper's Dining Room. Requires a lot of taste-testing."

"Everything still on track for opening the restaurant in August?" he asked.

Harper nodded. "We've had a few bumps in the road, but nothing dire."

"Oh?"

"You know about the fire. Someone also stole a lot of electrical wiring, which Luca says is common, given the copper in it. There was a near flood too."

Bradley frowned. "Near flood?"

"Someone poured cement down a drain and turned on the water. Fortunately, Luca, Conor, and I stopped by and heard it running. If we hadn't caught it quickly, it could have set us back weeks, maybe even more."

"Sounds like you've been fortunate."

"To have someone trying to sabotage my business?" she asked.

Bradley took another sip of wine, then set the glass down. "Of course, not for that. Just that none of the damage has been too bad."

Harper kicked off her shoes. "So you're in Philadelphia for business?"

"I am." Bradley leaned forward, resting his elbows on his knees. "We got the offer, Harper."

"We?" She tilted her head, completely confused.

"The swimsuit issue. The magazine came to me. They want you for the cover this year." Bradley was grinning from ear to ear —and Harper understood why.

The cover of the swimsuit issue had been Harper's white whale, the one goal she'd set for herself as a model that she'd never achieved.

"That's wonderful, but, Bradley—"

His smile faded quickly. "No." He raised his hand, cutting her off. "No, Harper. You can't turn this down. It's a seven-figure deal. Not to mention the prestige. This catapults you into the top tier of supermodels. Do you know how many more doors this would open? How many more offers would follow?"

"I get that, Bradley. I do. It's just—"

Bradley stood up, shaking his head. "Dammit, Harper. Enough is enough! I've indulged this midlife crisis of yours for too long."

Harper's temper piqued. "First of all, I'm twenty-nine, for God's sake. And secondly, what the hell do you mean, midlife crisis?"

"So you collapsed. I get that it was scary for you, but it was *one time*. It happens to every model at some point. It's time to get the fuck over it!"

"Get the fuck over it?" she yelled. "I modeled the entire time I was in culinary school. I didn't just quit."

"So you know you can do it. I don't understand why you're walking away from this. You were at the peak of your career. Leaving now doesn't make any sense."

"I'm never modeling again, Bradley. I don't know how to say that to you any more clearly."

He stared at her like she'd just announced she was carrying octuplets. "That's...*no*," he said in disbelief.

"Please tell the execs at the magazine I'm flattered, but I'm not taking the job."

His mouth opened and closed a couple of times, his face red. Typically, Bradley was a mild-mannered man. She could only recall a couple of times when he'd really lost his shit...one time being the night her mom had put her foot down at the hospital, demanding he cancel her attendance at the Milan fashion show. He'd cussed a blue streak—loudly—until a nurse and two orderlies showed up and told him he needed to keep it down or leave.

In the end, he left.

The second was when she'd first announced she was quitting modeling and going to culinary school.

Right now, she felt the need to brace herself because he was about to blow.

"Are you fucking kidding me?!" he yelled.

Harper started to reply, but Bradley didn't give her the chance.

"I can't go back and say no thanks. I'd be a laughingstock! Do you know how fucking hard I had to work to get you this deal?"

Harper set down her glass and rose. "Wait a second. Did they come to you, or did you go to them?"

"What does it fucking matter?"

Harper placed her hands on her hips. "It matters, Bradley, because I'm no longer your client. I'm no longer a *model*. You had no right to pretend you still represent me, to attempt to solicit work on my behalf."

"You ungrateful bitch!" he snarled. "Do you know how much of my life I've dedicated to your career, to making you into the success that you are?"

Harper felt her face flush with anger. "How dare you? I had a hell of a lot to do with that success you're claiming. But if you want to play it that way—fine. Do you know how much *my* dedication and success led to yours? Don't act like you were some self-less martyr. You got paid very well to do that job!"

Bradley ran a hand through his thinning hair, the action disrupting the work of his hair gel so that his comb-over became apparent. When he turned back to her, he looked somewhat calmer. "Harper...the agency is in trouble."

She frowned. "You said you'd hired a couple new models with potential."

"They're not taking off, not getting the jobs. They're not *you*. No one is."

Harper sighed. "That's not true, Bradley. It's just going to take some time."

"No," he insisted. "It's not. And besides, I don't have time.

We're not bringing in enough. At this rate...the agency is going to go under before the end of the year."

She didn't know what to say to that. She knew that she'd been responsible for a lot of the money brought in, but she hadn't realized she was the *only* thing keeping it afloat.

In the end, there was only one thing she could say.

"I'm sorry." Harper meant it, sincerely. But she couldn't return to a life she no longer wanted simply to save Bradley's business. Either he found a way, or he didn't. Ultimately, it wasn't her responsibility.

"You're sorry?!" Just like that, his anger was back. And it brought a couple of friends—fury and rage.

"I am."

"No." He walked closer to her...and for the first time ever, she felt afraid of Bradley.

Right now, she was looking at the man she'd spent almost half of her life working with and seeing the face of a stranger.

"I'm sorry," she said again.

He laughed viciously. "No. You're not sorry yet. But you will be."

Was he threatening her?

"You think that restaurant has seen some trouble before this? You just wait."

Harper froze as she considered the vandalism, the arson, the theft...

"It was you. You set the fire. You...did all the rest."

The smile he gave her was pure evil. "Prove it."

Her body went numb when she considered the lengths Bradley had gone to in order to keep his cash cow. The shit he'd put her through when she was juggling the modeling career and culinary school. The way he'd had a change of heart and was suddenly interested in hearing everything about the restaurant, including seeing pictures of the building and hearing about her business partner and her contractor.

"You asshole," she said through gritted teeth. "Get out! Get the fuck out!"

She started for the door, ready to kick him out on his ass, but Bradley spun her around, grabbing her upper arms, shaking her so violently her teeth rattled.

"You're coming back, Harper!"

He was fucking delusional. She tried to break his grip, tried to get away, but he was stronger than she would have expected.

"Let me go!"

"No!" His grip was crushing, leaving bruises.

"Get out!" she yelled again, just as she heard a knock on the door.

Thank God! Their argument must have caught someone's attention.

"Help!" she yelled, looking wildly toward the door.

"Shut up!" Bradley released one arm, but it wasn't until Harper turned her head back to look at him that she realized why.

Stars exploded behind her eyes as the back of his hand connected with the side of her face. Her neck twisted so hard, she feared she had whiplash.

She cried out in pain, trying to get away, as Bradley struck her again. This time with his fist.

The knocking on the door stopped, replaced by a loud —*really* loud—bang. Then another and another, until suddenly the door crashed open and Luca stormed in like an avenging angel.

Bradley pushed Harper away from him forcefully, ready to defend himself from Luca's attack. She had no chance of catching her footing as she stumbled backward into the coffee table, tumbling over it and hitting her head on the floor, *hard*.

It took her a few seconds to clear her vision and recover her wits enough to realize Luca had Bradley on his back on the floor —and he was beating the shit out of her asshole ex-manager.

She struggled to push herself upright, her head hurting, making her dizzy and nauseous.

"Luca," she said, too softly to be heard over her sexy protector, currently cussing a blue streak at Bradley.

"You don't. Ever. Lay a fucking. Hand on her. Again." Every few words were punctuated with another brutal punch as Bradley lay curled in a ball, his hands trying to cover his face as he pleaded with Luca to stop.

"Luca," she repeated louder.

That time he paused, her voice drawing his attention to her, his eyes going wide. She didn't know what she looked like, but it couldn't be good.

They stared at each other for just a second before two security guards rushed in.

"We had a call about a fight," one of them said.

They reached for Luca, but Harper stopped them. "No! He was helping me." She pointed to Bradley, whimpering on the floor. "That man attacked me."

One of the security guards pulled out his phone, calling 9-1-1. "No one is leaving here until the police arrive." He seemed to change his mind when he looked at her. "Should I call back for an ambulance?"

Harper lifted a hand to her face, shocked to discover blood on her fingertips. "Blood?" she asked, dazed. "What's bleeding?"

Luca reached for her hand, pulling it away. "Don't move." He walked to the kitchenette and grabbed a tea towel that he wetted at the small sink. When he returned, he knelt in front of her. "You've got a cut on your forehead, a split lip, and a bloody nose."

"Ouch," she said, only half joking.

Luca didn't laugh as he gently wiped away the blood. "Jesus Christ, Harper. I heard you screaming and... When he pushed you, and you hit that table..." He scrubbed his face with his hand. "Fuck me," he muttered.

"I'm okay," she lied. Her head hurt like a motherfucker, and she could now feel the sting from the bleeding cuts. "What are you doing here?"

"I grabbed your phone instead of mine. Didn't realize it until

I got to the restaurant. I'm glad the hotel and restaurant are so close."

It wasn't the first time the two of them had accidentally swapped phones. They'd even had a play fight this weekend, arguing about which one of them should have to buy a new case so they could tell them apart. It had been a silly debate, with Conor serving as judge.

"Thank God," she whispered, as it sank in how much worse things could have gotten if he hadn't returned. Bradley had been unhinged, and she didn't want to think about all the ways he could have hurt her.

The two security guards had helped Bradley to a sitting position, and a third man arrived, standing in the doorway of her broken-in door. Bradley's gaze kept sliding from the guards to the door, no doubt hoping for a chance to escape.

"What the hell happened?" Luca asked.

"He wanted me to come back to New York. To the agency. It's in trouble. He's the one who's been sabotaging the reconstruction."

Luca scowled. "Did he confess to that?"

She shook her head. "No. But I know he did it."

Luca glanced over his shoulder, cracking his knuckles as he glared at Bradley.

Bradley caught his malevolent stare and quickly looked away, obviously nervous Luca would come back for another round.

Harper tried to stand, but Luca placed a hand on her shoulder. "Stay there, Harper. Until the EMTs get here. Let them check you out to make sure nothing is broken."

She did her own small inventory, wiggling feet and hands, twisting a wee bit to check her ribs. "I don't think anything is." She suspected all her injuries were the ones already visible, except for the bruises he left on her arms when he shook her.

A few minutes later, the police arrived. Harper was relieved when Kayden walked in, quickly introducing her to his partner, Seth.

Kayden asked her a few questions as Seth stood next to Bradley. She told him about the surprise visit, his attempts to get her to return to New York, even her suspicions that he'd been the one sabotaging the renovation. After she'd given her statement, Seth reached down to pull Bradley from the floor. He winced, claiming he needed to go to the hospital.

Seth didn't respond. Instead, he cuffed him and read him his rights before leading him out of the room.

Kayden shook his head as he looked at Luca. "Looks like he needs medical attention."

"He was beating Harper," Luca replied darkly.

Kayden raised his hands in surrender. "Not saying you did the wrong thing. Just saying you Moretti brothers have a tendency to take matters into your own hands when someone threatens your girl."

Harper looked at Luca for an explanation, even though she was secretly thrilled by the way Kayden had called her Luca's girl.

Luca grimaced. "Jess was working as a maid in a seedy hotel when she first met Rhys and Tony. A guy attacked her, and Tony broke down the door and beat the fuck out of the guy."

Harper glanced at her destroyed door. "I'm sort of sorry my head hurts so bad because this knight-in-shining-armor thing you've got going on is a total turn-on."

Luca didn't laugh.

Kayden laughed. "Where's Conor?"

Harper wondered how on earth Kayden could know the status quo between her, Luca, and Conor had changed.

This time, it was Kayden who offered the explanation. "Luca, me, and a bunch of the guys have lunch together every Wednesday. Luca showed up this past week looking like the cat who ate the canary. It didn't take me three minutes to wear him down and get him to confess to what had put that shit-eating grin on his face."

"A good cop always gets his confession," she joked.

It was another miss, she realized, when Luca's frown grew more pronounced.

"Hey. I'm okay now." She reached for his hand and squeezed, stopping when he winced. Looking down, she saw his knuckles were split, bruised from the beating he'd given Bradley.

When the EMTs arrived, Luca rose. "I'll call Conor. Have him meet us at the hospital."

Harper wanted to tell him that wasn't necessary, but as the adrenaline began to wear off, fear was creeping in. She wanted both her guys with her, and she didn't care if that made her sound helpless or weak.

The EMTs confirmed what she knew. Nothing was broken, but they suspected the cut on her head would need a few stitches. They were also concerned about a concussion.

Luca returned. "Got his voicemail. Left a message. I'll try again when we get to the hospital."

Hotel security assured her they would secure the door—and all her belongings—and Luca rode to the hospital with her in the ambulance.

After three hours of pokes, prods, scans, and stitches, Harper found herself in a private hospital room, with Luca dozing next to her in the chair. She'd tried to convince him to go home, but he wasn't budging.

He tried to call Conor at least a dozen times, every attempt going straight to voicemail.

The two of them had decided Conor's phone battery was probably dead, and he had no idea they were trying to reach him.

It was a pretty lie they were telling themselves because one look in Luca's light brown eyes told her he was thinking the same thing she was.

Something still felt weird.

And wrong.

# Chapter Fourteen

The first thing Conor noticed when he woke up was the sharp pain in his neck. The second was the smell of coffee.

He slowly pried his eyes open, blinking a few times before twisting his head, grimacing as his stiff muscles protested.

Pushing himself upright from the living room floor, he frowned when he spotted Matt sitting on his couch, watching him.

"What are you doing here?" Conor asked, his voice husky, hoarse.

Matt sighed. "I was going to ask you the same thing. You always build a fort of books and sleep on the floor?"

Conor glanced around the room, aware how strange all of this must look. Given the concern on his brother's face, he'd guess it wasn't just odd, but alarming.

He'd spent the better part of two hours last night dealing with a killer anxiety attack. Once he'd managed to get his breathing under control, managed to convince his heart to stop trying to beat its way out of his chest, he'd given up on trying to sleep. After the panic stopped, his thoughts began to travel down some very dark roads, and rather than shut them down—as was his usual operating procedure—he let them in. Let himself wallow in every horrible memory, every frightening emotion, every defeatist bullshit thought.

And when he let it all go too far, he'd taken his pity party to the next level, trashing his living room in search of something that didn't exist.

"You let yourself in?" Conor asked.

Matt smirked. "I have a keycard to your place, same as you do to mine."

Because he and his brothers had all opted to live in penthouse apartments in Russo buildings, they'd exchanged keycards—the equivalent to leaving a key with a neighbor—in case of emergency.

"How long have you been here?"

"Long enough to make coffee and—" Matt was interrupted by the ping of the elevator, announcing someone's arrival. "Long enough to call him," he added as Gage stepped into the living room, his hair mussed and his shirt wrinkled. It looked as if he'd rolled out of bed, thrown on clothes, and come straight here.

"What's going on?" Gage asked as he walked in. "What's the emergency?" He frowned as he looked down at Conor on the floor. "Did you fall?"

Conor shook his head.

"No. Apparently, he slept on the floor," Matt replied.

"Why?" Gage asked.

Conor sighed. "Is there a reason you're both here?"

Matt took a sip of the coffee he'd helped himself to, bowing his head toward the table to indicate there were two more cups. Conor stood and reached for his before claiming one of the chairs. Gage did the same, though he opted to share the couch opposite Conor with Matt, his brothers sitting side by side.

Wonderful. That didn't make Conor feel even more self-conscious. At. All.

"Tony called me a couple of hours ago."

Conor turned toward the wall clock. It was eight a.m.

He'd destroyed his living room until nearly five before slumping down on the floor and falling into an exhausted sleep.

"That's early for a—" Conor stopped midsentence, his sleep-deprived mind finally waking up. "Luca. Is he all right?"

Matt quickly held up his hand. "He's fine. It was actually Harper who—"

"Harper? Fuck! Where's my phone?" Conor rose quickly, his heart racing as he glanced around the room, recalling he'd left it on the entryway table. Retrieving it, he tried to turn it on before he remembered it was dead. Scrounging around in his weekend bag, also still on the floor by the elevator, he pulled out the charger, plugging the thing in.

"Conor," Matt said. "She's fine. Sit back down."

Conor returned to his chair, falling into it heavily. "What happened?"

"According to Tony, her old manager showed up at the hotel last night to convince her to return to modeling."

Conor nodded numbly. That didn't sound so bad.

Until Matt continued. "When she refused, he got violent."

Conor bolted up again. "He *what*?"

Matt sighed. "He roughed her up a bit, then Luca kicked down the hotel door and—"

"Luca kicked down the door? Why was he there?" Between exhaustion and anxiety, Conor was struggling to wrap his head around anything.

"I don't know the answer to that. Luca subdued the manager until the cops arrived. Harper has a split lip, a few stitches, some bruises, and a minor concussion. They kept her in the hospital last night for observation."

Suddenly, there was a ping as Conor's phone came to life. Walking over, he looked at the screen, his heart thudding. There were twenty-two missed texts and a dozen voicemails, all from Luca.

She'd been attacked. Luca had saved her. Taken her to the hospital.

They'd needed him, and instead of going to them, he'd been here, falling apart.

No good to them.

No good to anyone.

"What's going on, Conor?" Matt asked. "You're worrying the fuck out of me."

Conor put the phone down, returning to the chair, bowing his head, uncertain how to respond.

He was too strung-out to come up with a lie.

Fuck.

He didn't *want* to come up with one.

When he lifted his face, he saw matching expressions of worry on his brothers' faces. For too many years after their parents' deaths, the three of them had been estranged, more colleagues than brothers. Lately that had changed, but not because of anything he'd done. He hadn't been the one to reach out. They had.

"I had a panic attack."

Gage's eyes softened as he shrugged. "Everybody gets those."

Conor could have left it there, grabbed the out his brother just handed him, but the way Matt remained silent, looking at him...

"It wasn't the first time I've had one," Conor said. "I actually have them...a lot."

Matt frowned. "What's a lot?"

Conor shrugged. "It depends on what's going on at work or in my life. When I was younger, I had them more frequently... five or six bad ones a month. But I've learned how to manage them better, so sometimes I can make it a month or two without one."

"Younger?" Gage muttered. "How young?"

Conor rubbed the back of his neck wearily, trying to work out the kinks. "I had the first one when I was twelve."

Gage's eyes widened, while Matt looked resigned, sad even.

"What triggered the first one?" Matt asked.

"I failed a science test. It was the first F I ever got, and the teacher called Dad, all concerned. He blew a gasket because..."

"Russos never fail," Gage said bitterly.

Matt frowned. "You were a straight-A student, Conor. What happened with that test?"

Conor swallowed heavily. He was shit at sharing personal stuff, and he was afraid some of what he had to say would hurt Gage.

"Mom always helped me study," he said quietly.

"Why didn't she—" Gage stopped suddenly, understanding dawning.

Their mom's depression became progressively worse as they got older. Conor couldn't remember her ever shutting herself in her room before he was nine or ten. In his mind, those early childhood years had been blissful. Mom read books to him and made him his favorite cookies whenever he came home with a good report card. Dad hadn't gotten his hooks into Matt yet, so he, Matt, and Gage were best friends as well as brothers.

Dad had been a dark shadow in Conor's teenage and adult life, but when he was young, his father left him and his brothers to their own devices, letting Mom do the lion's share of raising them since they didn't serve any purpose to him yet.

When Matt turned thirteen, that changed. Dad stepped in to begin molding his older son—his heir—into his own personal mini-me. Matt was resistant at first, but before long, the lessons took, and for years, it felt to Conor as if he'd lost his big brother.

Gage had always been the loose cannon, the black sheep, and a thorn in Dad's side because he was devoted to Mom, her constant companion. And while he and Dad butted heads, Gage seemed to get a bye from a lot of the pressure put on Matt because Gage was taking care of Mom, something Dad either didn't know how to do...or didn't *want* to do.

"She didn't help you because she was in her room, wasn't she?" Gage asked.

Conor nodded. "I was twelve, and more than old enough to

study for my own test. It was just..." The rest of that sentence wouldn't come. While he'd hated his father, hated everything he stood for, too many of his old man's lessons had stuck. If he finished his thought now, he would sound weak.

"Say it," Matt prodded. "It's just us, Conor. Dad's not here anymore."

He wasn't sure how Matt knew, but he let his brother's words bolster him.

"I hated it when she went away," he whispered. Mom didn't really go away, except in her head, but his brothers understood what he meant. "Dad yelled at me after he got off the phone with my teacher and sent me to bed without dinner. By the time I got to my room, my chest was so tight I couldn't breathe, and I swear to God, I thought I was having a heart attack. I lay on the floor for hours, sure I was dying."

"Jesus," Gage said, scrubbing his jaw with his hand. "Why didn't you come get one of us, man?"

Conor shook his head. "I don't know why. I... You were in Mom's bedroom with her, playing video games, talking to her, cajoling her like you always did, trying to pull her out of her sadness. And—" He glanced at Matt and stopped.

"And I had my head stuck up my ass, emulating the world's biggest prick," Matt said.

"I rode it out," Conor said. "Then I checked out a book on mental illness from the library."

Gage gave him a sad grin. "Of course you did. You and your damn books." As he spoke, he looked around at the utter destruction in his living room, but he didn't say anything.

Thank God.

Conor didn't have a clue how he was going to explain the mess.

"I researched what I could, found out it had been a panic attack. I guess I don't handle anxiety all that great. Over the years, I've found ways to deal with it. I've tried a lot of things, and some work with varying degrees of success."

"Like?" Matt asked.

"When I feel one coming on, I shut myself in, focus on my breathing, close my eyes, practice mindfulness. There's a three-three-three method that I like. I've got a shit-ton of lavender candles here and at the office because I read the scent is calming. I have a mantra I say over and over."

At Gage's curious head tilt, Conor answered the unspoken question. "I say, 'I'm okay. I'm okay. I'm okay,' over and over."

"You know," Matt pointed out, "a wise man once told me to go to therapy."

Conor smirked. That was exactly what he'd told his big brother to do when he confessed that *he* was the one who'd found Mom after she slit her wrists, admitting he blamed himself for it because he'd left her alone, knowing she was upset.

"Did it never occur to you to see someone?" Matt asked.

Conor crossed his arms as he leaned back. "Of course it did. I saw a therapist for a couple of years, but it didn't help. The guy just kept wanting to shove prescriptions into my hand, no matter how many times I said no drugs."

Gage took a sip of his coffee, making a face and putting the cup down. Like Conor, Matt liked his coffee strong and black. Gage, on the other hand, nursed his with so much cream and sugar, Conor wasn't sure it even classified as coffee. "Why are you so opposed to drugs? There's nothing wrong with taking antianxiety medicine."

"I didn't want to be a zombie like Mom. Sometimes I wasn't sure what was worse, the depression or the supposed cure."

Matt sighed. "Conor, she was on some seriously powerful medication—thanks to Dad's demands that the doctor 'fix her.' She wasn't receiving the right treatment because Dad refused to acknowledge her illness. He wanted her in that doped-up state because it kept her meek and quiet."

Conor frowned. "I didn't know that."

"All your memories of what Mom was going through were seen through the eyes of a boy. She was gone before you turned twenty. It makes sense you wouldn't have understood all the things you were seeing and hearing. It's not like anyone was trying to explain it to you." Matt lowered his head, and it was apparent he was taking on the burden of not talking to Conor.

"You were a kid too," Conor pointed out. "And my brother, not my parent. It wasn't your job to talk to me about any of that."

Matt faced him again, and though it took a few seconds, the clouds in his eyes lifted a bit. "Not sure I agree, but thanks for that."

Gage leaned forward, his elbows on his knees. "Are these attacks the reason why you keep your office at Enigma?"

Shit. All the dominos were falling today.

He nodded, then dug deep, desperately trying to lighten the mood. "You bastards barge into each other's offices all the time without knocking. I couldn't take the chance you'd come in when…"

"I get why you didn't tell us about this when we were kids," Gage started, "but lately…" He sighed, and Conor knew why.

"I'm sorry, Gage. I should have confided in you. In both of you. It's just…you'd spent the last decade wallowing in a shit-ton of guilt over Mom's death and I didn't want you to worry about me."

Matt rose, taking two steps toward him, stymied from making it all the way to his chair by several piles of books. "You're our brother, Conor. We're family. I know we haven't acted like one for most of our lives, but I want that to change. I *need* that to change."

Matt was typically a stoic guy, always playing his cards close to his chest. Lately, he'd been more open, laughing and smiling more than Conor had seen him do since when they were kids.

"Liza's been a good influence on you," he said, before turning to Gage and grinning. "And Penny's made you almost tolerable."

"Asshole," Gage tossed back, scoffing playfully. "I was always the handsome, charming, fun one. You guys were the miserable, brooding, sad sacks. Although, I have noticed lately…"

Gage and Matt exchanged a look, and Conor knew where this conversation was headed.

"What's the deal with you and Harper Branson?" Matt asked—before adding, "And Luca Moretti?"

"What makes you think—"

Gage raised his hand. "I pointed it out to him after the second hockey night here. The sexual tension radiating between the three of you gave me a sunburn."

Conor leaned back, too numb to even feel his exhaustion. Now that he'd opened the vault, he figured he might as well go for broke. "Did you know?" he asked them. "That I'm bisexual?"

Matt shook his head, while Gage nodded.

"You did?" Matt asked. "How?"

"I had a feeling. Back when we were in college, you went to California with some friend's family the day after Christmas."

Conor nodded, all of them aware of what Gage wasn't saying. Shortly after that holiday, Mom committed suicide.

"From the way you talked about the guy, I got the impression he was a boyfriend," Gage added.

"He was," Conor confirmed. "I wasn't sure how you would feel..."

"I hate that you thought you had to hide it from us," Matt said sadly.

Conor didn't want his brother taking that guilt on his shoulders. "I wasn't hiding it, Matt. I swear. I've just gotten damn good at living a very private life, and to be perfectly honest, there haven't been that many boyfriends—or girlfriends—in my past. I'm not great at forging relationships."

Matt twisted around the piles of books, tired of the distance between them. He placed his hand on Conor's shoulder and squeezed it tightly. "You don't have to say that for my benefit. I know why you kept it a secret. Dad was a fucking homophobic prick, but I'm not. All I want is for you to find someone who makes you happy. Or...maybe two someones?"

"Do you think it's crazy?" Conor asked.

Matt lifted one shoulder casually. "Not going to say I didn't raise my eyebrows when Tony and Rhys hooked up with Jess. Or when Gio moved in with Rafe and Keeley. By the time Aldo and Kayden decided to settle down with Hazel, it was less interesting, and I started chalking it up as a Moretti thing. But I've spent time with all of those throuples lately, and while it's not something I'd be comfortable with, I can't deny that it works for them."

"It does work," Conor said, now in possession of firsthand experience of just how well. "I was like you at first. I couldn't understand it, but after spending time with Harper and Luca, getting close to them, I can't imagine being with one of them without the other."

"Hey, you have to admit," Gage chimed in, "it's kind of the best of both worlds for a bisexual guy. You can have the peanut butter *and* the jelly."

"Jesus, never say anything that corny again," Conor muttered, though he chuckled.

"No promises," Gage said with a wicked grin, his eyes roaming around the room again. "So...what's the deal with the books?"

It was funny to Conor that admitting to his panic attacks was going to be easier than explaining this.

"At first, my intention was to purge. I couldn't sleep and I've run out of shelf space, so I thought I'd start making piles—of books to keep, to give away, regift. After an hour, I realized what I was really doing was looking for something."

"What?" Matt prodded.

Conor took a deep breath and rubbed his chest. Not because he felt a panic attack coming on, but more because that action had become a nervous tic. "Something from Mom."

Matt frowned. "Something you lost?"

He shook his head. "No. More like something I never found. You showed me the sketchbook she gave back to you the night she died." Matt had invited him and Gage over for happy hour at his place a couple of months earlier. While they were there, Matt showed them a sketchbook he and Mom used to swap back and forth when Matt was younger. Both brilliant artists, Mom had found a way to share that talent with her oldest son.

Matt had stopped drawing during his teen years when he began spending more time with Dad, giving the sketchbook back to her, telling her that he was done with it. Mom had returned it as a gift for Matt's twenty-third birthday. She'd killed herself just hours later, and Matt hadn't been able to bring himself to open the present until this year.

"And I told you about the cookbook," Gage said.

That same night, Gage admitted to finding some of his mother's drawings in a cookbook the two of them often used, whipping up masterpieces for dinner. Cooking—in addition to video games—was a shared interest between Mom and Gage, yet another way the two of them spent time together.

"I never found anything really special like that. The only things I have from Mom are the books she gave me over the years." Conor lifted his arms. "Countless books."

"You always had your nose in one," Gage said, though his smile this time was sadder.

"No inscriptions?" Matt asked, aware that was exactly what Conor had been hoping for.

"No. Nothing beyond 'Merry Christmas' or 'Happy Birthday' or 'Love, Mom'. I know it sounds stupid. To wish for something tangible. I have my memories of her, and I know deep inside how much Mom loved me. I do. It's just... Right now, it feels like all I inherited from her was this broken part in my brain." Conor tapped his finger on the side of his head.

"Fuck," Matt breathed. "Don't say that. Don't even think that. You're not broken."

"What if Mom's illness started as panic attacks?" Conor asked. "I've looked it up, read countless articles. Depression and anxiety attacks are often linked together. How do I know there's not a ticking time bomb inside my head waiting to go off? How do I know these anxiety attacks won't progress to something worse?"

Matt shook his shoulder lightly, cutting him off. "Stop, Conor. Breathe."

Conor rubbed his eyes wearily. "I haven't slept well the last couple of nights."

"Because of panic attacks?" Gage asked.

"Yes...and no. Things with me, Harper, and Luca have gotten pretty serious very quickly."

Matt gave him a crooked grin. "That seems to be the Moretti way. None of them have the patience for a long-term relationship. They jump from first date to serious relationship to marriage talk, all within the span of a few weeks."

Gage chuckled. "Suuuure. Liza's the one pushing for the two of you to take a trip down the aisle. Sell that to someone else, bro, because I caught you browsing the internet, looking at engagement rings two days after you and Liza made your relationship Facebook official."

Matt scowled but didn't argue.

"Luca and Harper are—God..." Conor raked his hand through his hair. "They're both so positive and upbeat and happy all the fucking time. I've never met two people who are always smiling and laughing and joking."

Gage picked up his coffee cup, started to take a sip, reconsidered, then put it down again. "I get that. I felt the same way with Penny when we first started dating. Conor, we grew up in a house where that shit didn't happen. I'm sure it *does* feel strange. Jesus, you should have seen me walking around Nonno and Nonna Moretti's house on Christmas Eve. Suffered some serious culture shock that night."

"That's not the problem. I like to laugh and cut up and have fun as much as the next guy," Conor said.

"Since when?" Gage joked.

Conor narrowed his eyes but forged on. "How can I ask them to be with me when..." For so many years, he'd eschewed relationship, dismissed the idea of marriage and children because he was determined he would not repeat the cycle. "I can't put them or future children through the stuff we went through."

"Put that out of your head right now." Matt crossed his arms over his chest. "Because there's no way in hell I'm going to let you throw away the chance at love, at marriage, and a family. We're fixing this."

"Aw shit, man. You did it now," Gage said. "You invoked the CEO."

Matt tossed Gage an exasperated look but continued. "You're moving your office out of Enigma and into the Russo Enterprises' building."

Conor already had an office there, right next to his brothers' on the top floor, but he'd never used it. Suddenly, the idea of being closer to them day in and day out didn't sound so bad. "Okay."

Matt looked slightly astonished by his quick agreement, then forged on. "That was the easy one. I'm going to give you the number of my therapist. I think you'll like her."

"You have a therapist?" Conor was surprised.

"I took your suggestion," Matt replied, making it clear he'd like to see Conor follow his lead. "I think you should discuss your concerns about the medications with her. If you still don't want to take them, fine, but listen to what she has to say with an open mind first. Put your damn Russo stubbornness aside."

Conor nodded. "Okay. I will."

"Can I have your therapist's number too?" Gage asked.

Neither Matt nor Conor knew how to respond to that because Gage—of the three of them—seemed like the one who had his shit together.

"Of course," Matt said slowly. "Can I ask why you need it?"

Gage looked away, the reaction unusual in his say-anything brother. "Penny's pregnant."

Conor snorted. "Not sure there's anyone in the state who doesn't know that by now."

Gage faced them, smirking briefly before the smile faded away. "I'm going to be a father. I don't..." He clenched his fists. "I don't know how to do that. I just know I don't want to be like ours."

Matt nodded. "I get that, Gage. Of course, I'll give you the number. I've talked to my therapist a lot about my childhood and about us. How would you guys feel about trying family counseling as well? It might help us sort some things out if we're all three together, sharing our memories."

Gage grinned. "I'd like that."

"Me too," Conor agreed.

Gage rose, looking around the room then back at Conor. "I don't know if this helps, Conor. But I can't stop thinking about that thing Mom used to say to us. What was it?" he asked. "Something like, you can't change what you are, just what you do."

Conor snorted. "You know she got that from a book, right? *The Golden Compass*."

Gage groaned. "Oh shit. I stepped into that one, didn't I? I know, I know," he said, waving his hand to ward off what he anticipated was coming next. "I'm really missing out by not reading it. You told me that a million times when we were back in high school."

"I did say that, and I stand by it."

"Yeah, well, it wasn't like I was going to ask to borrow your copy," Gage grumbled. "Only made that mistake once."

Conor narrowed his eyes. "You dog-eared the pages. What kind of monster does that?"

Gage shrugged, completely unrepentant.

Conor recalled that quote sticking with Mom enough that she repeated it whenever they were having trouble in college. He hadn't thought about those words in years.

Now, however...

He thought he'd been doing the right things since he couldn't change who he was, but considering last night's breakdown and after listening to his brothers, everything he'd done suddenly felt very, very wrong.

He should have kept going to therapy.

He should have talked to his brothers a long time ago.

He should have let Harper and Luca in, should have opened a vein—just like the two of them had done, countless times as they spoke of their pasts—and he should have truly shared himself with them.

The silence lingered as those hard truths sank in. When he looked up, he could still see the concern in his brothers' eyes, and he hated that he'd put it there.

"You know, I was the one who loaned Mom the book. Unlike you, Gage, she wanted to read it so we could talk about it." Conor rose and weaved his way around the stacks of books until he reached one of the shelves. He hadn't taken *The Golden Compass* off the shelf because he knew he was keeping that book, even though it was tatty as shit, the spine creased a million times over. He'd bought it at a used bookstore with his allowance when he was sixteen. It had been one of his favorite stories to escape into when things were rough.

"I haven't read this since high school." Pulling it off the shelf, he flipped through the pages, stopping when his eyes caught sight of something. Paging back, he stopped when he realized something had been underlined. "There's..."

"What is it?" Matt asked.

Matt and Gage walked over to him, looking over his shoulders. Conor used his thumb to mark that spot, then flipped through again, noticing that there were several more passages marked.

"She underlined things," Conor said excitedly. It hadn't occurred to him to look in this book because Mom hadn't given it to him.

"Thank God she used pencil," Gage joked.

Conor shoulder-bumped him, grinning.

Matt pointed to the page. "What did she highlight?"

Conor stared at the underlined words. "It's a quote that talks about being at peace. About not letting your thoughts turn traitor."

Conor stared at it, letting those words sink in. "Jesus. Do you think she knew?"

Gage shrugged as Matt murmured, "I don't know."

Conor had tried to talk to his mom about his attacks once—just once. It was the same day Luca had walked away from him in the library, hand in hand with Trina Paulson. He'd been in the throes of an attack and so fucking terrified. He had detoured on the way to his bedroom, opening the door to his mom's room. He'd called out her name, but he'd known the second he'd seen the drawn curtains, the darkness, her body a small lump buried beneath a mountain of blankets, that she'd disappeared.

Regardless of his fears, that day he'd walked into the room, sunk down on the edge of the bed, and reached for her hand. His had been shaking like crazy, while hers had been ice cold. He held onto it for only a minute or two before escaping to his own room.

Had she known?

Conor kept flipping, seeing more passages. He closed the book, suddenly anxious to read it again, impatient to discover which words spoke to his mother enough that she'd marked them for him to see.

"Looks like you found what you were looking for." Matt tilted his head toward the book.

Conor gripped the book tightly, smiling. "Yeah. I did."

"Feeling better?" Gage asked.

Conor didn't know how to answer that. He felt happy. Between finding something from his mother and unburdening himself of his secret, he was definitely lighter.

But there was still one big hurdle—one he'd placed himself—between Conor and true happiness.

"I don't know yet," he admitted.

"Yet?" Matt pressed.

"I need to talk to Harper and Luca. I need to tell them...all of it. What if—"

"There is no what if," Gage said. "You'll tell them, they'll understand, and then the three of you will have wild monkey sex. I'm not going to lie, I'm curious about the gymnastics it must require to get all those body parts together and in sync."

"Jesus," Matt said, shaking his head. "I'm going to cut him off before he starts asking you to draw diagrams."

Gage's eyes lit up as if that hadn't occurred to him, but he now wanted it.

"Forget it, Gage," Conor said, before looking at Matt. "I'm going to do what you said. I'll move into the office next to yours and I'll call the therapist."

"Great," Matt said. "And for what it's worth, I don't think you need to worry about Harper and Luca. According to Tony, they've been worried sick about you all night. He said Harper's going to be released from the hospital this morning. Now, I'm not a betting man, but if I were, I'd lay down every dime I have that they're going to pay you a visit today. Probably sooner rather than later."

"They will. They never leave me alone," Conor said, though his tone made it clear that didn't annoy him at all. Rather, it amazed him.

"Good. So stop pushing them away because of fear," Gage said. "I almost lost Penny and Matt came damn close to losing Liza because we'd been letting Dad live rent free in our heads. Evict him. It'll be the best thing you ever do. Then open the door and let Luca and Harper in. You need them in your life for the very reasons you said. They're happy and positive and they care for you."

Conor smiled, then felt the last of his heaviness fly away with Matt's next words.

"They won't let you get lost in the dark."

Chapter Fifteen

Luca parked on the street in front of Conor's building, but neither he nor Harper opened the car doors.

He'd tried to talk Harper into letting him take her to his place to rest after she was released from the hospital, but she refused, claiming she couldn't rest until she knew Conor was okay. Luca had tried calling and texting him last night, but eventually gave up when Conor didn't reply.

It was just shy of ten a.m., so there was a chance Conor was at the office. If he was, Luca was going to lose his shit. He'd been trying to hold it together for Harper, but between worrying about her and Conor and sleeping upright in an uncomfortable chair all night, he was riding the razor's edge.

"You mad at him?" Harper asked.

"Aren't you? Jesus, Harper. You went through hell last night, and he couldn't even bother to call to check on you."

"We don't know his side of the story," she started.

"You saw how he was yesterday, blowing us off. He keeps trying to push us away and it's making me—" Luca cut himself off, tightening his grip on the steering wheel until he was white-knuckling the thing.

Harper placed her hand on his forearm. "Let's go in and talk to him."

She was right. He knew she was. The problem was, he had experience with being dumped by Conor. Sure, it was a friendship forged in Spanish class rather than a relationship, but Conor had still walked away without any explanation. Sixteen-year-old Luca let him do it, but he wouldn't this time. Couldn't.

Luca took a deep breath, then nodded. "Okay."

Entering the building, they stopped at the front desk. Before they could ask the stickler-for-rules front desk attendant—who knew damn well who they were, after all their visits—to call Conor, he heard someone else calling their names.

"Luca, Harper." Gage waved at them, he and Matt crossing the foyer.

"You should have made that bet," Luca heard Gage say to Matt as they walked up.

"How are you feeling?" Matt asked Harper.

"I'm fine. Few bumps and bruises, but other than that," she said, in a cheerful voice Luca knew was fake.

Bradley's attack had shaken her. It stood to reason. After all, she'd worked with the man for fourteen years, and even if they hadn't exactly been friends, they'd always been friendly. At least, that was how she'd portrayed their relationship, and he didn't think she was lying. He'd been with her last night when Bradley approached them in the hotel lobby. She was genuinely delighted to see the man.

The *asshole*, Luca amended.

Kayden had called just before Harper's release to let them know Bradley was still behind bars, but likely to post bail by this afternoon. Kayden and Seth had been assigned to investigate the "accidents" at the construction site. Obviously, the fire had been scrutinized, as had the theft of the electrical wiring, but Luca stupidly hadn't reported the flooding, something that he could see in hindsight had been a mistake.

Kayden was taking Harper's allegations seriously that Bradley was to blame for all of the destruction. He was a good cop, and Luca didn't doubt Kayden would leave no stone unturned.

"Is Conor upstairs?" Luca was unable to hide the annoyance in his voice.

Matt nodded. "Tony called me this morning, said the two of you were concerned, so we came over to check on him. His phone was dead. He didn't receive your messages."

That didn't make Luca feel much better. "Did you tell him about Harper?"

Matt exchanged a look with Gage, one Luca couldn't begin to interpret. "We did."

"Is Conor alright?" Harper asked.

Matt rubbed the back of his neck. "We're going to let Conor explain what happened last night." He looked at Luca. "I hope you'll give him the chance."

There was something troubling in Matt's expression, and Luca's anger morphed to concern in an instant. Something wasn't right.

"Okay," Luca said, anxious to get upstairs. "We will."

Matt smiled, while Gage handed them a keycard. "Use this. And watch your step in the living room."

Before he and Harper could ask what the hell that meant, Gage and Matt headed for the exit.

At the same time, Harper and Luca's phones both pinged. Glancing at the screen, he saw it was a message on their group text thread from Conor, asking if they were still at the hospital.

She attempted a smile, but he could tell Matt's comments had bothered her too. "I'm worried."

Luca nodded and reached for her hand, leading her to the elevator. "Come on."

When the doors slid open to Conor's apartment, Luca understood Gage's warning. The living room appeared to have been bombed by a million books, the floor covered in stacks of varying height, some so tall they were defying gravity.

"Did you guys forget something?" Conor asked as he came

around the corner from the kitchen. His eyes widened in surprise when he saw them—clearly thinking his brothers had returned—then his expression morphed to concern mingled with anger when he saw Harper's face. "Jesus."

"It looks worse than it feels," she told Conor.

"Don't. Don't downplay it. I can tell it hurts." He walked over, gently cupping her chin, tilting her face this way and that as he took stock of her injuries. "I'm going to kill your manager."

For the first time since yesterday, Luca managed a grin. It was a malevolent one, but whatever. It worked because on this subject, he and Conor were in agreement. "We both will."

Conor's gaze traveled over to him, and Luca noticed the circles under the other man's eyes. Yesterday morning, those circles had merely been dark; today, they looked almost black.

"You haven't slept," Luca said.

"Not much," Conor admitted. "I... About last night..."

If guilt had a face, it would be Conor's right now. He raked a hand through his hair, clearly not for the first time as every strand was standing on end, completely askew. It looked as if he'd slept, or not slept, in his wrinkled clothes—and that was when Luca realized they were the same ones he'd been wearing yesterday when they dropped him off.

He didn't have a clue what happened, but he could tell it wasn't good. Just as he could tell Conor was struggling to explain.

When Luca played over the past couple of months, he wondered if he and Harper had made a mistake, letting Conor remain silent while they did most of the talking—about hopes, dreams, pasts, futures, childhoods. Conor had listened to all of it, but he'd contributed very little.

Harper must've noticed Conor's unease as well.

And because it was Harper and her love language was food, she found the right thing to say. "Come with me." She took off in the direction of the kitchen without even looking back to see if they were following. "I'm starving. Hospital food leaves a lot to be desired," she called over her shoulder. "I'll make us breakfast. We can talk after."

Conor's shoulders had been so tight, they'd practically hugged his ears, but the moment she offered him time, they slowly relaxed...a little. He was still strung tighter than a violin string, deep lines cutting grooves in his forehead and in that little space between his eyebrows.

He and Conor remained where they were for a moment, just staring at each other, before Luca followed Harper's lead.

If her love language was food, his was touching. Reaching out, he tugged Conor into his arms, his embrace firm, strong.

"It's going to be okay. Whatever it is, we're here. We're not going anywhere," he murmured when he felt Conor's stiff frame begin to sag, his arms slowly rising to hug Luca back.

"Thanks," he breathed.

When they parted, Conor sighed sadly, then headed to the kitchen, leaving Luca to follow.

Harper had already put a skillet on the stove, and she was rummaging around in Conor's refrigerator, pulling out item after item, placing it all on the counter.

"I'll whip up omelets. I found enough ingredients that I can make either a mushroom and sun-dried tomato or a bacon and brie. Preference?"

Luca and Conor said "bacon" in unison, and Harper laughed.

"Why did I even bother to ask? You guys and your bacon." She put the mushrooms and tomatoes back in the fridge then grabbed a bowl to whisk the eggs. The fact she knew where everything was in the kitchen proved just how much time she'd spent in this room cooking for them.

"Luca, I'll put you in charge of frying up the bacon. Don't burn it. Conor, can you grab the OJ and bottle of champagne from the fridge and pour us each a mimosa?" Harper began slicing the brie, and for several minutes, the three of them performed their assigned tasks, moving around each other in a well-choreographed routine. Which again, made sense. Luca had lost count of how many meals they'd made in here, Harper issuing orders that he and Conor followed.

While she was happy to let them take control in the bedroom, the kitchen was her domain. She was going to make an excellent chef.

Once the omelets and slices of thick, crusty toast were on plates, they each grabbed one, along with their drinks, and carried them to the kitchen table.

Before he picked up his fork, Conor spoke. "I'm so sorry about last night. I should have been there for you, Harper. For both of you. I can't tell you how bad I feel about—"

Harper reached across the table and placed her hand on his. "We saw Matt and Gage downstairs. They were the ones who gave us the key. They told us your phone died."

Conor shook his head. "It did, but that wasn't why I didn't come. I'm not sure...I could have..." He fell silent, and Luca imagined he could see the rest of his words lodging in Conor's throat.

"Eat first," Luca said, certain Conor hadn't had dinner last night. They'd all intended to fend for themselves, but after the attack, he and Harper had wound up sharing some crackers he'd grabbed from the snack machine at the hospital. He'd offered to bring her something from the cafeteria, but for the first time since he'd met Harper, she'd told him she wasn't hungry. "We can talk about it after."

Conor nodded. "Okay."

They dug into their omelets, and Luca was secretly relieved because some silly part of him figured if they could still eat with each other like this, they'd be just fine.

"Can I ask what happened with Bradley?" Conor asked.

"His agency is in trouble," Harper started. "He landed what had always been my dream shoot as a way to entice me to come back."

"Were you tempted?" Luca asked.

She shook her head. "Not even a little bit. Which was when I knew without a shadow of a doubt, I'd made the right decision. But when I turned the job down..." She shivered.

"Harper..." Conor said softly.

"He flipped out. Said he'd indulged my 'midlife crisis' long enough. Then he mentioned the restaurant."

Conor tilted his head, confused. "What about it?"

Luca and Harper took turns telling him about her suspicions regarding her manager's part in sabotaging their work on the restaurant.

"That son of a bitch," Conor seethed.

Then Luca filled him in on Kayden's investigation as well.

"Why were you at the hotel?" Conor asked him. "I thought you were just dropping her off."

Luca threw back the rest of his mimosa. "I was, but then she offered empanadas."

Conor rolled his eyes, good-naturedly.

"I accidentally grabbed Harper's phone from the counter when I left. Didn't realize it at first, and in truth, I considered waiting to make the switch until today, but then I remembered she had interviews, so I left Joey to do the walk-through at the restaurant, and I turned around. When I got back to her suite, I could hear her yelling for help."

Conor cursed under his breath.

"I would never have gone to that room alone with him, would never have put myself in a dangerous situation like that..." Harper started, her hands shaking with the memory of what she'd endured. Luca had seen that fear lingering in her eyes last night at the hospital. It was why he'd stayed with her.

"Christ, Harper. We know that," Luca reassured her.

"I've never seen him like that. So angry, so...scary. I don't know what would have happened if you hadn't come back, Luca, because I couldn't get away from him. I wasn't strong enough. I thought he was really going to hurt me or..." She sniffled, wiping at her eyes as she looked away, not wanting them to see her cry.

Luca reached out and took her hand in his, pulling her from

her seat and onto his lap. He hated the tears clinging to her lashes. Using his thumbs, he gently brushed away the ones that escaped, sliding down her cheeks.

"It's going to be okay." He gave her a soft kiss on the side of her mouth, avoiding her split lip.

"I should have been there," Conor said miserably, guilt radiating from every pore.

"You're here now, Conor," he said to him.

Luca had made a vow to himself that he would make these two people happy. Right now, he was zero for two. What they needed was a reminder that no matter how bad things were, they had each other. And if Luca had his way, they would *always* have each other.

Conor walked to where Harper and Luca sat. He ran his fingers over her arm, the gesture meant to comfort her. Neither man missed her slight wince.

Conor lifted the sleeve to her T-shirt, pausing when he saw the fingertip-shaped bruises on her upper arms.

Luca had seen them last night, and they'd made him feel murderous.

"He shook me," Harper said, her voice trembling.

"Never again," Conor muttered darkly, in that tone that reminded Luca of the captor in the woods.

"Once your stitches are out, Conor and I will teach you some self-defense moves."

"I'd like that," she replied.

Luca raised a finger. "But only if you promise not to use them against us the next time *that guy* visits." When he said *that guy*, he jerked his thumb in Conor's direction.

His joke—thank God—had the desired effect, as he managed to get a smile out of Harper...and Conor.

She gave them both a kiss on the cheek. "Deal."

Luca returned her kiss, placing a soft one on her lips and she sighed, the tension in her body loosening until she sagged against him, more relaxed than he'd seen her since they'd left the cabin.

"Talking to the two of you, being here with you..."

"It helps?" Luca asked.

Her contented sigh was all the answer he needed.

She nodded. "You make me feel safe."

"Safe," Conor whispered.

Luca turned to Conor. "Your turn. Talk to us."

Conor rubbed his neck wearily. "Okay."

# Chapter Sixteen

Conor followed his lovers as they headed to the living room, dodging the stacks of books, as they claimed their usual spots on the sectional couch. Harper took the corner, with Luca sitting right next to her. It wasn't lost on either of them that Conor had elected to put some distance between them by sitting at one end of the sectional.

He wasn't sure he could say the words with the two of them in such close proximity.

"Conor."

He knew Luca was going to demand that he shift closer, but Conor held up his hand to stop him. "I have some things to say—a lot of things, actually—and I..." Conor leaned forward, his elbows on his knees, his head bowed. "It's not easy for me, but I need to explain why I've been trying to keep my distance from you."

"What is it?" Harper asked softly.

"I didn't come last night because I had..." He swallowed heavily. "A panic attack."

Luca and Harper looked at each other, and Conor could tell they were at a loss for words. He didn't blame them because he hadn't given them enough. Panic attacks, like Gage pointed out, weren't exactly unusual.

He raked his hand through his hair. God. He had already said these words once today to his brothers, so he couldn't understand why this was still so hard.

Probably because there was a tiny part of him that was terrified they would decide he was too weak and move on without him. He knew that negative feeling was driven by his fucking father again, the man never once treating his youngest son as if he had any value. Dante Russo had his heir and his spare, which meant Conor was unnecessary. The only time Dad ever paid attention to him was when he screwed up.

"It was a bad one, probably one of my worst," Conor continued.

"*One* of your worst?" Harper asked.

He nodded.

"Do you know what brought it on?" Luca asked.

Conor glanced up and shrugged.

"Don't do that," Harper said. "If you're going to open up to us, then do it. All the way. Please."

"Show us all of it, Conor, because I can promise I'm not holding back. The two of you are going to get it all, the good, the bad, the ugly. There's nothing I don't want to share with you, even the bad stuff," Luca confessed.

Conor wondered what Luca considered the bad and ugly parts of himself because Conor sure as shit didn't see anything bad in the man. Or in Harper.

Rather than ask, Conor knew it was time to answer the question. "I was awake Saturday night at the cabin. I heard the two of you talking about having kids, and I... It freaked me out."

"Why?" Harper asked before lifting her hand and beckoning him. "Please slide closer. I hate that you're so far away from us."

He wanted to point out that there wasn't more than four feet between them, but he knew what she meant because he hated the distance between them as well.

Conor did as she asked, shifting until the three of them could touch each other easily.

"Why does the idea of having kids freak you out, Conor?" Harper repeated.

He took a deep breath, forcing himself to say the words he couldn't remember ever speaking aloud, even though he'd said them over and over in his head a million times. At first, he'd repeated them as a way of making that truth soak in. After a little while though, it was more to remind him to be careful. The words, his own personal cautionary tale.

"My mother committed suicide."

Neither Harper nor Luca replied, and Conor sighed. "From your lack of surprise, I assume you already knew that."

Luca grimaced. "Gage and I talked about our moms one night over a couple beers at the bar. This was last fall, before you and I—"

"It's not a secret," Conor interjected, sorry his comment had come across as an accusation. That hadn't been his intent. "It's just a hard thing for me to talk about."

"I'm sure it is," Harper said. "But what does that have to do with you not wanting kids?"

"Mom suffered from depression. Whenever she went to that dark place, she shut herself up in her room, pulled the curtains, and slept for days."

Harper linked their hands, then lifted them, kissing Conor's knuckles. "That must have been scary for you."

Conor nodded. "It was. I was around nine the first time she did it, and my brothers and I didn't understand what was going on. Dad said she was sick, that she was contagious and we had to stay away, but I didn't listen. Mom and I had a nighttime ritual, so I snuck into her room, armed with the chapter book we'd been reading together."

"What happened?" Harper whispered.

Conor let himself drift back there, let himself get lost in a memory he'd locked away, in hopes of protecting his sanity. "She wasn't asleep. She was just lying there, in the dark. I talked to her, but it felt as if she couldn't hear me. I put my hand on her forehead, like she always did for me whenever I had a fever, but she wasn't hot. Instead, she was cold. I shook her shoulder, and when she finally looked at me...it was like she wasn't there. It scared me so much I ran back to my room."

"I'm sorry, Conor." Luca's tone was full of compassion, and he saw understanding in the man's gaze. They'd both lost their mothers, and while the diseases were very different, he couldn't imagine it had been easy for Luca to see his mom slowly eaten away by cancer. Both deaths were brutal...and slow.

"I had my first panic attack when I was twelve. It was painful and terrifying, and I thought I was dying," Conor continued.

"What did your parents say?" Harper leaned toward Conor.

Conor looked at his and Harper's clasped hands. "They didn't know. Mom was shut up in her room at the time, and my dad...well, he wasn't known for his bedside manner. Truth is, he was the one who provoked it. I rode it out, then checked out a book on mental illness from the library."

"You were twelve years old, and you had to find out your own answers?" Luca was aghast. "Jesus, man. If I had a problem at that age, it wasn't a question of handling it on my own. It was a question of who do I ask for help. Where the hell were your brothers?"

Conor grimaced. "You're still looking at things through the Moretti lens, Luca. Dad had his claws in Matt, creating his own personal mini-me, and Gage was utterly devoted to Mom. He never left her alone during the dark days, always trying to cajole her out of it and bring her back to us."

"And that meant you were alone." Harper tried to covertly wipe away a tear, but Conor saw it, hated that he was making her cry, as much as he was moved by her tears on his behalf.

"That was by design. *My* design," Conor admitted. "When I was a kid, still living at home, I kept my attacks a secret because that was the Russo way. Don't ever admit weakness."

Luca scowled. "Panic attacks don't mean you're weak."

Conor shook his head. "My dad would have disagreed with you."

"I'm sorry that fucker is dead," Luca muttered. "I have a few things I'd like to say to him."

Conor grinned slightly, then forged on. "I moved out of his house when I was twenty-one, he died the next year. For the past eleven years, I've still made the choice to remain alone."

"Why?" Luca asked.

Conor lifted one shoulder. "I couldn't bear to put anyone—a spouse or a child—through what I went through. How could I ask someone I love to live with me with this ticking time bomb in my head?"

Luca scowled, clearly upset by Conor's choice of description. "Ticking time bomb? What the hell does that mean?"

"I never had the chance to talk to my mom about her mental illness. I don't know if it started as anxiety attacks or..." Conor hated that he'd never taken the time to talk to his mom during one of her lucid days. He knew why he'd kept quiet. At the time, he'd been terrified his admission would push her into a depressed state. He clung to the days when Mom was herself and happy, so he'd never wanted to take a chance on ruining any of them.

"So what's been going on here, Conor? Why have you been with us at all if your plan was to push us away?" Harper's tone made it clear she did not like that idea.

"I'm with you because I can't stay away. Besides, you two are damn hard to shake." He smiled as he said it.

Mercifully, Luca laughed. "We're not hard to shake. We're *impossible* to shake, and don't you forget it," Luca warned, reaching out to squeeze Conor's knee firmly.

Conor placed his free hand on top of Luca's. "I won't. I just... I thought it fell to me to be sure I lived a solitary life so no one would ever be hurt by my attacks. Then you two showed up, and I got swept away in this because...*fuck*. It's everything I'd never let myself dream of having."

Harper smiled. "I like the sound of that."

"But then you started talking about kids and my anxiety took over, like it always fucking does. By the time we got back to Philly, I'd convinced myself it was time to break things off."

Luca started to interrupt, but Conor held him off.

"Until my brothers broke into my penthouse this morning and staged an intervention," he said wryly.

"Intervention?" Luca chuckled. "Sorry I missed that."

"I guess turnabout is fair play because I've been on the other side of those Russo meltdown interventions. I should have reached out to Matt and Gage on my own, but the three of us weren't close up until a year or two ago."

"I didn't know that," Harper confessed. "You seem as close to your brothers as Luca is to his."

Conor liked that, liked that she thought that, because he longed for that kind of relationship with his brothers. "We're getting there. It's definitely a work in progress as we try to break free of those shitty lessons from our father. All of us succumbing to his voice in our heads, telling us we can't fail, we can't be weak, we can't be gay, we can't be mentally ill." Then he added another. "We *always* have to be in control."

"Did your brothers give you good advice?" Luca asked.

"Of course they did. Matt went hardcore CEO on me. Told me I was going to start using my office at Russo Enterprises to be closer to them both, and he recommended his therapist."

Luca nodded, clearly pleased. "I like the sound of that. Those are good places to start."

Conor looked at Harper. "I really am sorry I wasn't there when you needed me."

She squeezed his hand. "You already apologized for that, and I forgave you. Now that I know why...well, you didn't even have to say you were sorry. I'm the one who's sorry we weren't here for *you*."

Conor sighed. "I'm glad you weren't. I hate the idea of you seeing me like—"

Luca leaned over Harper's lap, cupping the back of Conor's

neck. "You're not hiding this part of yourself from us. Have you ever had an attack in front of someone?"

Conor shook his head. "Refer back to my father issues. I view the attacks as weak, something I can't let anyone see."

"Except us," Harper said. "Because that's what people in a relationship do. They hold each other up through the bad times, cheer them on through the good."

"Relationship," Conor whispered, trying out the word.

Luca, the confident bastard, as always, never missed a beat. "Yep. Harper's my girlfriend. And you're my boyfriend."

"Neither one of you is afraid this is going too fast?" Conor asked. "I mean, there's obviously still so much we don't know about each other."

Luca shook his head. "I don't think it's too soon to call this a relationship. I'm thirty-four years old, Conor. I've spent the past eighteen years dating with reckless abandon, all in the hopes of finding the person I want to spend my life with. None of those past relationships ever had me thinking forever. Not a single one. Except *this* one."

*Forever.*

Conor wasn't sure how one word could evoke such different emotions because as much as he loved hearing it, he couldn't ignore the tightness growing in his chest at the thought of it.

Before he could think of a response, Luca continued, "We may have only started fucking a few weeks ago, but we've been with each other nearly every day for over two months. I've never spent this much time with anyone. In the past, I'd only see the woman I was dating once a week—if that. But with the two of you, every time I leave you, I'm already texting to ask when we can get together again, and then I count down the minutes until that time comes."

Conor was the same. He hated every second he wasn't with them. He just wouldn't let himself admit that until now.

When neither Harper nor Conor replied to that, Luca narrowed his eyes, the man on a roll, speaking all the truths. "I also know I'm not the only who feels this way because, dammit, you two are texting me just as much, and stopping by with coffee and lunch and making up a bunch of other excuses so that we can be together. If you don't want to hear that yet, Conor, then fine. I'll hold my peace—for a little while. But I'm not going to lie about my end game here. It's the three of us, complete with vows and babies."

Conor was shaking his head through all of Luca's impassioned speech, but not because he disagreed. "I'm not sure if that's wonderful or utterly terrifying," Conor murmured, though he absolutely was *not* scared anymore.

Harper sniffled, then hugged Luca. "It's wonderful. Luca, that's the most beautiful thing anyone has ever said to me."

Then she turned to hug Conor as well. "Are you going to keep pushing us away?"

Conor shook his head. "God...no. I..." He decided to take a page from Luca's book and speak from the heart. "I couldn't stay away from the two of you if I tried."

The three of them smiled at each other for a long moment, then the floodgates opened and the need for words fell away as they began to kiss, touch, hug, revel in the miracle of them. Of *this*.

Conor had no idea how long they made out on the couch, but when Luca came up for air, he had only one thing to say.

"Bedroom."

Rising in unison, Conor led the way to his bedroom, overwhelmed by the need to pinch himself to make sure this was real.

He'd woken up on the floor, feeling as if the world had crashed around him. Given the state of his library, it was safe to say it had.

Now, Harper and Luca knew about the attacks, about his past, and they hadn't walked away.

Once they entered his room, he walked over to the bed, sinking down on the mattress. Luca followed but stopped in front of Conor's nightstand.

He frowned when Luca slid the drawer open. They'd stopped using condoms at the cabin, and he, for one, didn't want to return to them. Harper was the first woman he'd ever had sex with bare, and holy fuck, did it feel good.

He started to say as much until he realized it wasn't condoms Luca was looking for. His heart skipped a couple beats when Luca pulled out a tube of lubrication.

Conor started to rub his chest, but Luca grasped his wrist.

"We don't have to if you're not ready," he murmured.

Conor glanced down, realizing his lovers had clearly noticed his nervous habit.

"I want to." He had to clear his throat. "I'm not nervous about it. Fuck. I want to so badly," he repeated with more force.

Harper sank down on the mattress next to Conor. "I want to watch," she admitted.

Luca shook his head. "You're going to do more than watch, sunshine. It's the three of us now. Always. Get undressed."

Conor and Harper rose, helping each other strip out of their clothing. He pulled her T-shirt off gently, trying not to touch the sore spots on her face. The kisses they'd given her downstairs had been limited to her cheeks, her neck, her ears. Neither he nor Luca wanted to hurt her split lip.

Glancing over his shoulder, Conor saw that Luca had been more expedient, undressing himself while Conor and Harper were going slower, taking the scenic route.

Once they were naked, Conor drew back the duvet, helping Harper onto the mattress. He'd taken charge at the cabin for their captive role-play, but today, he didn't want to be anyone other than himself. While he'd enjoyed the control during their fantasies, when it was just the three of them like this, he loved that Luca was the dominant one.

Luca seemed to understand his hesitance. "Lie down on your back in the middle, Harper."

She did as Luca said, smiling at them so sweetly, Conor

thought his heart might melt. Her gorgeous, expressive blue eyes shone with excitement and joy and—fuck—love?

After hearing Luca's determined declarations, Conor had no choice but to follow suit, but he'd held back the last thing. Not because he didn't feel it but because it was something he'd never said. Not once.

Love.

He was in love with them.

He'd been in love with Luca since he was fifteen years old, his first crush, his first friend. Luca had brought fun and laughter into his life twice, both at times when Conor desperately needed them.

Harper had been claiming her half of his heart bit by bit every single day since she'd arrived in Philadelphia—with her amazing food, her insightfulness, her genuine joy for life. She once claimed he'd been her mentor as a restauranteur, but she'd been his as well, teaching him that the best life is one lived without regrets.

Luca touched his bare back. "Conor, turn around and look at me."

Conor twisted until he and Luca were face-to-face, close enough that their erections were doing a good impersonation of dueling swords. Harper giggled when their dicks smacked into each other.

Luca gave him a serious look. "Your pick."

Conor knew what he meant, and he was touched by the gesture. "But I'm not new here. You are."

"I want all of you, Conor. In all the ways. But today is about you."

Conor swallowed hard, the sentiment touching him deeply because as always, with these two, he felt seen, felt important. The lonely little boy inside heard those words, soaking them in like warm sunshine after a cold rain.

He and Luca reached out at the same time, each gripping the other by the back of their necks, pressing their foreheads together.

They remained there for a few seconds before Conor whispered, "Bottom."

Luca smiled, then gave him a hard, hot kiss. "Crawl on the bed. Over Harper. Hands and knees."

They released each other and Conor did exactly as Luca demanded. Once he was in place, he lowered his upper body so that he could press several kisses on Harper's cheek before sliding his tongue along her neck.

"You're so beautiful," Conor whispered.

She placed her palm on the side of his face. "So are you."

The mattress shifted and they looked over, watching as Luca joined them on the bed.

"Open your legs, Harper. Let Conor in between."

As her legs parted, Conor couldn't resist reaching down, running his fingertips along her soaking-wet slit. She moaned when he stroked her clit the way she liked. Sometimes he was amazed to recall this was still so new. The three of them already knew each other's bodies and turn-ons and hot buttons so well.

Walking on his knees, Luca took his place behind Conor, his dick brushing against Conor's ass.

Conor let a groan of his own slip when Luca ran his large, calloused hand over his ass cheeks, stroking them over and over, lulling him into a strange state between relaxation and arousal.

Conor continued to kiss Harper's neck, one of his hands cupping her breast, plumping, squeezing, teasing the nipple.

Harper wasn't idle as she ran her hands up and down his sides before reaching for his cock, stroking it in a slow but firm glide.

Jesus. They were seducing him with their touches, their kisses, their hungry sounds. It was heady, blissful. Conor never wanted it to end, though he knew he'd be lucky to hold out for long. This was too fucking good.

Conor jerked slightly when he felt the first drops of cold lube on his ass. He hadn't even seen Luca reach for the tube. He spread the lubrication around the ring of his anus, then slowly pushed it inside with one finger. Thrusting in and out slowly, Luca added more lube and another finger.

Fucking. Heaven.

"Tell me if I hurt you," he said. "Or if I do something you don't like."

Conor had to fight to remind himself that in this, Luca was a virgin. "You're doing everything right."

Luca stretched him even more with a third finger as Conor grunted, the slight pinch nothing compared to the pleasure he felt.

As far as male lovers went, Luca was thicker and slightly longer than any of the men in Conor's past, something that had his dick growing harder even as his ass clenched at the thought.

He groaned as Luca drove his fingers deep, stretching him.

Conor missed them the moment Luca withdrew, but he didn't have a chance to complain.

"Slide inside our girl," Luca murmured.

Conor didn't have to be told twice. Harper still had his dick in her hand, so she guided him to her opening, tilting her hips so he could slip in easily.

"Fuck," he muttered. There was nothing like being inside Harper. She was hot and wet and so sensitive, her inner muscles clenched as every inch penetrated.

Once he was fully lodged inside, he started to withdraw, ready to fuck her in earnest, but Luca stopped him with a strong hand on his lower back. "Not yet."

Conor forgot to breathe when he felt Luca's cock brush his ass. He'd dreamed of this moment for so many years.

He grunted as the head broke through the resistance of his ass, Luca's size a definite challenge.

"Okay?" Luca asked.

Conor nodded, words failing him.

Harper shifted slightly below him, her hands gripping his midsection. "This is so hot," she said, her voice more breath than sound.

He tried to smile at her, but Conor feared it looked more like a grimace as Luca slid in another couple inches.

"How does it feel?" Harper whispered.

"Perfect," Conor said. "So fucking perfect."

Luca was taking his time, clearly concerned about hurting him. But it was too slow, and Conor was too impatient, too ready for the next part.

He shifted backward, pulling out of Harper until only the head of his dick remained inside, while forcing more of Luca's cock inside him.

"More, Luca," he demanded, glancing over his shoulder, wanting to know how his lover felt about this, praying that he liked it.

The look on Luca's face said it all. He caught Conor looking at him, and a smile of wonder and lust filled his face.

"This feels so fucking good," he gasped.

Conor nodded. "It does."

Luca pushed his hips forward, driving the last few inches in until he was buried deep.

"Ready for the next part?" Luca asked them both.

Harper's hands moved from Conor's sides to his shoulders. "Need you," she said to both of them.

"Steady and strong, hard and fast, or slow and easy?" Luca asked Conor, winking at him.

"All of the above," he replied. He started to laugh, but it instantly turned into a moan as Luca took him at his word, withdrawing and returning with a force that drove Conor deeper into Harper.

After that, it was on.

Conor had never imagined anything could feel this damn good. Luca claimed his ass like a man on a mission while Harper's hips cradled him perfectly. Conor rocked between them, filling Harper on the downstroke, while Luca filled him on the upswing.

The only sound in the room was their panting breaths and the slapping of skin.

Harper, thank God, was the first to go over, her back arching as her pussy clamped down on Conor's cock so hard, his vision turned gray.

Resistance was always futile when she came on his dick like that. Even without the paradise that was Luca fucking his ass.

"Luca, I can't—" That was all Conor managed to say before he came as well. So much for warning him.

Not that the warning was necessary. Luca's climax was hot on the heels of Conor's.

He felt Luca coming, his steady thrusts devoid of rhythm now as he slammed in just three times more.

Conor melted, his upper body pressed flat against Harper, who placed soft kisses on the side of his head. He grunted as Luca withdrew, dropping next to them on the mattress.

"Jesus," Luca said, panting heavily.

Conor twisted, falling to the opposite side of Harper, his strength completely zapped.

They lay there together for so long, Conor wondered if they'd fallen asleep. God knew he was on the verge. They'd fucked every ounce of energy right out of him. A two- or twenty-hour nap sounded damn good right about now.

"That was incredible," Luca said softly. "Thank you, Conor. For being my first."

"Thank you for letting me be a part of it," Harper added. "And for trusting us enough to tell us about your mom and your panic attacks."

These two people.

Conor stared at them, marveling over the fact he was here with them, happier than he'd ever been in his entire life.

"I love you," Conor whispered, the words coming out before he could think about it. The second he said them aloud, he felt that familiar, horrible pang in his chest. "I'm sorry," he quickly backtracked. "It's too soon to say—"

"I love you too, you sexy nerd," Luca replied, leaning up on his elbow, cutting him off. Then he looked down at Harper and tapped the end of her nose, making her giggle. "I love both of you."

Harper didn't say anything at first, though Conor didn't think it was because she didn't feel the same way. It was more like she was struggling to speak through the happy tears sliding down her cheeks.

"So in love," she finally managed to squeak out. "I didn't know I could ever feel this happy."

They shared slow, soft kisses, sealing the words in, and the weight on Conor's chest flew away, leaving him here, floating on a cloud of bliss without a care in the world.

*Chapter Seventeen*

"I'm so glad you liked it," Harper said, reveling in Nonna Moretti's praise.

Tonight marked the soft opening of Harper's Dining Room. For the trial run, she and Conor had decided to host a private party, inviting family and friends as the first patrons.

The place was packed to the rafters—thanks to all the Morettis in attendance—and everyone seemed to be having a good time.

Her waitstaff was doing a wonderful job, and she was thrilled with the line cooks she'd hired. There had been only a couple of hiccups tonight, but overall, everything was running like a well-oiled machine.

In just one week, the restaurant opened to the public, and after this event, she felt confident they were ready.

"It's all just so perfect, Harper," her mother gushed. Mom and Luna had driven down from New York together.

Mom had lost her shit when she'd heard about Bradley's attack, arriving in Philadelphia exactly three hours after Harper had called to tell her about it, despite reassuring her mother she was fine. She had introduced Mom to Luca and Conor during that visit, but she hadn't come out and introduced them as her boyfriends. Her mom had been too distraught by the attack, so she and the guys agreed the time wasn't right.

Nonna had wasted no time hooking arms with Mom, taking her around the room to introduce her to everyone when she arrived.

Luna had attached herself to Harper instead, leaning on one of the counters in the kitchen, demanding all the details about Harper's not one but *two* hot-as-hell boyfriends. Harper had been a bit nervous coming clean to her mother and best friend about her relationship status because while threesomes felt normal when she was with Luca's family, it was pretty unimaginable for Mom and Luna and the rest of the world.

She'd finally had to shoo Luna out, with the promise they could do a long lunch tomorrow where she would "tell all."

"I'm so glad you're here. I've missed you." Harper reached out, squeezing her mom's hand, the two of them sharing a smile before Harper moved on, making her rounds of the tables, asking for honest opinions of things that needed to be tweaked.

Matt, Liza, Gage, and Penny—who was slowly rocking her one-month-old daughter, Willow—sat together at the corner booth she'd shared with Luca and Conor the night of their prom.

Conor was standing next to the table, the five of them in deep discussion.

"I told Conor that it looks like the two of you have a winner on your hands," Matt said as she walked up.

"Thanks," Harper replied.

Conor lifted his arm, tucking it over her shoulder, pulling her close. He gave her a sweet kiss on the side of the head. He'd begun seeing a therapist the week after he came clean to them about his panic attacks. The therapist had addressed all his concerns about medication, and he'd agreed to try taking something for antianxiety.

He'd suffered a few small panic attacks since then, but he claimed they'd been mitigated by the medication. And by her and Luca.

The first time he had one while they were there, it had woken him up in the middle of the night. His labored breathing had roused both of his lovers. Conor had tried to get out of the bed, determined to hunker down in the bathroom, but they'd refused to let him suffer alone.

Instead, they'd gone through some of his exercises together, taking slow, deep breaths, doing the three-three-three thing together, talked to him about what was bothering him.

It had passed relatively quickly—something that had amazed Conor—and since then, he sought them out whenever he felt an attack coming on, and they faced it together.

"So someone spill the tea," Harper said. "The five of you are looking way too serious for a party."

Liza grinned. "Oh, believe me, after what Matt just told us, we're about to kick this party up another notch or twenty."

Harper glanced at Conor, who explained. "Richard Eddington was ousted as CEO of his company. The board discovered he was engaging in some under-the-table deals that weren't exactly on the up-and-up. It was the last nail in the coffin, according to the chairman."

"Wonder how they found out about those deals?" Gage asked with a smirk, looking at Matt, who didn't even bother to play it innocent.

"He and Patricia tried to hurt Liza. That was a mistake on their part." Matt lifted Liza's hand and kissed it, drawing Harper's attention to the big-ass diamond on her ring finger. Matt had proposed a month earlier, and the two were now planning a huge wedding for September. According to Liza, Matt was demanding they make a honeymoon baby. Not that Liza looked too upset by that demand. In truth, given the way Liza's gaze kept slipping to Willow, Harper would be surprised if the baby-making didn't start pre-wedding.

"Everything was delicious," Penny said, polishing off her dessert one-handed, licking the spoon with a contented smile. "Four thumbs-up," she said, jokingly adding Willow's thumbs to the count, before Gage gently reached for their sleeping daughter. According to Penny, she never got to hold Willow for more than ten minutes at a time before Gage snatched her away.

"Thanks, you guys." Harper grinned, then gave Conor a kiss on the cheek. "I'm going to keep making the rounds."

He gave her a wink, then turned to continue talking to his family.

Harper made her way to the middle of the dining area, where they'd pushed several tables together for Luca's siblings and their significant others. Tony was at the head, flanked by Rhys and Jess, as Gio, Keeley, and Rafe took one side, and Luca's sister, Layla, and her guys took the other.

"Thanks so much for the invitation," Layla said as Harper approached. "We're having a blast and the food is out of this world."

This was Harper's first opportunity to meet Luca's little sister, who lived in Baltimore, and Harper absolutely adored her and her men, Finn and Miguel, who were hilarious and fun.

"I'm just so glad I finally got to meet you," Harper said. "Luca talks about you all the time."

"We've all got lots of stories about this one. She was a real handful growing up," Gio teased.

Layla rolled her eyes. "I was an angel, and you know it. I think you must have me confused with you. *You* were the one who was no stranger to the principal's office."

Tony laughed as he said to Harper, "Gio went through a class clown phase in middle school. One that wasn't appreciated by his math teacher."

Gio snorted. "Josh Banks bet me twenty bucks I couldn't get the humorless woman to laugh. It took me three weeks and four trips to the principal's office, but eventually I wore her down and won that money."

Luca walked up behind her, wrapping his arm around her waist. "God. Are you all seriously talking about Ms. Woodward? Still bragging about winning the bet?"

Gio smirked. "Hell yeah! No one in all the classes before or since mine ever heard that woman laugh. I gave my class the gift of a goddamned unicorn."

Luca snorted. "You and the damn unicorn." He gave her a kiss on the cheek. "You have a second? Kayden just got here, and he wanted to talk to you, me, and Conor."

"Sure. Excuse me," she said to everyone at the table.

Harper followed Luca over to where Conor and Kayden were standing near the front door.

"Hi, Kayden. I'm glad you could make it," she said, giving him a hug. She'd grown quite close to Luca and Conor's families and friends over the past four months, all of them welcoming her with open arms.

"I intended to be here earlier, but I got a call that resulted in some last-minute paperwork. I thought you might like to know that Bradley was arrested in New York a couple of hours ago," Kayden said.

"*What?*" Harper said.

Kayden had been trying to find evidence that Bradley was behind all the sabotage, but the man had airtight alibis for the nights of the fire and theft, as well as the afternoon of the near-flooding.

"NYPD arrested Bradley's cousin yesterday for possession. Apparently, the guy has already spent some time behind bars. His rap sheet reads like a grocery list—DUIs, assault, petty theft, low-level dealing. According to the arresting officer, he called Bradley to bail him out, and he refused. Probably not the wisest decision because the cousin—not the brightest bulb—went the revenge route, confessing to setting the fire, clogging the drain, and stealing the electrical wire. Said Bradley paid him to do it. And he had a bunch of incriminating texts and emails from Bradley to back up that story."

"Wow. Talk about family love," Conor muttered.

"Yep," Kayden agreed. "Guess the cousin decided since he was going down anyway, he'd take Bradley with him. Bradley has lawyered up, but the detective in New York says it doesn't matter. They have enough evidence to put him away for a while."

Harper suddenly felt lighter, something Conor and Luca clearly realized as they both turned to her, smiling. She'd confessed after Bradley posted bail for assault that she couldn't stop looking over her shoulder. She'd been told he'd returned to New York, but that hadn't helped. Knowing he was behind bars now, and likely would be for some time, felt incredible.

"They got him," Conor said, hugging her.

She let those words sink in and soothe her.

Luca reached around from behind her, drawing both her and Conor into his arms. If she lived to be a thousand, she would never tire of being wrapped up in these men's arms.

"What a great night." Harper thanked Kayden, then pointed out where Hazel and Aldo were sitting with Gianna and Elio. "They all waited for you, to eat. I'll send the waiter over to take your drink order right away."

Kayden gave her a grateful nod, then went to join his partners and friends.

"Happy?" Luca asked.

"So happy I'm not sure I can hold it all inside. It's too big," she confessed.

Conor kissed her cheek. "I feel the same way. We did it," he said as the three of them looked around the restaurant, busting at the seams with family and friends, all having a good time and enjoying their meals.

"Dream come true," she whispered.

The rest of the night passed far too quickly as Harper moved between the kitchen and the dining room, preparing the meals and chatting with her guests.

Matt and Liza were the last to leave, Conor locking the door behind them.

Harper's apartment above the restaurant had been completed a few weeks ago. And while she'd moved her furniture out of storage, she hadn't spent a single night in her own bed, the three of them always sleeping at Conor's.

"Ready to go up?" Luca asked as he turned off the lights. They'd decided to spend the night here rather than drive back across town to Conor's.

She nodded, and they walked to the kitchen, where she checked that everything was turned off and cleaned up. Luca made sure the back door was locked, set the alarm, and then they climbed the stairs.

When they reached the top, Luca paused. "You know, I hate to put a damper on the night, but we've got a big problem."

"We do?" Conor asked.

Luca nodded. "Yeah. We need to decide where we're going to live. My place is out, obviously, because it's too small. Which leaves us choosing between Conor's penthouse or here."

"We're moving in together?" Harper asked, excited by the prospect.

"Of course we are."

Conor shook his head. "We've been officially dating all of two months. Typical Moretti. Always rushing to the next part."

Luca punched Conor on the arm. "Typical Moretti, huh? Gage was married to Penny about five minutes after they said I love you, and Matt and Liza are currently trying to set some record for shortest engagement in history, planning a big-ass wedding in two months. So if you ask me...you should be saying typical *Russo*."

"You really want to move in together?" Every now and then, Conor still seemed as if he couldn't quite believe what the three of them had was real.

"I definitely want to," Harper said. "To be honest, Conor's place feels more like home to me than this apartment. We could always rent it," she said. "Joey mentioned he and Miles were thinking about finding a place together. I wonder if they'd like to live here?"

"That's a great idea," Luca said. "I'll mention it to them tomorrow. As long as Conor's okay with us invading his home."

Conor smiled. "I can't think of anything I want more."

Harper clapped her hands. "Awesome!"

"Now that that's settled," Luca said, "I think we should celebrate tonight's success with something special."

"Like what?" Harper asked.

Luca's eyes twinkled with mischief. "A visit from *that guy*."

*That guy* hadn't made an appearance since the cabin.

Harper had missed *that guy*.

Conor didn't seem to mind the request because, he never missed a beat. "That can be arranged easily," he said in that deep, dark, sexy voice that had her panties soaked in a second flat. Pointing down the hall toward her bedroom, he said, "Get to your room, baby girl. Now."

Harper didn't need to be asked twice. She quickly led the way; aware her guys were hot on her heels. Stepping across the threshold, she turned toward them, feigning fear as she resumed her role as their captive.

"What are you going to do to me?" she asked timidly.

Conor put his hands on his hips. "Whatever we want. Take off your clothes."

Harper wasted no time stripping off her clothing. Her arousal had been set to simmer the last couple of hours, as her men kept sneaking over to whisper sexy innuendoes in her ear, or covertly stroke her ass, or steal kisses—one after another.

"Get on the bed, sunshine," Luca said once she was naked.

She did as they asked, curious when Conor drifted over to her closet. Her heart skipped a beat when he returned with two scarves in his hands.

"Lift your hands above your head," he demanded.

She had always—ALWAYS—wanted to be tied up in bed, but she'd never dated anyone she trusted that much. That desire had ramped up following her sex-in-the-woods fantasy, when Luca had tied her with a jump rope. Being rendered helpless should be a terrifying thing, but the truth was, it felt freeing in a way. Without the use of her hands, she didn't have to worry if she should be doing something, and if so, what. It meant she could concentrate solely on what *they* were doing to *her*.

Harper considered putting up a fight, making them work for it, but in the end, she didn't have the patience to wait. Raising her arms, she squeezed her legs together, seeking friction, as Conor bound her wrists together, then secured them to the headboard.

Luca stood at the end of the bed, stripping off his own clothes as he watched. "Stop moving," he demanded. "And open your legs. Let me see how wet you are."

Harper had more trouble following that command, her body already shifting into overdrive.

When she failed to obey, he stopped undressing, reaching out to force her knees apart.

She started to close them again, but he pierced her with a glare. "Close those and we're starting tonight with a spanking."

Harper was so fucking tempted. Because as much as she enjoyed being tied up, she loved being spanked even more.

Conor shook his head. "No spanking. She likes it too much. Hold those legs open for us, baby girl, or we're going to tie your ankles apart...and force you to watch us have sex without you. No orgasms for bad girls who don't do as their told."

She kept her knees open, letting Luca look his fill as he finished taking off the rest of his clothes. Conor followed suit. They took their damn time about it, something she knew was intentional. They were testing her ability to obey.

Her body was demanding to be touched, rubbed, filled.

God.

*Anything.*

After too many minutes, Conor ran his finger down the center of her chest. "Good girl," he purred. "I think she deserves a reward." Glancing at Luca, he pointed to Harper's pussy. "Go down on our girl. You're going to make her come with your mouth while I fuck you."

Conor's words were the equivalent of sucking all the air out of the room. None of them breathed as he and Harper both studied Luca's face.

So far, Luca had firmly resided in the top spot when it came to him and Conor fucking. Conor had confessed his penchant for being the bottom, but she wasn't a bit surprised that *this guy* wanted it the other way around.

"Okay." Luca's voice was gruff. He swallowed deeply.

Conor walked around the bottom of the bed, gripping Luca's arm to turn him so they were facing. "Okay?"

"You're not exactly a small guy, and I've never shoved anything up my ass," Luca confessed with a wry grin.

"I'll go slow."

She noticed Conor didn't offer him an out, which told her just how much he wanted this.

Luca nodded. "I want you."

One side of Conor's mouth crooked up. "Do you have lube, Harper?"

She tilted her head toward the nightstand. She'd just unpacked her sex toys a few days earlier. Not that she'd used them since crawling into bed with these two men.

Conor opened the drawer, his eyebrows rising in shock...or maybe amusement. "Trying to decide if this arsenal means you're a bad girl or a very, very *good* girl," he joked.

Curiosity killed the cat...and Luca, who walked over to take a peek. His eyes widened, his smile huge.

"Damn, Harper. Just when I thought I couldn't love you any more," Luca said.

Her heart tripled in size every time one of them told her they loved her.

"We're moving all of this stuff to my place tomorrow," Conor said. "I want to use that butt plug on you."

Harper had spent too many years either alone or in unfulfilling relationships. As such, she'd become a maestro when it came to playing with her own body. She'd always known that with the right lover—or lovers, in her case—she would be sexually adventurous, willing to try anything.

Conor grabbed the lube and started to shut the drawer. Thinking better of it, he reached back in and grabbed a vibrator, tossing it at Luca. "Use your mouth *and* that."

Luca nodded, clicking the toy on, testing out all the speeds as Harper fought hard not to hump the air.

Returning to the bottom of the bed, Luca bent over, tugging Harper down as far as the ties would allow so that he could taste her. He wasted no time, drawing his tongue along her slit from her ass to her clit, as she moaned—partly in relief, partly in desperation. She needed more. A hell of a lot more.

Luca toyed with her, licking her over and over, never remaining in the right place for long. She began to struggle against the ties around her wrists, suddenly not such a big fan. She wanted to grab Luca's hair and hold him where she wanted him. And the bastard knew it. Lifting his head, he gave her a shameless wink.

"Please, Luca," she started. "I need—"

"Quiet!" Conor snapped. "You're going to take what we give you and be grateful for it. Keep complaining, Goldilocks, and you'll find yourself gagged."

Oh *fuck*. Why did that sound so hot?

She mentally added gagging to her list of sexy things she wanted to try with them. It was a good thing they were moving in together sooner rather than later because she wasn't sure a lifetime would be enough to do all the things she wanted to try with her men.

Luca took mercy on her—sort of—the next time he lowered his head, circling her clit with his tongue. It felt better, but it still wasn't enough.

Then his tongue disappeared completely, his hot breath the only thing that remained as she saw his ass shift. While she couldn't see what was happening, she knew what Conor was doing. Especially when Luca hissed.

"How many fingers?" she asked Luca.

"One. Just one," he said through gritted teeth.

She knew what he was feeling because she recalled the first time she'd tried out the butt plug. It had taken her a few tries, a lot of lube, and a fair amount of pep talking before she was able to push the largest part inside.

"It's going to feel good," she reassured him. "Trust me."

Luca gave her a grateful look, then returned to her pussy, sucking her clit into his mouth until she gasped at the powerful suction. It hurt in all the best ways.

Luca grunted, and she suspected Conor had added another finger. She glanced at Conor's face, saw determination and lust radiating from him. Obviously, he wanted Luca to like this enough that he'd be willing to do it again.

She was distracted from watching Conor by a buzzing noise. Her hips jerked when Luca placed the tip of her vibrator against her clit.

"Oh my God!" she cried out. It felt amazing, and again, like not enough. While her clit was her magic button, it only worked in conjunction with something inside her.

Luca held the vibrator in place, driving two fingers deep into her pussy.

Harper's body reacted as if she'd touched a live wire, and she came.

Just. Like. That.

It was a quick orgasm because the second she came, Luca pulled the vibrator away from her clit, shaking his head. "Bad girl. No one told you that you could come."

She huffed out a breathy laugh. "My bad," she said without an ounce of remorse.

Luca chuckled, but it was short-lived. "*Fuck*," he cursed.

Her eyes flew to Conor, who was roughly thrusting his fingers into Luca.

"How many?" she asked again.

This time, it was Conor who answered. "Three." Pulling his fingers out, he lubed up his dick, then positioned it at Luca's ass.

Luca held perfectly still, even though he still had two fingers inside her. It looked as if every bit of his concentration was focused on what Conor was doing to his body. He breathed out several shaky breaths and small gasps as Conor seesawed in and out, going a little deeper with each pass.

Luca pounded his free hand on the mattress. "Jesus Christ! Too tight, too..."

Conor stopped for a moment, looking not at Luca but at her. She was confused until she realized that she could see what he couldn't...Luca's face.

His brow was furrowed, but there was no genuine pain in his features.

She gave Conor a smile and a wink.

He grinned, then started working himself in and out again.

When both men released deep groans and stilled, she realized Conor was there. All the way inside Luca's ass.

Luca looked over his shoulder. "Fuck me, Conor," he breathed. Then he turned back to her, picked up the vibrator, turned it on high, and slammed it inside her.

Harper's back arched as Luca fucked her with the toy, his tongue flat against her clit, the pressure just perfect this time.

Conor had begun to move as well, taking Luca hard and fast. Harper came again—without permission—but neither man called her out. Both of them were too focused on themselves, on their own pleasure.

Conor came next, cursing while calling out Luca's name, then hers. Luca pulled out the vibrator, Harper's pussy clenching in an attempt to hold it in, even though she'd already come twice.

For a minute, Conor held still as his climax waned. Then he slowly withdrew. The second he was free, Luca climbed on the bed, shoved Harper's legs even farther apart, and thrust in fully, roughly. He was claiming her, using her, and she was here for it.

"God! Yes!" Harper called out as Luca fucked her like a man

possessed. Less than two minutes later, both of them were coming together.

Gasping for air, Harper didn't even realize Conor had walked to the head of the bed and untied her until he drew her arms down, gently massaging her shoulders.

Luca fell to her side, his arm resting on her middle. Conor climbed in, resting his hand on Luca's arm.

They lay there in sated bliss for ages.

Words unnecessary.

Until Harper broke the silence.

"Better than a Quarter Pounder with Cheese."

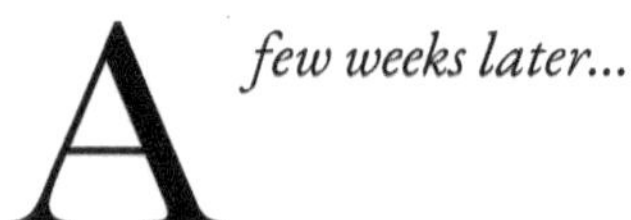

# Epilogue

A *few weeks later...*

"What a place!" Joey did a complete three-sixty, spinning around to take in the gorgeous sights around him.

He and Miles had just made the three-and-a-half-hour drive from Philadelphia to Northern Virginia in order to start filming the second episode for their third season of *ManPower*. The closer they got to their destination atop the mountain, the more blown away Joey had been by the view.

The large wooden sign with the colorful words Stormy Weather Farm—the t's in stormy and weather shaped like lightning strikes—told them they'd arrived.

Joey felt like he'd stepped back in the past as he took in the giant white farmhouse with large navy-blue shutters, surrounded by countless well-kept outbuildings, including an honest-to-God red barn. The place was storybook perfect with rolling green hills, a view that stretched for miles, and beautiful spring flowers adorning the wraparound porch.

"Shit, man. That was some climb. I wasn't sure the truck was going to make it," Miles muttered. "We're not in Philly anymore, Toto."

Joey chuckled. The rest of the *ManPower* crew would be arriving tomorrow, but they'd made plans to meet Levi Storm and his brew master, Lou, this afternoon for a tour of Stormy Weather Farm, as well as the two businesses located on the massive property—Rain and Shine Brewery and Lightning in a Bottle Winery.

Joey had been doing some research on the farm in preparation for the show. The Storm family had settled here over six generations ago, and they created a pretty amazing legacy.

After the tour, Levi, the oldest of the latest generation, had promised them a home-cooked dinner and the chance to meet the rest of his siblings and cousins. He and Levi had spoken a couple of times on the phone in preparation for the filming, and the man had mentioned the fact he had six brothers! Joey, who was one of five, had been awestruck by the thought. The branches on the Storm family tree seemed to be weighed down by as many relatives as the Moretti's tree.

Levi reminded Joey a lot of his older brother, Tony—friendly and easygoing. The kind of guy who'd never met a stranger. For most of Tony's adult life, the family had called him the mayor because the dude seriously seemed to know every single person in Philadelphia.

"Never gave much thought to the farming lifestyle but, damn, Miles, imagine getting to wake up here every morning of your life," Joey said, staring into the distance.

"No thanks," Miles grumped.

Joey rolled his eyes. Miles was taking in the same view he was, but there was no denying his best friend was much less impressed. A city boy from the word go, Miles viewed the mountains and woods and all nature in general as wasted space simply waiting to be "civilized" with houses, stores, restaurants, and a fucking Starbucks on every corner.

Levi had mentioned on the phone that on a clear day, they

could see all the way to Washington DC, their view from up here completely unencumbered by other houses or trees or anything, and Joey found himself searching the horizon to see if it was true. They were so high up, he could almost believe that if he was only an inch or two taller, he'd bump his head on the sky.

"Should we go knock on the door?" Miles asked after another cursory glance at the view Joey couldn't take his eyes off.

Before Joey could respond, they heard a female voice calling to them from the porch of the house.

"You made it!" she said.

Joey spun around, blinking several times and even shaking his head, trying to convince himself he was seeing...her.

His shocked gasp was audible, drawing Miles's attention.

"You okay, man?" Miles asked.

"It's her," Joey whispered.

"Her who?"

Joey watched as the petite strawberry-blonde woman descended the stairs, walking their direction, intent on greeting them. She wore faded overalls over a hot pink tee and her long, wavy hair was pulled back in a high ponytail, though a chunk of it had fallen out on one side and she kept tucking it behind her ear each time the breeze blew it loose again. She wore the girliest Doc Martens he'd ever seen, the boots covered in pink and purple flowers.

She was smiling at them as she approached, and Joey knew without a doubt, he'd never seen a more beautiful woman in his life.

"Joey?" Miles prodded. "Who is she?"

Joey grinned, unable to look away from her as he said, "The woman I'm going to marry."

Are you ready for more Italian Stallions?
Down and Dirty
Hard and Fast

Rough and Ready
Wild and Wicked
Hot and Heavy
Naughty and Nice (a holiday novella)
Tempted and Taken
Steady and Strong
Kiss and Tell

Calling all fans of Mari Carr AND Facebook! There's a group for you. Come join Mari Carr's Facebook group for sneak peaks, cover reveals, contests and more! Join now.

And be sure to join Mari's mailing list to receive a **FREE** sexy novella, Midnight Wild.

# About the Author

Virginia native Mari Carr is a New York Times and USA TODAY bestseller of contemporary romance novels. With over three million copies of her books sold, Mari was the winner of the Romance Writers of America's Passionate Plume award for her novella, Erotic Research. She has over a hundred published works, including her popular Wild Irish and Italian Stallions books, along with the Trinity Masters series she writes with Lila Dubois.

Follow Mari:
www.maricarr.com
mari@maricarr.com

Join her newsletter so you don't miss new releases and for exclusive subscriber-only content.